THE WAY WE WERE

For more information on Marcia Willett and her books,
see her website at www.marciawillett.co.uk

THE WAY WE WERE

MARCIA WILLETT

McArthur
&
Company

First published in Canada in 2009 by
McArthur & Company
322 King St. West, Suite 402
Toronto, ON
M5V 1J2
www.mcarthur-co.com

Library and Archives Canada Cataloguing in Publication

Willett, Marcia _   The way we were / Marcia Willett.

ISBN 978-1-55278-768-7

      I. Title.
PR6073.I277 W39 2009   823'.914   C2009-900779-7

Printed in Canada by Webcom

Jacket design by Michael Storrings

Jacket illustration by Vitali Komarov

10 9 8 7 6 5 4 3 2 1

To Yvonne Holland

ACKNOWLEDGEMENT

A History of St Breward provided some crucial insights into the village and its surroundings. My thanks to the editor, Pamela Bousfield, and all the other contributors.

PROLOGUE

February 1976

'TO THE WEST'. The road curls round in a steep bend and forks unexpectedly. The old sign, almost obscured by the bare, out-thrusting branches of an ancient thorn hedge, is barely legible but she drives confidently on; both road and sign are familiar to her. 'TO THE WEST': the words always have the power to thrill her. When she was a child the phrase conjured up mysterious, mountainous landscapes, tall pinnacles and towers showered with powdery golden light and lapped by the shining tides of aquamarine seas; a magic place where she might escape the confusion and unhappiness of her own small world. Romantic tales of courtly love in castles and courts across Shropshire and Herefordshire and along the Welsh Marches, and stirring stories of fierce battles and bloody ambushes in the stony mountain fastnesses, were told to her by her grandfather, a descendant of the great Roger de Mortimer, Baron of Wigmore, Earl of March and Lord of Brecon, Radnor and Ludlow. There were other, older, stories reaching further into the west, to Tintagel on the wild north Cornish coast, of King Arthur and his knights, of Guinevere, his queen, and the magician Merlin.

Involuntarily she glances quickly at the small bronze figure on the passenger seat: the boy Merlin with the falcon on his wrist. She has set him up as a talisman; someone to watch over her and the Turk on this long journey to the west.

'Take the little Merlin,' her grandmother says earlier, appearing beside her as she swung her tapestry holdall into the camper van and settled the terrier on her rug. 'Go on. Take him. You've always loved him.'

She takes it unwillingly. The bronze is smooth and heavy in her hand, the delicate detail giving the boy the same intent expression as that of the falcon. His tunic swirls as if he is in perpetual motion, invoking an urgency of purpose that hurries him forward to some unknown destination, his chin lifted and unafraid. Her heartbeat quickens at the prospect of her own journey; the bronze would give her courage – yet still she hesitates.

'To please me.' The older woman, breathless from the quick, last-minute dash into the house to fetch the charming little statue, speaks pleadingly – and uncharacteristically.

'It belongs to my father,' she replies reluctantly.

Her grandmother gives a cry of angry impatience. 'Everything belongs to your father now. It's how your grandfather arranged it years ago, and I didn't give a thought to how it might be for you when he died. It never occurred to me that your mother would die soon afterwards, or that your father would remarry. I must be grateful that he allows me to stay here, I suppose. A custodian of his treasures, which will all go to his son by that Frenchwoman. At least take the Merlin. He's been standing on the shelf in the Red Room for years and nobody will miss him. Take it, Tegan.'

Always Tegan: never the little name 'Tiggy' that her friends use. She opens the passenger door and places the little figure – no more than six inches high – amongst the impedimenta on the seat: a rug, maps, some chocolate. Nestled in the warm folds of the rug, he stares forward, his profile as imperious and compelling as that of her grandmother. Tiggy settles him more firmly, shuts the door and takes the frail old woman in her arms.

'Thank you,' she says. 'You'll look after yourself, won't you? I might not be able to get away for a bit.'

For a moment the old woman holds her tightly; then she kisses her granddaughter and stands back. She is not demonstrative and the need to give the Merlin, an impulsive but oddly necessary gesture, has taken her by surprise.

'I'm glad you're going to Julia,' she says. 'Such a good friend. Give her my love.'

'Of course I will. I'll let you know I've arrived safely but I might stop overnight on the way down so don't worry about me.'

'I've long since given up worrying about my family,' is the tart response. 'Goodbye, darling.'

She turns abruptly, crossing the gravel and disappearing towards the house, leaving Tiggy to climb into the VW and set off down the drive. She's not hurt by that sudden departure: she knows quite well that they're both feeling churned up inside and that, though she would never show it, her grandmother is near to tears.

Has she guessed the truth? Tiggy shakes her head. Surely not. There has been no indication, no change in her grandmother's behaviour – except right at the end in the giving of the bronze: an uncharacteristic neediness that absolutely required that gift should be accepted, overwhelming Tiggy's own strong instinct to reject utterly anything that belongs to her father. And after all, she tries to persuade herself now, the Merlin might have been collected in the first place by her grandfather – the Red Room has always been full of beautiful and unusual pieces to which his son now continues to add – and this thought somehow makes it easier to accept one small object from among so many. Her grandfather, who had told her so many stories of Merlin and the court of King Arthur, would not have begrudged her this artefact from his collection. Odd that now, at the time of her greatest need, she should be travelling west. Julia lives a matter of miles from Tintagel.

'Of *course* you must come to us,' she said. 'Oh, poor you. This is so awful. Losing Tom is bad enough but . . . Look, of course you must come down to Trescairn straight away. . . Pete? Pete won't mind a bit. He's going to sea next week for three months, so he'll be delighted that I shall have some company. Don't fuss, Tiggy, just come whenever you're ready.'

Oswestry, Shrewsbury, Ludlow, Leominster: the miles are slowly eaten up beneath the trundling wheels. She stops on Wenlock Edge to make coffee, and to give the Turk a run, and again at Hereford to fill up with petrol. They have an early lunch in the winding Wye valley, beside the river, and all the while Tiggy is conscious of the wild bleak country to the west and north, stretching away to Snowdonia where Tom died four weeks earlier, attempting to complete the Horseshoe under snow. Snow still lies on the Black Mountains and the Brecon Beacons, and even here, deep in the valley, the wind is icy and the February sun is a chilly glimmer in the veiled grey sky.

Tom: she sees him clearly in her mind's eye as he would have been now. Lighting the little gas stove, filling the kettle, the tall strong length of him leaning at the van's door with his hands in the pockets of his jeans, whistling beneath his breath. How he loved travelling: making plans through the short winter term for the long summer holidays, with maps spread over the floor of his small flat on the university campus, showing her the roads they would take and discussing the places where they'd camp.

'Why did you decide to teach?' she asked him.

He took a few moments to answer, running his long brown fingers through his short dark hair, his light grey eyes thoughtful. 'Probably because I'd spent all my life in institutions,' he answered. 'It seemed the natural thing to do. What about you?'

'I love small children,' she said. 'Perhaps it's because we never had families of our own. Not proper ones, anyway. We surround ourselves with other people, the more the merrier.'

'But not always,' he said. 'Sometimes I need to be alone or, at least, away from the crowds. That's why I like climbing.'

Tiggy shivers as she bundles the Turk back into the van. The Dandie Dinmont's large dark eyes gaze at her with bright intelligence and Tiggy buries her head suddenly against the wiry coat, longing for Tom and wondering if she'll have this sharp pain in her heart for the rest of her life. The initial disabling numbness, which at first had affected her whole body, has dwindled gradually into a hard central core of anguish. How does such grief work and who can she ask? For years after her mother died, she felt slightly at a disadvantage with children of her own age. They knew things she didn't, hinted at behaviour she couldn't understand; sometimes, when she asked an outright question, they'd scream with embarrassed laughter. Slowly she pieced together her experiences into a mosaic she could make sense of: for instance, her father's unexplained absences and her mother's tears, resulting in bitter words and long silences, began to make a pattern. Much later, remembering how she wakened to hear his footsteps crossing the landing to the au pair's bedroom, another shape in the picture fell into place. Some of the girls were told to go;

they protested, drenched in tears, begging to stay and talking of promises of marriage; some were angry, shouting threats, whilst others looked frightened and ran away without giving notice. She never understood why – and some of them she missed terribly – but her father banished them all with a shrug and a shake of the head that said simply that women behaved inexplicably: it was nothing to worry about. It was a relief to reach an age where no more au pairs were needed. After all, she was away at school now for most of the year and at her grandmother's home in Herefordshire for a great deal of the holidays.

Then, one night he came to her room, a glass of whisky in his hand, swaying a little as he watched her from the doorway as she sat brushing her hair.

'You've grown, haven't you?' he said. 'Little Tegan. Come and give your old pa a kiss.'

The ensuing scene was undignified and confusing: eventually he withdrew, liberally splashed by his whisky and cursing beneath his breath. She decided to think no more about it, putting it down to his being lonely and drinking too much. On the second occasion he gave her some wine at dinner and this time the struggle was grimly determined and frightening. The third time he struck her hard, knocking her to the floor, but she scrambled away from him in time to lock herself in her bathroom before he could catch her. She stayed there all night and, in the morning when he went to the gallery, she packed some things into a suitcase and telephoned Julia, her dearest, closest friend.

'Of *course* you must come,' she said at once. 'You don't want to spend the holidays alone in a flat in London. Hang on a sec.' And, as Julia consulted with her mother, Tiggy was able to hear the usual cheerful, reassuring sounds of Julia's family life in rural Hampshire, siblings shouting and wailing, dogs barking, and her mother's warmly practical voice – 'Of course she can come and stay. Now do ask about trains, Julia,' – and all the while Tiggy clutched the receiver, her knees trembling lest her father should return unexpectedly.

Only Julia knew the truth, though Tiggy guessed that her grandmother suspected something akin to it. Less than a year later, during which time Tiggy never stayed at the London flat unaccompanied, her father sold the London gallery, married his partner at the gallery in Paris and moved to France; six months later their son was born.

Now, Tiggy slams the side door of the van and climbs into the driving seat, hugging her long sheepskin coat around her. Tom bought the coat for her in the King's Road and its all-embracing warmth reminds her of him. Once she met Tom it seemed that her life had properly begun – even the simple act of breathing took on a deeper, fuller quality – whilst lovemaking, something to be avoided since her father's forced fumblings, became with Tom a joyful and fulfilling delight. Knowing Tom, travelling with him in the old orange camper, loving him, had given her exactly the same sensation as the warmth and light the sun bestows when it breaks out from behind dark, rain-heavy clouds. Her muscles relaxed at last, she grew supple and free and at peace. His love enabled her, encouraging without attempting to possess her; his friendship showed her unexplored paths of knowledge and discovery. Now she must learn to do without it.

The little Merlin stares resolutely forward, showing the way. Tiggy switches on the engine and drives up on to the road leading to Chepstow and the Severn Bridge: to the west.

It takes well over an hour to negotiate her way through Bristol and it is with relief that she picks up the A38 again, heading out of the city and wondering where to park up for a much-needed break. In the end, she stops twice to make tea and to stretch her legs; the first time in a little lane just north of Taunton and the second time beside the entrance to a bridle path between Whiddon Down and Sticklepath on the winding A30 west of Exeter. This time, after a walk, Tiggy makes toast on the grill while the Turk continues to explore, her scimitar-curved tail waving excitedly. It's nearly four o'clock. The northern flanks of Dartmoor are powdered with fine snow, the sun has disappeared long since behind thickening cloud, and wet sleet hisses softly against the windscreen.

'Pete said the journey might easily take you seven or eight hours,' Julia told her rather anxiously. 'Should you do it in two stabs, d'you think?'

'I'll see how I get on,' she answered. 'If I make an early start I should be OK. I'd rather get it over with in one go if I can.'

Now, with her hands wrapped gratefully around the mug of hot tea, she wonders whether it would be sensible to stop for the night while it's still light enough to find a good camping site. Despite the fact that her back aches and she's very tired, she feels despondent at the prospect and is seized with new determination to press on. The Turk comes back and barks to be let in; Tiggy takes one last look at the map and then climbs into the driving seat.

'Not far to Okehampton then straight on to Launceston. We should be with Julia in about an hour and a half,' Tiggy says aloud, as much to comfort herself as to reassure the Turk. She is filled with an overwhelming longing to be at the end of her travelling; sitting with Julia beside a fire recounting the long day's journey to the west.

'You'll love it here,' Julia told her. 'Trescairn has been in Pete's family for ever, something to do with the mining, and you can see for miles. We're just about settled in, although it's a bit of a hike into the base. Still, Pete thinks it's worth it and the children just love the space. After that quarter in Gosport it's utter heaven.'

Tiggy touches the little Merlin for luck, pushes her foot down on the accelerator and switches on the windscreen wipers; when she stops for petrol just outside Sticklepath she notices a sharp drop in the temperature.

'More snow coming,' the attendant remarks cheerfully. 'Going far?'

'Down into Cornwall,' she tells him. 'Near St Breward.'

He draws down the corners of his mouth, shaking his head doubtfully. 'You might just make it before it comes on really thick,' he says. 'It's already settling on the tops.'

As she leaves the lights of Okehampton behind her and travels around the northern edge of the moor, the sky brightens and, away in the west, long fingers of sunset light probe down between the layers of dense cloud so that the mysterious peaks and uplands of the distant landscape are revealed just as she remembered it earlier when she saw the sign: 'TO THE WEST'. A line or two of a hymn hums in her head and she sings it aloud to the Turk, who beats her tail politely upon her rug:

> The golden evening lightens in the west,
> Soon, soon to weary warriors cometh rest.
> Sweet is the calm of Paradise the blest . . .

The vision and the words hearten her, bringing a much-needed surge of energy, as the brief sunset glow leaks into the gathering clouds. Soon the slopes and tors of Dartmoor drop away and they're through Launceston and into Cornwall at last, approaching Five Lanes and Altarnun. Snow is falling on Hendra Downs as she pulls into the side of the road to look again at Pete's map. It is very clear: 'Leaving Jamaica Inn on your right, pass through Bolventor and take the next turning right signposted to St Breward. Pass over the cattle grid on to open moor.'

The light is dying now, and the wind is beginning to rise, but Tiggy sees the sign clearly and swings the camper off the A30, rattling across the cattle grid. The snow has already settled across the narrow moorland road and a tiny spasm of fear shakes her heart. The wild sweep of land glimmers ghostly and chill; small scattered clumps of gorse show smudgily black against the faint covering of snow. A larger smudge suddenly detaches itself and moves out into the road. Tiggy gasps with fright and then breathes deeply with relief as the pony trots away. She drives very slowly, leaning forward a little so as to scan the landscape more clearly, noting a signpost pointing away to the left, remembering the next part of her instructions: 'Follow the signs for St Breward: all right-hand turns.'

The lane is running down off the moor now, between granite walls on either side; the headlights slanting across great boulders and showing up the thick sturdy roots of the thorn trees, and the falling snow whirls and dazzles. Tiggy holds tightly to the wheel, following the twisting lane as it climbs again, and she sees how easily she might lose sight of the track and plunge on to the moor. The lane swings left so abruptly that she's brought up almost against a wall and the high blank side of a house, and she wrenches the wheel violently, feeling the camper skid; and all the while a deeper, almost atavistic kind of fear is growing inside her; a foreboding that something terrible is about to happen. She's noticed the familiar shape of a telephone box a little way back, its lamp glowing in the darkness and snow gathering on its ledges, and wonders whether she should stop and telephone Julia. Yet how can she ask Julia, with three small children, to come to her aid on such a night?

All the while the strength of the wind is increasing, buffeting the sides of the van, driving the snow before it so that it heaps and drifts against the stone walls. With relief she sees the granite post with its sign pointing to the right and she jolts onward, hardly able now to distinguish the road from the rough moorland in the dim snowy twilight and occasionally bumping the two offside wheels up on to the uneven grass. Ahead of her she can just make out the shape of a bridge and remembers that this is mentioned in her instructions as Delford Bridge; she approaches slowly, driving carefully between the iron railings, glancing briefly, fearfully, down into the swirling black water of the De Lank River. The unexpected jolting rumble of the wheels over a cattle grid startles her but at last the lights of St Breward twinkle ahead in the gloom and she turns right again, away from the village, knowing she is now on the very last leg of the journey.

Yet all the while the formless panic grows and clutches at her heart and churns in her stomach, and it is with instinctive misgiving that she plunges down the narrow lane between high banks; a black tunnel where the remaining twilight is shut out and the headlights reflect back off the dancing snow, almost blinding her. Another cattle grid, with a high wall to the left and the snow-covered verges strewn with huge boulders; and almost too late she sees the lane leading off to the right. As she hastily manoeuvres the van she feels its huge bulk begin to skid out of control, and she stamps on the brakes, screaming with terror as it slides sideways into one of the granite blocks.

Trembling violently, not capable even of comforting the Turk who has been flung to the floor and is whining piteously, Tiggy covers her face with her hands. She is rendered powerless by fear, unable to move lest something more terrible should occur; yet all the while she has the impression that Julia is beside her, comforting and encouraging her. She raises her head and sees a distant light shining steadily through the blizzard that whirls across the high moor: Trescairn.

Slowly she stretches her cramped muscles, breathes deeply, and turns to reassure the Turk. She realizes that the engine is still running; with trembling limbs she presses her left foot down gingerly on the clutch pedal and very carefully pushes the stick into bottom gear, then treads gently, very gently, on the accelerator. Vibrating loudly, its wheels spinning to get a purchase on the small stones and slippery surface, the van slowly begins to move; still shaking, Tiggy steers carefully into the mouth of the lane, heading into the blinding snow and up on to the moor. The five-bar gate stands wide open and with little sobs of relief she turns on to the smoother surface of the drive and up towards the house.

As she comes to a halt beside an open-fronted barn, the front door is flung open, light streams across snowy yard, and Julia is beside her, opening the driver's door, almost dragging Tiggy from her seat, embracing her.

'Oh God, I've been so worried,' she cries. 'I thought you might be stuck somewhere . . . I hoped you might telephone . . . could have warned you about the snow . . .'

With Julia's arm around her, supporting her, her voice in her ear, Tiggy is assailed by another strong sense of déjà vu. All this is familiar.

'Come on,' Julia is saying. 'Let's get inside and give you something to eat and drink. Everything's all right now you're here. Oh, there's the Turk. Good girl, then. Come on,' and they all cross the yard, heads bent against the wind and the snow, and go together into the house.

The little room is filled with an eerie light: snowlight. It reflects off the pale walls and flows across the narrow bed where Tiggy is curled beneath the quilt with the Turk comfortably asleep on her feet. Tiggy raises herself on one elbow, frowning at the square of window, puzzled as much by the deep silence as by the quality of the light. Pushing back the quilt she steps shivering out of the bed and goes to the window. Holding aside a curtain in each hand she stares out in amazement at the scene. The moor flows away from the house in a snow-covered tidal sweep that washes against grey granite peaks and laps at green-black stands of fir. Almost hidden in a fold of land, the square tower of St Breward's church stands starkly outlined amidst bare tree-tops and, beyond again, a sinuous curve of silver water snakes its way out to the distant sea.

The tranquillity and beauty of the scene hold Tiggy spell-bound; gradually she is possessed with a profound sense of peace and contentment. Here, in this immense landscape, the barriers between past and present, the living and the dead, seem non-existent and, unexpectedly filled with this new joyful awareness, she believes that she is on the brink of discovering a great truth: something that will sustain her during the months ahead. Pushing back the curtains wider still, she realizes that this is the first morning since Tom's death that she hasn't wakened to a sense of despair. This thought, once admitted, presses in upon her brief remission from the pain of loss, crowding out the peace, and fear settles into its now familiar position in her breast. Still she gazes out; willing herself back into that place of tranquil joy, but the spell is broken: so is the silence. A door opens and voices are heard; two are raised in a protesting, wheedling duet, whilst the third – Julia's contralto – runs beneath the childish treble in a placatory but firm continuo.

The Turk jumps down from the bed and runs to the door, whining to be let out. Dragging her dressing gown around her, Tiggy opens the door and looks out on to the landing. Imme-diately the voices cease, two heads with butter-blond mops of hair, swivel; two pairs of blue eyes stare at her. Tiggy smiles at the twins, Andrew and Olivia: Andy and Liv. Julia raises a despairing hand.

'Sorry,' she says. 'I'm sorry they woke you. I *told* them you needed to sleep in but of course they're simply dying to see you. Now, you see.' She addresses the twins. 'You've woken poor Tiggy.'

'They didn't wake me. I was already up.' Tiggy watches the twins crouch down to embrace the Turk and then smiles at Julia. 'I can hardly believe I made it when I look out at all that moorland covered with snow.'

Julia shudders a little. 'I was out of my mind,' she admits. 'It could have been a disaster. I've promised the twins a ride in the van but not today.'

Another voice, increasing in volume, roars behind a door along the passage.

'Poor Charlie's feeling left out of things. He'll break the cot to pieces.' Julia looks hopefully at Tiggy. 'Could you make some coffee while I get him up? The twins will show you where everything lives.' She hesitates, looks back over her shoulder. 'Are you . . . you know . . . still OK?'

'Oh, yes,' says Tiggy. 'Very OK.'

'Good,' says Julia uncertainly. 'That's good, then, isn't it?' She glances at the twins. 'Off you go, then, and help Tiggy with the coffee. Don't forget to let Bella out.'

The twins set off down the stairs, arguing as to which of them should let Bella and the Turk into the garden, and Tiggy follows more slowly. She understands the reason for Julia's uncertainty but there is no question in her own mind and instinctively she spreads one hand over the place where Tom's baby is hidden, still clinging on, despite the terrors of yesterday. She could easily imagine the conversation Julia and Pete might have had: Julia defensive, wheedling Pete into a sympathetic frame of mind, and Pete slightly impatient, his paternal instinct roused, planning how to sort it all out.

'It's all very well, darling, but how will the poor old love cope with a baby and no father? They should have been getting married instead of swanning round the Continent in that camper van all last summer,' Pete might have said.

'But they were always going to get married, Pete. It's just so typically Tom and Tiggy, isn't it? They live in their own little world. Well, they did . . . Oh God, poor Tom.'

'But honestly, Julia, how is she going to manage?'

'Well, we've agreed she can come here to begin with and then, when the baby's born, she'll go back to teaching . . .'

As she follows the twins downstairs Tiggy wonders if Pete would have seen the flaw here: the headmistress in her own little school had picked up on it at once. Mrs Armstrong had remained unmoved by the undignified and disastrous combination of shock at Tom's death and morning sickness that had forced Tiggy's confession in the first place, or by the protestation that she and Tom had planned to marry at Easter. The rules were clear, she'd said: Tiggy, as an unmarried mother, was no longer a good example to her small charges and she must leave. Tiggy knows that these rules will hold just as firmly once the baby is born.

'I can't give the baby up,' she cried to Julia on the telephone that evening – and Julia's generous response filled her with overwhelming gratitude and relief. It offers Tiggy a respite; meanwhile she schools herself to deal with her fear by looking no further ahead than the birth of her baby, but she isn't always successful. The reality is stark: how will she manage to support them both?

The narrow staircase opens into a big sitting-room dominated by a granite fireplace that takes up almost the whole of one wall. Tiggy draws back the curtains and looks around the room. It is here, before a blazing fire, that she and Julia spent the evening – just as she had imagined on the journey – talking over the events of the day. The hearth, with its stack of logs at either side, is cold now, the pale ash feathered and heaped around half-blackened logs, but Tiggy guesses that a core of heat remains deep at the heart of it. She crouches beside the hearth, pulling some of the half-burned logs together and, picking up the bellows, blows gently into the ash. It whirls and floats, rather like the snow last evening, but soon a spark blossoms on a charcoal flake, grows and flowers into flame that catches at the fragments of charred wood and soon is burning steadily. Tiggy piles on more wood, sets the guard in place and goes into the kitchen.

Bella, Julia's beautiful brown field spaniel, comes to greet her whilst the Turk follows the twins into the back porch and whines impatiently as they wrestle with bolts and locks. Tiggy goes to help them, opening the door on an unfamiliar world into which both dogs plunge regardless. The three of them stand together, silenced by the glory of the translucent blue-green sky, with its streaming rosy clouds, and by the million tiny points of brilliant light reflecting back from the snow-covered moor. Just briefly Tiggy glimpses once more the ineffable delight she'd experienced earlier; then an icy breeze snakes down from the stony heights of Rough Tor and curls around their ankles, so that the twins shiver and huddle into their dressing gowns.

Tiggy hurries them back into the warm kitchen and gives them mugs of milk. She riddles the Rayburn, fills it with coke and puts the kettle to boil, and by the time Julia appears, with Charlie astride her hip, coffee is ready. He stares in amazement at Tiggy and is seized by a sudden shyness, burying his head in Julia's neck whilst peeping coyly with one eye at Tiggy, though nobody is really convinced by his performance.

'You remember your godmother perfectly well,' Julia says firmly, putting him into his high chair and ignoring his tendency to cling. 'Say hello to Tiggy while I get your milk.'

The twins begin to chant, 'Hello, Tiggy,' encouragingly in unison, giggling wildly, and Julia gives Charlie his bottle, seizes her mug and pours some coffee. The dogs come bursting in, their coats caked with snow, and she picks up an old towel and, going down on her knees, begins to rub them dry, laughing at their antics, her thick fair hair falling over her face.

Tiggy, looking at her with huge affection, is surprised by an unexpectedly painful stab of envy. How wonderful to be Julia: pretty, beloved and secure, with three beautiful children and this delightful old house. Suddenly Tiggy sees with a bleak clarity the difference between them: Julia, wise and beautiful, giving generously to her foolish friend. Tiggy feels humiliated and very much alone. Dismayed by this unfamiliar emotion, she speaks quickly in an effort to dispel it.

'This is an amazing house. What luck that Pete's uncle and aunt have decided to move out.'

'I can't get over it.' Julia finishes a game of tug of war with the Turk, hangs the towel in the back porch and comes back to the table. 'It simply got a bit too much for them to manage though they hated leaving it, Uncle Archie especially. I think Aunt Em is very happy to be in a small cosier house. The point is that Pete and his brother were going to inherit it anyway, so Uncle Archie decided it might as well be now. Luckily, Robert has no desire to live in the middle of Bodmin Moor so we raised a mortgage and bought him out. Pete and I love its irregularity. It was three cottages, as far as we can tell, but there have been lots of changes over the years though it's easy to see the original structure when you know what you're looking for.'

As she talks, Tiggy remains aware of her own isolation: it

separates her from the chattering twins, from Charlie, drinking his milk with an eye fixed unwaveringly on her face, from Julia herself, who is now describing how the cottages had been converted into one big house. She feels quite separate, as if this simple drama of family life, instead of including and comforting her, is serving merely to point up her own aloneness.

Andy looks up at her and smiles his sweet serious smile. 'Mummy says we can go for a ride in your van,' he says rather shyly. 'She says it has a little cooker and we can make our own lunch.'

His small face, expectant yet hesitant, is so rosy, so perfect, that she wants to cover it with kisses.

'Of course we shall go,' Tiggy says at once. 'Though not until the snow has melted. We shall go to the beach and have cheese on toast for lunch. Do you like that? And we shall make tea. Will Charlie like it, d'you think?'

Andy and Liv stare anxiously across the table at Charlie. He's just put down his empty bottle with a great gasp of repletion and is now waving at Tiggy – a rather Episcopalian gesture that involves the use of his whole arm – whilst beaming benevolently upon her, and Tiggy smiles back at him, oddly touched and feeling as if indeed she has been in some way blessed. Her pain recedes a little: optimism regains its tenuous hold.

Julia wipes Charlie's milky chin and drops a kiss on his head.

'Charlie will love it,' she says firmly. 'We all shall. But today we shall have to make do with building a snowman. Go and get dressed and then we'll have some breakfast.'

The twins slide off their chairs and run shrieking up the stairs. Julia begins to collect the mugs and, as she piles them on to the draining board, Tiggy gets up and slips a hand into the crook of her friend's arm.

'Thanks, Julia,' she says.

Julia responds to the gesture by pressing her elbow against her side. 'It's going to be such fun,' she says.

It is more than a week before the snow clears sufficiently for Julia to be confident about Tiggy driving the camper through the narrow twisting lanes that lead down to the sea.

'The main roads will be clear,' she says, 'but I wouldn't want to chance some of the lanes,' and Tiggy, remembering how the van had skidded and slid, is quite happy to agree. Very little damage has been done on inspection: a bit of a dent, some scraping of paint, but nothing really to worry about.

'Tom drove it very hard,' Tiggy tells Julia, 'and he'd have thought it all rather fun. His old cousin, the one who brought him up, came and took everything away except the van. Tom and I bought it between us and shared the costs so he said I could keep it.'

It is cold; very cold. Julia blesses Pete for his foresight in stocking up with coke for the Rayburn and logs for the fire, though she longs for central heating in the bedrooms. The twins undress each evening in front of the log fire in the sitting-room and are hurried up the stairs to cuddle under their quilts and extra blankets with hot-water bottles. Charlie is allowed the one small electric radiator. Neither Bella nor the Turk is discouraged from curling up with Julia and Tiggy on the ends of their beds.

'If it goes on like this,' says Julia, 'I shall get another dog. Of course Aunt Em and Uncle Archie are simply Spartans so I'd never dare complain to them about the cold.'

Tiggy takes to herself the task of dog-walking. She studies Julia's Ordnance Survey maps, as Tom had taught her, and each day she goes a little further into the wild country that lies at the door. The snow isn't deep; the wind scrapes unceasingly across the grasslands and over the granite tors, sweeping the powdery snow into gullies and valleys, leaving on these higher slopes a thin icy covering that creaks and cracks beneath her boots. From her high vantage point she can pick out greyish, sheep-shaped objects straying about below her in the shelter of the hills, and all the while the chilly fingers of the wind tweak at her cheeks and pick and pluck at the stones. She discovers tiny pools of water, each with its crumpled, puckered surface, instantly frozen into pleats and folds in the very moment that the wind's cold breath had touched it, and once, standing on Alex Tor, she hears the drumming of small hard hoofs and suddenly a group of skewbald ponies appears, skittering amongst the rocks with the dogs panting behind them.

The landscape dips and drops away to the pyramids of St Austell's clay works to the south and culminates in the sea that rims the world with silvery gold away to the north; the sheer immensity and the sense of infinity it implies brings Tiggy comfort. Here, it seems, Tom walks beside her; here she is able to commune wordlessly, to share with him, and there is no misery but instead the deep-down instinct that, after all, they can never be separated.

It is in the small minutiae of the day to day that she continues to feel the agony of loss: making coffee, baking scones, holding Charlie's warm, wriggling foot as she inserts it into a sock, feeding the dogs. Later, alone with her own baby, these little humdrum tasks without Tom to share in them would be empty; simply jobs to get her through the day. Yet when these disabling thoughts threaten her she strives to remember the way she feels out on the hills and deliberately directs her mind towards the baby she carries: Tom's baby is her reason for hope. Meanwhile the twins and Charlie keep her occupied by day, and each evening she and Julia sit by the fire watching television or talking; planning for the warm spring days and all that they will do together.

Yet, despite the brilliance of the sun that blazes each day from a clear blue sky, the temperature continues to stay below freezing. The tiny garments pegged out on the line by an optimistic Julia ('Surely it must be warmer today!') slowly stiffen like the cardboard clothes for Liv's cut-out dollies and are brought inside to be thawed out on the wooden rack above the Rayburn.

Then, one afternoon, the wind shifts; it veers to the west where ramparts of soft, grey cloud bank and tower along the horizon. The thaw is swift, icicles dripping, pools defrosting, whilst water runs and flows over the surface of the moor, pouring into the deep lanes and swelling the streams. Freed from its icy restraint, the land begins to show tentative signs of the cold sweet spring.

PART ONE

CHAPTER ONE

April 2004

The cold sweet spring: ivy leaves shivering on the trunk of an old tree, and the sticky black buds of the ash outlined starkly against a pale, dazzling sky. On the high moor, half hidden amongst the bleached grass where larks nest, tiny pools brimmed with water – blue eyes winking each time a cloud crossed the sun. Deep down in the lanes, sheltered and secret, primroses and celandines glimmered amongst the roots of thorn and oak in the steep stony hedgerows.

In the car, travelling between Port Isaac and Blisland, Liv drove slowly, revelling in the glory of it all. This sparkling day, coming after weeks of rain and cold winds, was a gift that she accepted gratefully. She sang beneath her breath, window down, braking sharply as a little party of sheep stampeded and panicked ahead, imprisoned in the high-banked lane. Lambs at heel squeaked little plaints of fright whilst the old ewes trampled against a field gate, forcing their woolly skulls against the unyielding bars.

Liv skidded past in a wide arc and, peering in the mirror, saw them scrambling up the muddy bank and back into the field, barging their way between the strands of broken wire. She couldn't blame them for seeking freedom; it was that kind of day.

'Just dashing over to see Aunt Em,' she'd said to Chris, shutting down the computer, pushing back her chair. 'Shan't be long.'

He'd grinned at her across the desk. 'You've always been the same,' he'd said. 'I remember when we were at uni, the first ray of sunshine and you had to be out in it.'

She'd ignored the reference to their past – long past – intimacy. 'Why do you think I said I'd help you and Val out?' she'd retorted. 'My sunshine fix was part of the package. Anyway, there's nothing for me to do at the moment. Aren't you feeling good? You should be. We've weathered our first bank holiday and everyone's happy. See you later.'

She hadn't waited for his reply; it was so necessary for her to be outside, with the chill April wind sliding over her skin and the warmth of the hot sun on her face. She'd hurried into her annexe to pick up her jacket and the bag of cakes for Aunt Em, and then into her little car and away on the road to St Teath. At once her spirits soared; passing through a landscape she'd known for thirty-two years she was so happy she felt frightened.

Testing herself, she thought about Chris. How much of her happiness was because she was working with him, living in the annexe next door to him and Val, seeing him each day?

'Are you sure it will work, darling?' her mother had asked anxiously. 'I know that you and Val are friends too, but you and Chris were so close when you were at Durham. There was a time when we really thought you would make a go of it together.'

'Honestly, Mum,' she'd answered impatiently, 'it's no big deal. We're all good mates, that's all there is to it. It's ten years since Chris and I were at uni together. He and Val have had enough of London and they want to sell up and move to the country. They've seen this place at Port Isaac and want to have a go at holiday letting. I can help them.'

And she had: making ready for letting the three little modernized barns that were grouped round the old farmyard, and planning and stocking up the little shop and restaurant complex which, in its prime position on the edge of Port Isaac, was bound to bring in visitors. Penharrow, the original house now occupied by Val and Chris, had a tiny apartment for Liv.

'Stop fussing,' she'd told her mother, 'and tell Dad too. I always wanted to do something like this, only it would have been even better if it had been my own project rather than Val and Chris's. It's a terrific challenge and I'm loving every minute of it. I know Dad thinks I should be a lawyer or a doctor or something he can brag about, but I always wanted to stay here, in Cornwall, just like Charlie always wanted to work with horses on Uncle Robert's farm in Hampshire and Zack wanted to be in the navy. Out of us all, only Andy is a city person and Dad worries about him too.'

'He wants you all to be happy and secure. That's reasonable, isn't it? And he's not really fussing. It's just that he doesn't want you to be living at Penharrow with Chris and Val for the rest of your life.' Her mother had hesitated. 'It can be dangerous,' she'd said at last, 'when two people have had a very close relationship.'

Now, driving to Blisland, Liv remembered her mother's expression; as if she were remembering something particular – and painful.

'But I'm not in love with Chris any more,' she argued to herself. 'It doesn't apply.' Yet she felt uncomfortable, knowing deep down that there was a tiny remnant of real affection, and knowing that Chris felt it too. Part of her happiness was due to the knowledge that she would see him later; sitting together at the big refectory table with glasses of wine, talking over the day. Val would be there, of course, but it *was* fun, something extra, that sense of past intimacy.

The fresh sweet air was intoxicating and she took one hand off the wheel to lift the thick fair hair from her neck so as to feel the cool breeze flow like water on her skin. She shivered, remembering how, a few nights back, Chris's hand had rested lightly there on the back of her neck: a casual gesture made as he'd passed behind her chair to pour some wine, whilst at the same time addressing a remark to Val as she'd bent, flush-faced, at the open oven door. Before Val had straightened up he'd already moved on, filling his own glass now with the bottle he'd held in his other hand, and she, Liv, had sat for one heart-stopping moment as if immobilized by his touch. Something had happened then, for her at least, as if he'd shown that they weren't just good friends but that something more still existed between them. He'd made no other sign, no indication that anything had changed, and later she'd told herself that she was attaching far too much importance to what had, after all, been nothing more than a friendly gesture as he'd leaned to fill her glass.

But why, she asked herself, had it excited her, filling her with a new kind of mad exultation? Because it reminded her of other more intimate caresses?

'It can be dangerous,' her mother had warned.

Liv shook her head in refutation: she would never do anything to hurt Val.

She drove for a while, thinking about Val. If she were to be absolutely honest, Val wasn't exactly doing herself any favours just at the moment. The strain of having Penharrow ready for

Easter had taken its toll on her patience: she'd panicked at the least thing, snapped at everybody and developed a series of bad headaches. It was to protect Val from nervous strain, Liv reminded herself, that she and Chris had spent even more time together, working every spare minute – and relaxing together too, while poor old Val lay on her bed in a darkened room knocked out by painkillers.

Liv experienced anxiety, guilt and defiance all in one burst. Pee po piddle bum. She remembered the silly nursery jingle that she and Andy still chanted in moments of frustration, and grinned to herself. She was imagining things, letting the stress of the last week addle her brain. She turned down the lane into Blisland, driving slowly round the village green where daffodils blossomed beneath the trees, and parked outside Aunt Em's small pretty house. Picking up her bag and the cakes, she got out, locked the car and began to climb the steps up to the garden.

Since Liv's telephone call ('It's such a fantastic day, Aunt Em. Can I come and have coffee later on? I'll bring the cakes'), Em had been enjoying the especial pleasure that an unexpected treat bestows on the recipient. She was touched that Liv should want to spend such a morning with her when she might have gone shopping to Wadebridge or Truro, or simply spent it with friends of her own age. In the early months of widowhood after Archie's death she'd imagined such visits to be the result of kindness, even pity, though she'd been grateful nevertheless. Now, ten years on, she was able to accept that the young came to see her because they actually wanted to; she'd ceased to ask why. She'd quickly realized that such questions merely demanded a constant reassurance from family and friends, which was tiresome for them: much better to accept without question and simply enjoy it.

How difficult it had been to make that act of acceptance: what a shock to realize that *taking* required a particular kind of generosity on her part. It was so much more satisfactory to be the bestower of gifts, the good fairy dispensing kindness, than to be the one who was obliged to be grateful. Gradually it occurred to her that it was her own perception of herself that influenced other people: she need not enter into a mindset that implied that because she was old and alone she was no longer worthy of other people's time or friendship. She *was* still worthy of love: gratitude was not needed here; with her work in her garden and greenhouse and in her little studio she was always busy.

She still missed Archie quite dreadfully but she'd learned to manage the loneliness: twenty years as a naval wife had given her plenty of practice. Em smiled reminiscently, remembering how she'd clung to Archie in the early years of marriage, almost smothering him with thankfulness for loving her. Her own lonely, loveless childhood hadn't prepared her for Archie's brand of generous affection. Even after their relationship had settled into the normal pattern of a naval marriage – periods of separation punctuated by leaves and the occasional shore job – the joy of loving and receiving love had been tinged with anxiety. She'd settled into the routine but, despite her natural self-reliance that carried her through the long periods of loneliness, she'd still looked to Archie to fill that aching need for family, especially when it became agonizingly clear that they would have no children of their own. She'd waited eagerly for his retirement, when they would spend time together; the long, lonely hours would be filled with companionship, that tiny aching need would be satisfied and she'd be content at last.

She'd learned, however, that contentment was not some-thing that could be supplied by other people: it couldn't be grappled with and twisted to her need. On the contrary; she'd realized that it was achieved only by letting go; by accepting that she could not control Archie or force him into the pattern she wanted him to fit.

It was when she and Archie had moved from Trescairn to the cottage that she'd taken up a long-abandoned hobby. She'd unearthed her painting equipment, made a space for herself in the small spare bedroom and, once she'd proved to herself that she was still able to produce an adequate watercolour, she'd joined the local art class. One of the members was a retired art master from Truro who was glad to share his experience with the group, and Em enjoyed these sessions and the painting expeditions to Padstow to sketch the fishing boats in the harbour or to the Jubilee Rock to attempt to capture the golden flowering furze. She'd bought a small rucksack to hold her paintbox and a few brushes, along with a bottle of water to clean them, and a pad of watercolour paper. On such mornings, she'd make sandwiches and a Thermos of tea, pack a waterproof jacket and set off for a happy day sketching and painting. Sometimes the group would pay for a professional artist to give them an inspiring demonstration and celebrate it with a small party to which they'd all contribute some delicious teatime treat and a little gift for a lucky dip. It was fun, and Em liked her fellow artists; it was her own special thing and Archie encouraged her in it.

He'd been impressed by her work and had persuaded her to submit a painting for auction at a fund-raising event for the RNLI. When it was knocked down at forty-five pounds Em was shocked into silence whilst Archie was openly jubilant.

'It's simply because it's for charity,' she'd said on the drive home from Padstow. 'Forty-five *pounds*. Madness!'

'Not a bit of it,' crowed Archie delightedly. 'You had those ponies off to a T. And the clouds massing just behind the Tor.

It was excellent. I wish we'd kept it. And to think I never knew you had all this talent.'

'Nonsense,' muttered Em.

A few days later she'd been approached by a local architect who asked her to design a Christmas card for his company.

'It's just because he's one of your cronies,' she'd said uncertainly to Archie. 'I haven't got the nerve to design a Christmas card.'

'It's nothing to do with me,' Archie had replied. 'He loved your painting and he thinks you've got talent. Have a crack at it.'

Nervously she'd made a sketch of Delford Bridge under snow, with a dipper perched on a boulder mid-stream, and washed it with soft colours of blue and grey. It was delicate, charming, and though she was privately pleased with it she was sick with anxiety lest it should be rejected. The architect had loved it, insisting on paying her for the original, which he'd had framed and hung in his office. She had felt a little thrill of pride; her small skill was raising her self-esteem and confirming her determination to work towards allowing Archie his freedom for charity work or to go sailing without any resentment on her part.

How exhilarating it had been to discover that by giving Archie freedom from what might have been a crushing affection she'd become the recipient of an even deeper love. Over the years, as her confidence had grown, so a new measure of happiness had developed between them. It had come as a shock, after his death, to realize that she must now apply all that she'd learned to the new painful, lonely business of being a widow; accepting kindness and love without being choked by the insidious creeping tentacles of self-pity.

Em went out through the garden room into the courtyard to see if it might be warm enough to have coffee in the garden

– she knew how much Liv loved the sunshine – and decided that it would be. The little south-facing court, ringed by fields and sheltered from the chill breeze, was bright with tubs of daffodils and sweet-scented narcissi and the pretty flowers of the 'Lady Clare' camellia blooming on the tree by the wall.

'Camellia,' Archie had always cried impatiently. 'It's pronounced camellia. Not cameellia! How do you pronounce b e l l? Bell. How do you pronounce m e l l? Mell. Right, so it's camellia.'

The whole family, impressed by his passion, had abided by his dictum.

Em set out the French wrought-iron table and chairs, heard the car approaching and went swiftly inside and through the house to meet Liv. Standing at the top of the flight of steep stone steps, watching her getting out of the car, Em's heart gave a little painful tick: how like her mother, the young Julia, this beloved child was. How often Julia had come smiling up these steps, sometimes with Andy and Liv running ahead and Charlie astride her hip, or carrying some little offering as Liv did today.

'Hi, Aunt Em.' Holding the cakes aside, Liv leaned to kiss the older woman. 'What a magic day. Can we be outside?'

'We can indeed, my darling. Go on through. I'll switch the coffee on and be right with you.'

As she decanted the cakes on to a plate, Em watched Liv as she stood for a moment in the sunny courtyard. Slender and supple, she tipped her face towards the sun, rising on her toes, stretching out her arms: the gesture reminded Em of some ancient ritual. Picking up the plate, she went out to her.

'So how is life at Penharrow this morning? Clearly not *too* busy.'

Liv sat down. 'I shouldn't really be here,' she admitted. 'But it was such a fantastic day I simply couldn't resist. I can always work on later if I need to.'

Em nodded: she understood. From childhood onwards, the twins, Andy and Liv, had been subject to these mood swings; a sudden need to be outside in the sun and wind, free from constriction, would seize them. Frustrated by routine, easily bored, they'd conformed, up to a point, but still the wild adventuring spirit would come upon them, driving them on to new places or new jobs. Em could see that helping to get Penharrow up and running was exactly the kind of project that appealed to Liv: a new challenge, new ideas, new people to meet. All her energy was focused on it just as, at present, Andy's was concentrated on his rapidly expanding Internet company. However, Em knew how much Julia and Pete worried about the twins so she was always alert to any way in which she could encourage Liv and Andy towards the more conventional path whilst respecting their individualism and nurturing the particular essence of their creative spirits.

'Have you thought what you might do after Penharrow?' she asked. 'You've always given the impression that it's a short-term project.'

'Well, it is.' Liv settled comfortably, face to the sun, eyes closed. 'I think they'll need me for a bit longer but, to be honest, I'm a kind of comfort zone they're not quite ready to move out from, if you see what I mean. The tourist industry is a totally new way of life for them and, after all, they've only been at it for a few months. I thought that I might look for something else after the summer season but I don't know where yet. Something will turn up, I expect.'

Em looked at her with amusement. This was so typical of Liv – and the odd thing was that something generally did turn up. Liv had a wide-flung web of friends owning hotels, bars, leisure centres across the West Country, one of whom always needed someone to help out at short notice, and Liv was not afraid of hard work so long as she could surf and sail and swim.

'Did you watch *Antiques Roadshow* last Sunday?' Liv was asking. 'No? I didn't see it either but I had an email from Andy about it. Someone had brought along a little bronze and one of the experts was talking about its similarity to *The Child Merlin* that's in some German museum. Apparently there's some question whether the *Merlin* is a fake and Andy was asking if we still had our little statue. Do you remember the little Merlin, Aunt Em?'

Em drank some coffee and thought about it. 'Yes, I do. Though I haven't seen him for years.'

'We loved him when we were little.' Liv smiled, remembering. 'He was rather sweet with the falcon on his wrist. It wasn't ours though, was it? It was Tiggy's. She brought it with her when she came to stay that summer. Can you remember Tiggy? Sometimes I think I can and then I think it's more what we were told about her than actually remembering.'

'Of course I remember Tiggy. She was such a romantic figure, arriving in a snowstorm after that long journey from the Welsh Marches with her little dog.'

'I remember the camper van,' said Liv. 'Gosh, we loved that van. I must ask Mum about the little Merlin when she gets back. She and Dad have gone to Tavistock to help Caroline with the unpacking. Anyway, I doubt it's very important. There's bound to be hundreds of copies of it.' She stretched and sighed. 'I suppose I'd better make a move or Val will be getting twitchy.'

'I should think she ought to be used to you by now,' suggested Em. 'You and Andy were never ones to be ruled by the clock.'

Liv chuckled. 'I know we're hopeless but we do our best work at odd times. Val's the complete opposite: everything by the clock. Poor old Chris has to hold the balance between us.

Thanks for the coffee. And don't forget I need some new cards for the shop. Have you thought about it? I know we can reproduce the old favourites but I hoped you might be inspired to paint something new.'

'I'll think about it,' promised Em.

CHAPTER TWO

2004

At Penharrow, Val and Chris were having another row.

'She must see that it's just not on to dash off whenever she feels like it.' Val's face was pinched with frustration. She thrust her short dark hair away from her face with thin fingers. 'The trouble with Liv is that she's never grown up. She sees herself as a free spirit who isn't subject to the ordinary rules that other people live by. And you encourage her.'

Chris sat at the table, his eyes on his empty plate, gently pushing the fork handle to and fro. He felt irritated: after all, he could have hardly ordered Liv to stay and work.

'She does more than her fair share,' he said coolly. 'We'd never have got Penharrow up and running without her and, just occasionally, she needs to let off steam. She'll probably work until late this evening.'

'You always stand up for her.'

'Oh, for God's sake,' he said impatiently, 'I'm simply saying that this isn't some nine-to-five office job. It's a twenty-four seven project—'

'You're telling me. And if I'd realized what a strain it was I'd never have let you talk me into it.'

'Talk you into it? Come off it!' He shoved the plate to one side. 'You were just as keen as I was. It was you who wanted to live the good life, if you remember.' A little pause. 'And it was you who'd lost your job.'

She stared at him angrily, arms clenched and folded tightly beneath her breast. 'Thanks,' she said. 'Thanks for that.'

He made a gesture of conciliation. 'I'm sorry. But—'

'Always a "but". Never just "sorry".'

Chris stood up quickly, snatched up his plate, but then stood for a moment, considering.

'We asked Liv to help us,' he said at last. 'We both wanted to try this holiday letting business and Liv was here, on the spot, knew the area and the locals. All of that. She's had a great deal of experience in getting new projects off the ground. Don't forget she's got a very good reputation for it and we were very lucky she agreed to help us. She found Debbie and Myra for us, talked to the local craftspeople about stuff for the shop, designed the layout for the café. She takes a very small wage because she knows we need time to build things up, and she grafts damned hard and doesn't mind what she does. Every now and then she freaks out and dashes off to go surfing or to the pub with her mates. She told us she would and we accepted it because we both know how Liv operates. She worked her way round Australia; she temps; does odd things because she doesn't like to be tied down. But you know as well as I do that she is putting in much more than she's taking out and neither of us is in a position to tell her what to do. It's not that kind of set-up. We'd have looked a right pair of fools without her, I can tell you that much.'

'And meanwhile who's going to help Debbie this afternoon now that Myra's got some kind of drama at home?'

'I will,' he said briefly. 'It's fine. I can manage.'

Val was silent, fingers balled into fists, out of her depth for the first time in her well-ordered life. Chris watched her, his irritation dissolving into compassion.

'Val's finding it hard,' Liv had said to him privately. 'She always needs to be in control and it scares her when she isn't. She's too high-handed with Myra and Debs because she's frightened that they'll take advantage but she'll have to learn to trust them a bit more. Meanwhile she needs lots of hugs.'

Chris thought: The trouble is I don't feel like hugging her at the moment. Right now I don't even like her very much.

The thought shocked him into action. He went round the table and put an arm round Val's stiff, unyielding shoulders.

'Come on, love,' he said. 'Let's not make a drama out of a crisis. Or is it the other way round?'

She wouldn't look at him or acknowledge his feeble joke, but he sensed a wavering and he bent and touched his lips lightly to her temple.

'I'm going over to help Debbie out,' he said. 'I enjoy it actually, chatting to the visitors. What do the locals call them? Emmets? It's good fun. Part of why we're doing this. Don't lose sight of that, Val.'

'I'm so tired,' she said defensively, 'and these headaches are wearing me down.'

'It's just the stress of getting everything in full working order in time for Easter,' he told her. 'And we've done it. The units are booked up way ahead and the café is picking up lots of passing trade. I know we can't sit back and put our feet up but we can try to enjoy parts of it.'

'I'm not so good at fooling about with the staff as you are.'

Val moved slightly away from him. She picked up his plate and began to load the dishwasher.

He watched her dispassionately: she'd lost weight and this new thin tautness didn't suit her, made her face look too sharp, rodent-like. And for heaven's sake, did she have to call Debs and Myra 'the staff'?

'Well, it's a good job that one of us is,' he said lightly. 'Helps to get the work done. See you later.'

He went out, crossing the yard to the café, reacting with pleasure to the warmth of the sunshine and the crying of the gulls. The small kitchen was clean and smelled delicious. Myra and Debbie were conferring together and looked up anxiously at him as he came in.

'I'm ever so sorry,' Myra said at once. 'It's just the school's phoned. Gary's been sick and they want me to collect him. I've been trying to get hold of Mum but she's not answering.'

'It's fine,' Chris said reassuringly. 'Not a problem, Myra. You dash off and I'll give Debbie a hand. We can manage, can't we, Debs?'

'Course we can.' Debbie beamed at him. 'I was just telling her to get off.'

Chris went through into the high-raftered room and looked around. Four of the six tables were occupied and two women were lingering at the far end amongst the shelves and tables that held hand-painted cards, delightful pieces of pottery, guidebooks and a display of silk scarves. Everything was made locally; all the food products locally sourced. Chris felt a great surge of pride and smiled at a woman who was now approaching to pay her bill.

'That was scrumptious cake,' she said appreciatively, taking out her purse.

'Glad you enjoyed it,' he said, 'and here's the cook,' as Debbie came out of the kitchen.

'How do you manage to stay so slim with all this temptation about?' asked the woman saucily, looking him up and down as he rang up the till. She winked at Debbie. 'I expect you keep him busy.'

'Oh, I do,' agreed Debbie promptly. 'Night and day. Never let up for a minute.'

They all laughed, enjoying the simple joke and the sunny day. Through the window Chris saw Val crossing the yard. Head bent, lips pursed, she seemed unaware of the sunshine; preoccupied with anxiety and weighed down by care. Another woman approached the counter; she carried a pretty hand-painted silk scarf, two cards with scenes of Port Isaac and a pottery candle-holder. He totted up her bill whilst an elderly couple came in and ordered two cream teas from Debbie: more jokes, more friendly chatter. When he looked again Val had disappeared.

Val checked out the laundry-room, wiped down the machines and swept the floor. It was important that it should be spotless at all times; everything must be tidy. Debbie or Myra were supposed to give it the once-over each evening after the shop and café had been cleaned but she wondered if they always remembered it. Liv usually gave them a hand; she often heard them laughing and exchanging backchat; Liv never minded helping out with the most menial tasks.

As Val came out into the yard she saw Liv climbing out of her car, bag over her shoulder, holding a spray of flowers. It occurred to Val that Liv was so often carrying something – a bag of cakes, flowers, a bottle of wine – something received or to be given.

Watching her waving a greeting, her face flushed by the sun, Val resentfully wondered why Liv should be the re-cipient of so much generosity. There was a lightness about her; an air of spontaneity to which people responded with delight.

'It's all right for Liv,' she'd said crossly to Chris. 'She has no responsibilities. No wonder she does as she likes.'

'It's not that,' he'd answered – he always defended Liv. 'It's just that Liv, unlike the rest of us, doesn't hanker after things. She doesn't want to possess and she doesn't need to own or control. She likes to sit light to the world.'

'It's a good job that we don't all think like that,' she'd answered sharply.

Chris had shrugged, pulled his mouth down at the corners. 'Oh, I don't know. Perhaps we'd be better off if we did. It's not as if she doesn't pay her way. She's always had some kind of job. It's just that she doesn't set the same store that most of us do by possessions. And she doesn't get upset if other people have other views about life that are different from her own. She believes in live and let live.' He'd laughed suddenly. 'That's why her name suits her so well.'

Val hadn't responded to his joke; she'd been silent, thinking it over. She'd suddenly realized that Liv's rejections of her, Val's, values irritated her. Chris was right: Liv didn't crave a house of her own or a new car or the latest fashions. She seemed to be too busy simply enjoying life.

'I don't know why you split up if you think she's so wonderful,' she'd said sulkily.

'Oh, give it a rest,' he'd replied wearily.

Now, raising a hand in response to Liv's wave, Val wondered what it was about her that she liked so much. However much Liv irritated her, Val still continued to need her friendship. To be fair, it was only in the last few weeks – since she'd been so stressed out – that this irritation with Liv had arisen. To begin with, making plans for Penharrow, moving down to Cornwall, had all been fun and Liv had been such a strength: she still was, of course. Perhaps she, Val, should be anxious that Chris might feel attracted to Liv again but she never seriously considered it: ten years was a long time and Liv and Chris never behaved other than as good friends. It was only occasionally that she felt a tiny dart of jealousy. Like now, for instance, when she felt exhausted and weepy and irrational – but she mustered a smile as Liv advanced towards her, though reproving words were forming in her mind.

'Aren't they pretty?' Liv proffered the flowers before Val could speak. 'Camellias from Aunt Em's garden.'

Even as she nodded, acknowledging the prettiness of the spray, Val felt a spasm of irritation at Liv's affected pronunciation of their name.

'I thought they were called ca*mee*llias,' she said.

'Not if you'd known Uncle Archie,' chuckled Liv. 'Aunt Em sent them with her love and said, "Come to tea sometime when you're not too busy."'

She whirled away, leaving Val holding the flowers and wondering if she should say that she didn't have the time to go off for tea just because she felt like it; but Liv had already gone into the shop and wouldn't have heard her.

Having seen the exchange, Chris tensed slightly as Liv came in. He wondered if Val had been tactless – or even just plain rude. Liv gave no sign of any altercation; she smiled at Debbie and raised her eyebrows at Chris.

'Learning to cook?' she asked. 'Aunt Em loved the cakes, Debs. She says she'll be over to see you soon.'

Debbie looked pleased. 'I like your Aunt Em,' she said. 'We sold one of her paintings this morning. Did Val tell you? Gary's ill and Myra's had to go and fetch him from school. Chris is helping out.'

'Shit!' said Liv. 'Poor Myra. Never mind. I'll carry on here, Chris, if you want to get on.'

'I'm rather enjoying it,' said Chris. He was relaxed again: relieved that Val hadn't challenged Liv and made oddly happy by her presence, which both comforted and energized him. He realized with a shock that he wouldn't want to be tackling this project without her; that she was necessary to him. 'I like meeting the punters,' he said. 'But I ought to be in the office, I suppose. End-of-month accounts and the VAT return.' He made a face. 'It's more fun in here.'

'Tough,' said Liv firmly. 'You know that Marx thing? To each according to his need. From each according to his ability. You do the accounts because of your ability and Debs and I eat cake and chat because of our needs.'

'What about my needs?' he demanded indignantly.

Debbie laughed. 'He's already had some cake,' she told Liv. 'And as for chat,' she rolled her eyes expressively, 'you should hear him with some of the customers, especially a couple of girls who were in just now.'

'Too much information,' said Liv severely. 'Go on, Chris. Back to the treadmill.'

He shook his head mock-complainingly and went away.

'He's nice, isn't he?' said Debbie, watching him cross the yard. 'Great legs. It's a pity Val doesn't lighten up a bit. She makes real hard work of it.'

'It's early days,' said Liv placatingly. 'Bit scary for her till it's all up and running properly. She'll be fine when she sees it's going to be OK.'

CHAPTER THREE

2004

After Liv had gone, Em pottered for a while in her greenhouse; tweaking up some weeds, pinching off unwanted leaders, thinning out a tray of seedlings. She relaxed in the humid warmth, liking the sensation of the crumbly earth between her fingers, and snuffing up the sharp, green, vegetal smell. All the while she was thinking about Liv. There had been a luminosity about her, as if she'd been lightly dusted with a glittering of happiness. Liv was usually good company; quick with a jokey response, intuitive, ready with some amusing little anecdote about her life. Yet this morning there had been an extra quality that had made the simple act of drinking coffee and eating cake a celebration.

The obvious deduction was that Liv was in love. Pleased with this idea, Em began to invent the scenario, allowing her romantic imagination free rein; she pictured a handsome fellow coming into the café for coffee, chatting with Liv, coming back the next day. He might invite her to go for a walk on the

51

cliffs, or to the pub for a drink, or to Rick Stein's. Perhaps he'd be a bit older than Liv, late thirties, mature but not stuffy. He'd been in a long relationship (no children), which had now fallen apart – not his fault, of course – and he was looking for a career change. Em fretted over this point for a while: he mustn't be unstable nor yet a stick-in-the-mud, and she couldn't quite decide what career he might pursue in Cornwall. Liv didn't want to leave Cornwall. Em pictured the handsome fellow: dark-haired, not over tall, with a nice twinkly sexy appeal.

Realizing that quite unwittingly she'd cast Chris in the role of this desirable man, Em put down her little watering pot and went into the courtyard, sitting down again at the table feeling rather dismayed. Of course, she'd always been far too romantic. Quite suddenly she remembered how she and Tiggy had once laughed together on this very subject. Tiggy had told her how she'd longed for a tough, strong-jawed Georgette Heyer-type male to save her from her loneliness, and Em had described how, through all those years of aching boredom caring for her elderly aunt, she'd daydreamed of the handsome war hero who would rescue her.

'It worked for you, Aunt Em,' Tiggy had said.

And so it had: on a fine winter afternoon Archie had turned up at one of those interminable bridge parties so beloved by her aunt and she, Em, had fallen in love with him and he with her. She and Julia often discussed the possibility of Liv meeting someone and falling in love.

'Of course, nobody will ever be good enough for Pete,' Julia had said. 'You know how he adores Liv. I worry about her working so closely with Chris again after all these years, Aunt Em. I know she says it's all over but there's something so dangerous about the whiff of nostalgia, isn't there? Chris represents Liv's youth. Oh, I know she's only thirty-two but, even so, there's something special about the late teens and early twenties. And then, if you've had a fling with someone and they come back into your life, you might wonder if things would have been better if you'd stuck with them. Can you really be entirely indifferent to someone you've been to bed with?'

Em hadn't answered; she had no experience to call upon. Neither of them had mentioned Angela Lisburne but Em knew that Julia had been thinking about her.

Now, despite the warmth of the late April sunshine, Em was aware of a tiny chill shivering her skin. It would be terrible if Liv were to undermine Chris and Val's relationship in the same way that Angela had once tried to destroy Julia's marriage. Em reviewed the morning's conversation, anxiously looking for tell-tale signs or explanations of Liv's condition. She'd talked easily about Chris and Val, as well as Debbie and Myra, but had there been anything particular that denoted a renewal of that past love? Em thought not, but her daydream had ceased to bring her pleasure; all she could think of was Angela's sly, secret smile, and Julia stumbling up the garden steps with tears on her cheeks, one cold February day nearly thirty years before.

'I think Pete's having an affair with Angela,' she'd said.

Sitting in the April sunshine Em was filled with a sense of frustration. The joy that Liv had brought trailing in her wake diminished a little: Liv and Andy, Julia and Pete, Charlie and Zack. They were all her dear children and she wanted them to be happy. She was reminded of how much Liv had looked like her mother; the young Julia, Zack astride her hip, the twins with Charlie between them, helping him up one step at a time. Now Charlie was married with two children of his own and Zack's wife, Caroline, was expecting a baby in the summer. Where had the years gone?

'Do you remember the way we were that long hot summer

of 'seventy-six, Aunt Em?' Julia had asked her not so long ago. 'How careless we were about our happiness! We took so much for granted. Oh, I know that there were all sorts of problems but when I look back it seems to have had a special magic that whole time Tiggy was with us. I remember her arriving in the snow and the twins building a snowman the next morning. And that glorious spring and all those jollies in the camper van. How the twins loved it. Do you remember that summer? It seemed to go on for ever. We didn't know how lucky we were. We didn't appreciate it.'

'I think Tiggy did,' she'd answered. 'She'd lost her lover and I think she'd learned exactly how ephemeral happiness is and treasured it accordingly. Whatever guilt you still feel, Julia, try to set it against the comfort and happiness you gave Tiggy. You provided her with a family and a home at a time when she had nothing. No wonder it was a special time for all of you.'

The breeze fell away and the sun was hot. Em closed her eyes, breathed in the heavenly scent of the narcissi. The warm sunshine and Liv's visit had given her new vitality and courage: the summer lay ahead and there was work to be done. To begin with she must give consideration to painting some new cards, perhaps even a bigger canvas.

Yet still she sat in the sunshine, thinking about that first meeting with Tiggy twenty-eight years before.

1976

'Damned cold out there,' Archie says at breakfast one chilly morning. 'Shouldn't be surprised if we had some snow. Isn't Julia's friend arriving today? Funny name, Tiggy.'

Buttering her toast, Em looks at him rather vaguely; she hasn't been concentrating. A few days earlier she had a rather startling idea and all through breakfast she's continued to brood on it; conning it over in her mind. Last week she received a letter from an old friend; no, not a letter but a notelet, that was the name for it. On the front is a pretty painting of a butterfly, a very accurate depiction of a marsh fritillary, and Em is beginning to wonder if she might be able to design a cover for a set of these little cards – perhaps several different covers – and offer them for the next RNLI fund-raising event. She's already decided that the first painting should be a montage of spring flowers: daffodils leaning almost protectively over the smaller blooms; violets and snowdrops and primroses, all set against a pale blue sky. Her thoughts speed forward: the cliffs in summer, cushioned with pink thrift, and the rich purplish colour of the heather . . .

'Snow,' repeats Archie loudly, as though Em has become suddenly deaf. 'I think snow's on the way.'

She nods intelligently, trying to look alert, but her reaction both startles and amuses her: she's had a horrid stab of anxiety that the prospect of snow might prevent him from going out. Her one ambition is to go up into her little room and get to work, and she knows from experience that it is much more difficult with Archie around. He tends to hover, offering coffee, or wondering how she is getting on with the work in progress. Em reaches for the honey.

'I doubt it will amount to much,' she says cheerfully. 'It's a glorious day. Wonderful to see the sunshine after all those endless weeks of rain.'

'Heard the early forecast,' he tells her triumphantly, 'and it's more than possible later on. Make a shopping list and I'll get a few extra supplies while I'm in Bodmin. Just in case.'

Em is almost shocked at the extent of her relief. 'Good idea,' she says warmly.

She pours more coffee thoughtfully, her mind straying back to her project, wondering if she will be able to strike a good deal with the printer in Bodmin. Archie has spoken again.

'Sorry, darling,' she apologizes. 'Just thinking about that shopping list.'

When Archie has gone she sits on for a little longer with her mug of coffee, still brooding. She is pretty certain that the printer in Bodmin will give her a good deal once he knows that the notelets are for charity, and if she is lucky she'll be able to sell the original paintings.

With excited anticipation Em climbs the stairs to her little studio, the small back bedroom that has become her own special place. As she opens the door the warm glow of the electric fire, which she has turned on earlier, welcomes her. It is a pity that the pretty little fireplace has been blocked up but it would be tiresome to carry wood or coal upstairs each time she wants to work. She turns off one bar of the fire and looks about her with satisfaction. The worn lovat-green carpet needs a rug or two so as to hide the worst of the rubbed areas but the rather arty effect of the paisley shawl draped over the wine-coloured velvet of the old wing chair is very pleasing. Sometimes she brings up her cup of favourite Darjeeling tea and sits here beside the fire, planning her next painting without interruption, and enjoying the atmosphere she's created. Her small mahogany bookcase holds some of the tools of her trade: reference books, sketch pads, photographs and camera. On the top shelf are her favourite photographs: she and Archie on their wedding day; the twins clutching her hands as she kneels between them on Polzeath beach, laughing at the camera with eyes screwed up against the sun and wind; a rather formal study of Julia and Pete, with Charlie in his christening gown. Beside them a potpourri of rose petals in a blue Wedgwood bowl gives off a faint, sweet-smelling scent.

The divan bed is pushed against the wall, covered with the

pale green and cream chintz that match the curtains, and piled with bedding and curtains from Trescairn, yet to be sorted. The basin to the right of the sash window is a bonus; water to hand saves journeys to and from the bathroom not only when she is painting but each time she needs to stretch her watercolour paper. She does this on the old blue Formica-topped table that they'd brought from Trescairn, soaking the paper, then placing it on her drawing board and securing the edges of the paper with wet strips of brown gummed paper so that once it is dry and taut it won't bubble or buckle when the colour wash is applied.

This morning her board is on the table ready for use, along with her brushes, looking like some kind of zany flower arrangement in their ancient chipped china vase. She's bought the best sable brushes: some rounds with good points, a few flats for all sorts of washes, and a mop that holds a lot of paint and is a favourite for painting skies. Very carefully she moves the table just a little so that it is at the most advantageous angle for the light coming in through the window. Earlier she's picked a tiny bunch of snowdrops and put them in a mint sauce jar so as to copy them. Looking at their delicate veined petals and drooping heads she wonders how they are able to survive the biting January winds. She assembles her other props: two Cornish honey jars filled with clean water and some photographs and sketches of spring flowers that, unlike the snowdrops, are not yet in bloom; a biscuit tin, with a picture of a mare and her foal on the lid, in which she keeps little tubes of watercolour paint; her white palette, and the little sponge, which, when dampened, she uses to lift colour out of a sky so as to give the effect of scudding clouds. Some tissues and an old tea towel for drying her brushes complete her equipment.

On the back of a pine chair – brought up from the kitchen

because it is just right for working – hangs one of Archie's old checked shirts, which Em now uses as a smock. As she pulls it on she is assailed by a pang of remorse for the relief she'd felt earlier when he'd said that he would be going to Bodmin; she hopes he is keeping warm, wonders briefly if he's remembered his gloves and then, putting everything else out of her mind, settles down to work.

She plans her palette: manganese blue with a touch of cobalt for the sky, very watered down; then the various shades of yellow for the daffodils and the primroses. She chooses cadmium yellow, Windsor lemon, yellow ochre and cadmium orange. Ultramarine and burnt umber mixed with cadmium yellow will make different shades of green, with sap green for the brighter leaves of the primroses. Last of all, she selects magenta to mix with ultramarine for the pretty violets.

Em squeezes some of the rich pigment from the little watercolour tubes into the wells of her palette. She mixes the palest blue, uses the lid of the biscuit tin to tilt her drawing board, and with her mop brush she begins to paint the background. The flowers are already lightly sketched in and she grades the sky carefully lest the paint should touch the heads of the flowers, creating green daffodils when she adds the yellow paint later on. She's decided that whilst the background dries she will paint a little card for Julia's birthday; perhaps a colourwash of the snowdrops against a wintry sky.

Em works happily, utterly absorbed, hardly aware of the dimming of the sun as the clouds bank up and drift from the north-east on a light chill wind. It is much later that she remembers that Tiggy is due at Trescairn, and nearly a week before the lanes are clear enough to be able to drive up to Trescairn to meet her.

*   *   *

The really strange thing Tiggy remembers about that first meeting is that she recognizes Aunt Em: not the woman who comes hurrying into the sitting-room, arms held wide to the children and a smiling welcome for Tiggy. No, not a physical recognition, Tiggy tells herself afterwards, but a gut-twisting shock that she is looking at somebody she knows deep down inside.

'You looked so surprised,' Julia tells her later, chuckling – and Tiggy grimaces guiltily.

'You might have warned me,' she says.

Aunt Em, wearing Levi jeans and a navy-blue Guernsey, doesn't look like anyone's aunt: very slender, very tall, with straight, fine ash-coloured hair, she has a bred-in-the-bone elegance and a charm that immediately captivates. The twins fall upon her with cries of joy whilst Charlie, corralled in his playpen, stamps round and round, clinging to the rail and roaring with frustration. Aunt Em kisses Andy and Liv, passes them a package each and goes to the playpen.

'May I?' she asks Julia – and then, lifting him out, she swings Charlie up and up, high, into the air while he chuckles with delight. She sets him down again gently, then quickly, before he can protest, produces a small soft toy: a black and white penguin whose beak and huge feet are the colour of egg yolks. He sits quite still, turning the toy in his hands, examining it closely.

'Crayons!' shriek the twins, wrapping paper all over the floor. 'Colouring books!' and they run into the kitchen and scramble up at the kitchen table with their presents.

Aunt Em gives Tiggy a little wink. 'That'll keep them quiet for a moment,' she says. 'Long enough for us to say hello, at least.' She holds out her hand. 'I'm Em and you're Tiggy. Or should we be very formal and call ourselves Emily and . . .' a little hesitation, 'Tegan, is it?'

'Tiggy will do just fine.' She takes Em's thin hand. 'Only my grandmother calls me Tegan these days.'

'That's rather a pity. It's an unusual name.'

'It translates as "beautiful" or "blessed". I prefer Tiggy.'

'And I prefer Em.' The older woman smiles but there is a more searching scrutiny hidden behind the smile, as if she is making some connection at a deeper level, and Tiggy's clasp involuntarily tightens before she releases Em's hand. 'And this is Archie.'

Archie is definitely uncle material and Tiggy greets him almost with relief. His thick silver hair brushes the low, heavily beamed ceiling, and he ducks his head automatically. He has a broad-shouldered, bear-like quality, exaggerated by his Norwegian jersey and baggy cords, and Tiggy is seized by an odd desire to throw herself and all her problems and fears into his arms. He looks so capable, so calm – rather like a much older Tom, she suddenly realizes.

His greeting is friendly, if slightly preoccupied, and, as soon as he relinquishes her hand, he returns to his conversation with Julia, which has to do with some damp on the ceiling in Charlie's bedroom.

'I'll go up and take a look,' he says, 'while the kettle boils,' and disappears up the stairs.

Tiggy watches him go, turns to see Em studying her curiously and is visited by the familiar anxiety of the attractive young girl when confronted by an older and possibly jealous woman.

'Neither of you is the least bit how I'd imagined,' she says quickly. 'Do you do that? Make mental pictures of people you're going to meet?'

Em chuckles. 'I always do it and I am invariably wrong. So how did you see us? Rather elderly and wizened, wearing shabby but well-cut tweeds and being kind but firm with the children?'

Tiggy bursts out laughing. 'Well, I did, if you want the truth. Julia might have warned me.'

'So she might if she'd thought about it. Julia's too used to us by now. What a darling she is! Pete is so lucky. I'm very glad she's got you to keep her company while he's at sea.'

'I'm lucky too,' mutters Tiggy, suddenly confused, wondering how much Em knows. Julia has promised that nobody else knows the truth but Tiggy instinctively guesses that it would be foolish to underestimate this woman's intelligence.

Julia appears. 'Is it OK if we have tea round the kitchen table? It's so much easier to keep the children under control. Great. I'll shout for Uncle Archie.'

'It must be a comfort for Julia to have Uncle Archie so near at hand when things go wrong, especially since you both lived here and know the house so well. It's a bit daunting all on your own with three small children.' Tiggy follows Em into the kitchen.

'Oh, Archie's everyone's uncle,' Em answers lightly. 'Not just Julia's.'

She bends over Liv's colouring book, exclaiming at the brightly coloured picture, and Tiggy stands still, for a moment, feeling faintly uncomfortable and wondering if she's heard her correctly.

'What did she mean?' Tiggy asks later. They've already discussed Tiggy's surprise at Aunt Em's appearance and Uncle Archie's Paddington Bear-like attraction. 'About Uncle Archie being everyone's uncle?'

'Well, it's true. Poor Aunt Em. Uncle Archie simply can't resist a cry for help and everyone knows it. He loves to be organizing and fund-raising and in the thick of it. I think it's because she's waited all these years for him to stop going to sea so that they can be together and it's been a bit of an anticlimax.'

'She seems quite a bit younger.'

'Oh, she is.' Julia kneels down on the rug in front of the fire and begins to pull the logs together, prodding them with the poker to make a blaze. 'It was a tremendous romance, Pete says. Uncle Archie was a typical career officer, confirmed bachelor and so on. And then he met Aunt Em and she completely knocked him sideways. Although she was brought up by some dreary old aunts she's such a live wire and everyone loves her. The kids absolutely adore her. It was a great shame that she couldn't have any of her own.'

Tiggy feels a twinge of anxiety. 'Does she know about me?'

'Of course not.' Julia looks up reassuringly from her crouching position. 'But she's bound to find out before too long.'

'I know. It's stupid of me.' Tiggy shivers, edging closer to the warmth, remembering Mrs Armstrong's shocked and disgusted expression. 'It's just that I can't bear the thought of how people will react.'

'But you were going to be married at Easter. It wasn't just a one-night stand,' says Julia. 'And if you'd told Tom about the baby, you'd have been married by now and nobody would ever have known.'

'I wasn't certain, you see,' says Tiggy wretchedly. 'You kid yourself that you've got the dates wrong or it's because you're worrying about it. You know how it is.'

She breaks off, knowing that Julia has never been in such a frightening position, experiencing the earlier sense of isolation. Julia watches her sympathetically, remembering Tom's striking good looks but also his faint air of unapproachability. Pete had really liked him.

'After all,' she says, with unexpected intuitiveness, 'even when you're engaged it's a bit tricky coming out with that kind of news, isn't it? And Tom was just a tad intimidating, wasn't he, being that much older? He was so terribly . . . complete.'

Tiggy looks at her with surprise. 'That's exactly right,' she agrees. 'He was very self-contained. Oh, not in a cold way, but he didn't *need* people in the way I did. Do. I needed reassurance that he really loved me. When I first guessed about the baby I was immediately frightened that he'd see it as a nuisance. Or a threat or something. When I was sure, I held back from telling him because he was so set on doing the Horseshoe under snow. It was a big thing with his climbing group and I didn't want him to have anything on his mind.' She bends forward so that her forehead rests on her knees. 'I wish I'd told him,' she says, muffled.

Julia pokes at the fire, rather at a loss for words; anything will sound trite.

Presently Tiggy raises her head. 'It's wonderful being here,' she says. 'You've saved my life.'

Julia looks embarrassed but pleased. 'It's nice for us too, you know,' she says.

'What did you think of Tiggy?' Em asks as she and Archie drive back to Blisland.

Archie reflects on the question. He liked the girl; very pretty with all that long dark reddish-brown hair. There's probably some fancy word for it. Auburn? Too light. Anyway, it's pretty hair. And she had a nice straight way of looking at you. Good eyes too. Greeny-blue, like the sea on a hot day. And that little dusting of freckles is rather attractive. Bit on the thin side for his taste, not like Julia who is a good armful when you give her a hug.

'I liked her,' he says – and sees Em smile. He's thankful that Em isn't one of those jealous types who goes all grim and silent each time he looks at a pretty girl. Couldn't have coped with it. No, Em's more likely to say 'Isn't she pretty?' or 'Do you like that woman's frock?' or something like that. Not that she's ever had anything to fear; until he met her he'd never liked a woman enough to make any kind of change to his life. Em took him aback all standing: caught him right off guard. He knows he lets her down a bit; he still needs time to himself, to go off on the boat or have a run ashore with his chums at the sailing club. After all, by the time he and Em met he'd got rather set in his ways. Even now that he's retired, Em still spends quite a lot of time on her own. Archie feels a tiny twinge of guilt.

Em smiles and touches him lightly on the arm. 'I think you made a hit.'

'Who, me? Nonsense.'

'Tiggy said that she thought that Julia and Pete were lucky to have you for an uncle and I said you were everybody's uncle. Was that rather bitchy of me?'

Archie chuckles. 'If you mean I'm a bossy interfering bugger, well, I can't really argue with you.'

'Tiggy was rather shocked,' says Em ruefully.

'That's the trouble with the young,' says Archie. 'They're so easily shocked. I expect she'll get over it.'

'I liked her too,' says Em. 'She reminded me of myself at that age.'

'What, to look at? Can't see that.'

'No, no. Not physically. There was just something. A kind of wistful eagerness.'

Archie unexpectedly catches a little glimpse of what she means; he's not overly imaginative but he can remember that rather attractive hopefulness in the young Em. Despite her overbearing elderly relations she retained an optimistic view of the future; a readiness to believe that there was more to life than she'd been shown.

As they drive into the village and round the little green, Em wonders whether to tell Archie that she suspects that Tiggy is pregnant – but decides not to; after all, it's pure instinct and

Archie can be a bit strait-laced. She gets out so that Archie can park the car in close against the stone wall, still thinking about Tiggy and the odd sense of recognition she experienced, and wondering if Tiggy felt it too.

The next time Aunt Em visits Trescairn she goes alone. Uncle Archie is busy with fund-raising for the RNLI. After lunch, whilst Julia is upstairs putting Charlie down for his sleep and the twins are in their bedroom setting up the hand-painted buildings of the little wooden village that Aunt Em has brought for them, Tiggy tells her that she is expecting Tom's baby. To Tiggy's relief she looks neither disgusted nor shocked; instead, an odd, rather wistful expression passes fleetingly over her face.

'At least you have something of him,' she says gently. 'I was so sorry to hear that he had died.'

'I was dismissed from my job. The headmistress said that I was a bad influence on the morals of the young. I expect everyone will feel like that so I wonder how I shall manage for us both.'

'Not everyone,' says Aunt Em firmly.

Tiggy smiles gratefully. 'It's silly to be frightened. Only I rather depended on Tom, you see. He was quite a bit older and he always took charge when there was a crisis.'

'That sounds like me and Archie.' Aunt Em hangs the damp tea cloth over the Rayburn rail to dry. 'I think that's often the case in any relationship where the man is quite a bit older. Archie is fifteen years older than I am and I feel that I shall never quite catch up in the experience stakes. It can be frustrating.'

'Yes, it was rather like that. But in a way it was often a relief too.'

'Perhaps what we were looking for was some kind of stability. Julia told me that your mother died when you were very young and that your father remarried. I was brought up by elderly relatives, passed round amongst them like an unwanted parcel. It was such a relief to meet someone who really loved me. I felt so grateful. Maybe you felt the same.'

Before Tiggy can answer, the twins appear crying that everyone must come – must come *now* – to see the little wooden village set up, and Tiggy and Aunt Em go upstairs to exclaim and admire.

That night, Tiggy dreams about Tom and the baby. She seems able – as is often the case in dreams – to be both present in the dream but also watching it from the outside. She wakens suddenly, her heart beating fast, putting out her hand to touch the Turk's rough warm coat. It is very early morning and, beside the bed on the little table, she can just make out the figure of the little Merlin, hurrying forward to whatever the future holds.

'It was so odd,' she says to Julia later. 'We were all there. You and me and Tom. First of all, I was holding the baby and Tom was beside me and then you were holding her and I was standing beside you. Then there was someone else.' She frowns, trying to remember.

'Holding *her*?'

Tiggy smiles. 'I remember saying, "Her name is Claerwen, Clare for short," and then I woke up. It was all very strange. It seemed so real.'

'Claerwen,' repeats Julia. 'It's rather a nice name. Is it Welsh?'

'It's my grandmother's name,' says Tiggy. 'It means "clear white". If I do have a little girl I shall call her Claerwen. Clare for short.'

CHAPTER FOUR

2004

The hall of the small terraced house in Chapel Street was crammed with tea-chests.

'I'm keeping the sitting-room and our bedroom as clear as I can,' Caroline told Julia, as they unpacked the kitchen boxes. 'I need somewhere I can go to relax between bouts.' She took the narrow silk scarf from around her neck and tied back her shiny brown hair. 'It's really kind of you to help. I thought that later on we'd wrestle with all the sheets and towels and things.'

Julia straightened up and put some plates on the working surface. 'This really takes me back,' she said. 'How I dreaded moving. All those wretched inventories and the married quarters' officer telling me that I hadn't cleaned the cooker properly. Though I must admit that I gave up on moving round with Pete very early on compared with lots of naval families.'

'I don't blame you,' said Caroline fervently. 'This is only my second move and I'm tired of it already.'

'Well, being pregnant doesn't help. We went to Trescairn when Charlie was about a year old and after that I stayed put except for the posting to Washington. Look, I'll take all this stuff out and put it on the table and then you can tell me where you want it to go.'

Caroline looked round the small kitchen rather despairingly. 'Just imagine if it were a real house move. We haven't any furniture of our own but we seem to have so much stuff.'

'We were just the same,' Julia assured her. 'Even when we were moving between furnished places there was always boxes of books and china and all the things you need to make the place feel like your own. Pictures and cushions and ornaments and lamps. And clothes, of course.'

'I think it looks as if we've got so much because the house is rather small. What about a sandwich? I bet Pete's getting hungry.'

Julia went out into the hall and into the room that doubled as a study and dining-room. Pete had been hanging some paintings and was now unpacking books and stacking them on to the bookshelves.

'Zack will have to put these in order when he gets home,' he said. 'I know he has a pathological passion for having them in alphabetical order but I haven't got the time for that. I'd like to do as much as we can before we go so that Caroline isn't tempted to try anything silly.'

Julia grinned. 'Nothing changes, does it? Remember all those years ago, Pete? It seemed that every time we moved house the submarine sailed at exactly the same hour that the removal van was due at the door.'

Pete laughed. 'It was all planned, of course. We weren't stupid, you know.'

'I believe you. I was remembering the move to Trescairn. All those lovely men eating pasties and drinking tea in the kitchen and playing with Charlie and the twins. They were very kind.'

'I expect you did your helpless female thing and got them to do all sorts of things they weren't paid for.'

'Well, of course I did. I wasn't stupid either. Caroline wonders if you'd like a sandwich.'

'Oh, I think we can do better than that. Why don't we stroll over to Brown's Hotel and have lunch?'

'Oh, yes,' said Julia at once. 'Now that's a very good idea. Caroline loves Brown's.' She smiled at him and then on impulse leaned forward and gave him a little kiss.

He raised his eyebrows. 'Any special reason? Apart from the fact that you're mad about me.'

'Just remembering,' she said. 'You know. The way it was all those years ago.'

He looked at her ruefully. 'It wasn't all jam, was it?'

She shook her head. 'But there were some very good bits.'

Pete put some more books on to the shelf. 'I need to wash,' he said. 'And then I need a pint.'

Caroline came in. 'Are you starving? I've got some delicious things from Creber's, and I could make a sandwich. Oh, and I remembered to get some Doom Bar in for you, Pete, in case you get seriously thirsty.'

'Pete wondered if you'd like to have lunch at Brown's,' suggested Julia. 'It would be rather good, wouldn't it? A civilized moment amongst all the chaos.'

Caroline beamed with pleasure and relief. 'Oh, yes. Fantastic. I'll go and tidy myself up a bit.'

She disappeared; Pete looked thoughtful.

'I approve of our daughter-in-law,' he observed. 'She gets her priorities right.'

'I imagine you aren't referring to her desire to be tidy?'

'Don't be foolish,' he said. 'I'm talking about the Doom Bar. I like a girl who recognizes a good beer when she sees one.'

*　　*　　*

'It's a nice little house, isn't it?' Julia said later, as they drove back to Trescairn. 'Gosh, my back aches. Still, I think we cracked the worst of it and Caroline can relax. I wish Zack was home to help her.'

'It's only a couple of weeks to go before he joins *Seraph* but I doubt he'll be around much anyway. This next job as Jimmy is crucial if he wants to be recommended for Perisher and drive his own boat. He won't want to be stuck alongside the wall in the dockyard.'

'Poor Caroline.' Julia stared out of the car window. 'I hope he's home when the baby comes. It'll be wonderful to see him again. At least he's got a fortnight's leave when he gets down. I'm glad that Caroline and Liv are such friends, Pete. I wonder what Liv will do when she leaves Penharrow.'

Pete shrugged impatiently. 'We've had this conversation. None of us ever knows what Liv will do next.'

'I suppose that being brought up at Trescairn with all of Cornwall on the doorstep makes it hard to settle to a nine-to-five life in the city,' said Julia placatingly.

She wished she hadn't brought up the subject. Pete was always touchy about Liv's lack of ambition. Julia pondered on how odd it was that it should be Zack who had followed Pete into the navy whilst neither Andy nor Charlie had any close affinity with the sea; but then Andy had never shown much affinity with any kind of career until just lately. Zack and Charlie had always been more focused: Zack on the sea and ships, Charlie on the land and horses. She and Pete had been so pleased when Charlie joined his uncle on the family farm in Hampshire, gradually building up the livery stable that he and Joanna now ran so successfully together. There was a stability about Charlie that provided an area of peaceful relief amidst the turbulence of the twins' activities; though Andy's Internet company seemed at last to be making progress, even if she and Pete couldn't quite understand what it was all about. Neither of the twins placed any great value on status or security, which bothered their father, but at least Charlie was well and truly settled and Zack was happy, first in his naval career and now in marriage with darling Caroline.

'The trouble is, you spoil her,' Pete was saying; he who'd always adored his only daughter and was putty in her hands. 'No wonder she won't settle down.'

Julia smiled to herself: Liv always rolled her eyes and made fearful faces behind his back whenever he talked of her getting a sensible job or starting a serious relationship.

'*Why* should I, Dad?' she'd demand. 'Yes, but *why* should I?' Just as if she were still four years old.

He could never think of any good answer: after all, she was usually solvent, always happy, generally busy.

'It's about the same size as Andy's flat in Hackney,' she'd said, when Pete complained that she could be doing much better for herself than living in a friend's annexe, 'and without his crippling rent. And just look at my view! A million times better.'

There was no arguing with this: the wild coastal sweep across Port Quin Bay towards Rumps Point was breathtaking.

'After all,' Julia said to Pete, 'it's not as if she's never done anything else. She did that gap year teaching in China before she went to university and she worked her way across Australia. She's perfectly capable. In fact, she's got quite a reputation for setting up projects, and she's got every right to choose where she wants to be.'

'That's the whole point. She could have been a lawyer. Or a doctor,' he answered crossly.

The fact was that Pete wanted to see Liv fulfilling her potential.

Julia gave a little shrug: she simply wanted her daughter to be happy.

'I hope something really special will turn up for her,' she said. 'I think it's a mistake for her and Chris to be working together. Old relationships can cause problems.'

There was an uncomfortable little silence and Julia wondered if Pete was thinking about Angela. She sought to change the subject.

'So what do you think about a trip to see Charlie and Jo and the babes?' she asked. 'In fact, we could see everyone if we make a big effort. What a relief that most of the family live in Hampshire. We could fit it in at the end of the month. What d'you say?'

'Don't see why not. What about Frobes?'

Julia frowned, considering their very lovable but enormously neurotic flat-coated retriever, Frobisher.

'I think he's too much for Aunt Em,' she said at last. 'Those garden steps could be a bit dodgy. Liv might have him again, though she said that Val hadn't been very keen last time. She's not a dog person. Perhaps we'd better take him. He's not much trouble really and he gets on with Charlie's dogs OK.'

'Fair enough.' He put out a hand and touched her knee. 'It'll be good to have Caroline and Zack a bit closer, won't it?'

Julia smiled happily. 'It'll be great.'

1976

Although March is a wild stormy month there are often mild, gentle days when Tiggy and Julia can take the children and the dogs off in the van for wonderful adventures. Bouncing around on the brown moquette-covered bench seat, Charlie wedged in beside them in his pushchair with the dogs at his feet, the twins are ecstatic. They picnic by little fords with tumbling streams, on high cliffs overlooking dramatic seas, and on sandy beaches in the shelter of rocks that demand to be climbed. They paddle in icy, peat-brown moorland water and in sun-warmed rock pools, and jump great green curling waves that foam and sink to nothing in the golden sand. Charlie staggers after them, restrained by Tiggy or Julia on the end of his reins, shouting with frustration or suddenly bewitched by a shell or a snowdrop or some other tiny miracle.

The twins adore the camper. They never tire of swishing the orange curtains to and fro, pretending to sleep in the bunks and helping to make toast on the small cooker. It is a mobile playroom, a little house on wheels, and on each sunny morning they beg to be taken out in it.

'I must admit that it's the greatest toy ever,' Julia says. 'They never get bored with it.'

Easter arrives with a freezing wind and a scattering of snow. Unexpected hail showers clatter down, cracking like shot on the granite slabs, and dwarf daffodils the colour of lemon ice gleam in the hedgerows. Then, one April morning of almost Mediterranean warmth, Tiggy drives them to see Tintagel Castle. She's told the twins the legend surrounding the little Merlin, and they often walk on King Arthur's Downs just below the house, but the visit to the castle is rather more special. Tiggy is eager to see the great stronghold on the north coast; she is rereading Mary Stewart's books *The Crystal Cave* and *The Hollow Hills*, and the descriptions of the castle are vivid in her mind.

This morning, for the first time, the child moves within her: a strange butterfly vibration that first puzzles her and then floods her with amazed joy. She goes into the kitchen where Julia is timing the children's eggs and slips her hand into the crook of her arm.

'The baby moved,' she whispers. 'I felt it.'

Julia turns swiftly, her face glowing with such inexpressible delight that Tiggy is filled with gratitude and love for her; and they stand together, Julia's elbow pressing Tiggy's hand against her side, sharing in this miracle. Then the twins start up with one of their protests from some earlier injustice, '*Why* can't we . . . ?' 'Yes, but *why* can't we . . . ?' and the moment passes.

They drive through narrow lanes sheltered by high banks of new-flowering gorse, through small villages, where bright-faced camellias flower behind garden walls, through the village of Tintagel looking out towards the bleak cliffs where the gaunt remains of the medieval fortress stand on its high crag. Even on this sunny day, the ruined castle, with its stout walls and steep stone steps, retains all its aura of mystery and power. Yet Merlin's story cannot hold the twins' attention for very long and soon they are asking for something to drink and presently they drive out to the church to eat their picnic on Glebe Cliff in the sunshine.

Later, on the cliff, walking ahead of Julia and the children, with the dogs racing to and fro, Tiggy feels again the movement of her baby, and is seized anew with happiness; these flutterings present her with her first true awareness of the living child and her awe outweighs any of the more familiar fearfulness. Today the aquamarine sea leans gently against the cliffs, its taut, silky surface barely rising and falling, as if it breathes quietly mid-tide, waiting. The warm sweet-scented wind, drifting from the west, washes over Tiggy and she gladly lifts her face to it. Once more she is filled with the certainty that Tom is close to her, that nothing separates them, and then Liv comes panting up behind her, seizing her hand, and the spell is broken.

One day in late April the girls have another visitor. They've slept late after a disturbed night, first with Charlie, who is teething – big double teeth breaking through his tender gums, causing him great anguish – and then by Liv who's had a bad dream and needs a great deal of comforting. In the end they all get up to sit around the kitchen table, Julia's eyes streaming with tears as she yawns and yawns, whilst Tiggy makes tea for everyone, including Charlie. He downs his sweet, weak, beakerful with delight and holds the cup out again, his wet-lashed eyes huge with exhaustion, his cheeks red with the hectic flush of teething.

'When's Daddy coming home?' Andy asks fretfully – and Tiggy sees Julia's expression, just for one moment as she is caught off guard, and how her mouth turns down exactly like the twins' when they are unhappy.

'Soon,' says Tiggy quickly, leaning between the twins, smoothing Andy's blond mop of hair as she gives him a biscuit. 'Very soon. Have you got a picture for him to go with Mummy's next letter?'

She dribbles more tea into Charlie's mug, pours in some milk, adds a small quantity of honey and gives it to him whilst the twins scramble to find their colouring books so as to select a picture.

'I miss him too,' murmurs Julia, as the twins squabble over the rival merits of their artwork, and Tiggy sees how hard it must be for her with Pete at sea so much. She knows that Julia hates being without him, yet most of the time she is so cheerful and capable that it is easy to forget that she is making a tremendous effort to hide her own particular loneliness and anxiety. Submariners are doing a dangerous job and there has been a rumour, just the faintest whisper, that the boat has been deployed to a Russian anchorage off Libya.

'There are always rumours,' Julia says after this particular phone call from another anxious wife. 'Of course Pete never says a word, and quite rightly, but it explains his touchiness.

He needs a while to come off the boil when he gets home from most patrols.'

Now, Tiggy pushes the biscuits towards her and Julia grins reluctantly.

'Wouldn't it be wonderful,' she asks, 'if we could be four years old again and have all our problems solved by the prospect of a chocolate biscuit?'

In the morning the children are fractious: all through breakfast Charlie grizzles, the twins bicker, and Julia moves about, tripping over the dogs and still yawning ceaselessly. The twins, unable to decide which of their pictures are worthy to be sent out to Pete, settle down at Tiggy's suggestion to make a drawing of the little Merlin, which is brought down and set before them as a model. It is an ambitious scheme but it keeps them busy while Tiggy chops vegetables for soup and Julia does the washing-up. Charlie, maintaining a steady jabber, makes his way cautiously round the kitchen, clinging to the furniture, until he topples into the dog basket, startling both dogs. The Turk jumps up on to the sofa out of harm's way but Bella simply licks Charlie's face until he explodes with giggles and Julia whisks him up and puts him back, protesting loudly, into his high chair. The twins, distracted from their drawing, begin to bicker again.

'Maybe we should go down to Delfy Bridge and have a paddle,' Tiggy is suggesting, when they hear the sound of a car's engine.

'Damn!' says Julia wearily. 'Damn and blast! Who can that be?' She peers from the window. 'Oh, *no*,' she mutters. She looks cross, even angry, and her cheeks flush pinkly.

Surprised at her reaction, Tiggy joins her at the window. 'Who is it?' she asks curiously.

'It's Angela Lisburne and the ghastly Catriona.' Julia keeps her voice down lest the twins should overhear. 'Angela's husband, Martin, was with Pete on *Orestes* and since then she's absolutely determined that we need to be best friends.' Julia ducks back so that Angela won't see her. 'Her family's known Pete's for ever and she had a bit of a thing with Pete when they were both quite young. She doesn't like me – or him – to forget it. And Cat is such a spiteful child. We all try to like her but she makes it very difficult. She always manages to upset Charlie or the twins somehow.'

Tiggy feels a strong surge of partisanship for Julia. Already she dislikes Angela, and she cranes to get a better look at the young woman who has climbed out of her car and is now releasing a small girl from her chair on the back seat. She lifts her out and tries to set her down but the child clings, her legs firmly wrapped about Angela's waist. Julia heaves a sigh, combs her fingers through her hair and goes out into the hall; Tiggy waits in the kitchen, listening. The twins, who are now playing with the dogs, seem to sense the quality of the silence and look up.

'Where's Mummy gone?' asks Liv, her arms round Bella's silky brown neck. Bella pants, smiling fatuously in her embrace; her long spaniel ears fall down over Liv's arms like thick curling plaits.

'Angela's here.' Voices can be heard in the hall and Tiggy keeps her voice low. 'Angela and Catriona.'

Andy makes a face; he screws up his nose in distaste. 'We don't like Cat. She's horrid. We hate her, don't we, Liv?'

Liv nods, hugging Bella even tighter. 'She's a silly baby. Scaredy Cat.'

Before Tiggy can remonstrate, the door opens and Julia comes in followed by Angela with Cat clinging to her, limpet-like.

'This is Angela, Tiggy,' says Julia in a bright, hostessy voice. 'And this is Cat.'

'Hi, Angela,' says Tiggy. 'Hello, Cat.'

Angela smiles a greeting but the child merely buries her head in her mother's shoulder and takes a renewed grip with her knees.

'She's shy,' says Angela. 'Aren't you, little Cat? Look, pussycat, there are Andy and Liv. Aren't you going to say "Hello"?'

She makes as if to set Cat on the floor but the shrill scream that this produces makes her shrug and instead she sinks down on one of the chairs beside Charlie's high chair.

'Do be quiet, Cat,' she says. 'You're frightening Charlie.'

The child raises her head and Tiggy glimpses a small narrow face with close-set eyes that peer slyly at Charlie. He stares back, seraph-like, wide-eyed and curious at this intrusion but not unduly upset.

'Coffee?' Julia says to nobody in particular, assembling mugs.

'Thanks,' Angela says. 'We're on our way to see my mother at Rock and couldn't resist dropping in to see how you are.'

With her free hand, she puts her bag on the table and roots for her cigarettes. She shakes a few loose, offers one to Julia and then to Tiggy, who refuses with a shake of the head. It is interesting to her that the narrow-faced, slant-eyed look should be so sexy on the mother when it is so unattractive on the child. She is aware of an uneasiness but can't decide whether it is emanating from Julia or herself, though she is very glad that she's wearing a baggy shirt over her jeans: she knows at once that Angela wouldn't miss a trick.

Julia is filling the kettle for coffee, talking easily enough, but Tiggy senses that the focus has changed and somehow Angela is now in control. She sits with the child clamped to her lap, the centre of attention, smiling her secretive, slant-eyed smile, as if she and Cat have some kind of right of ownership here, and Tiggy has a strong desire to break this odd spell. Clearly

Andy feels the same. He begins to play noisily with the Turk
so that she barks and, when Julia tries to hush him, he shouts,
'Pee po piddle bum,' whilst Liv shrieks with hysterical laughter.
Tiggy sees that, though this might have made Julia laugh if
they'd been on their own with the twins, with Angela here she
is flustered and upset. Tiggy decides to take control.

'Oh, shut up, Andy,' she says calmly. 'That isn't remotely
funny. And where are your pictures for Daddy? Have you
written on them yet so he knows which is which?'

Somehow she manages to get them back to the end of the
table, creating a small area of activity that catches the attention
away from Angela and Cat, who now raises her head to watch
the twins busily at work.

'How *is* Pete?' asks Angela, blowing smoke sideways, hefting
Cat more comfortably on to her lap. 'Are you getting letters?
He's in the Med, isn't he?'

Her voice carries a faint inflection of affectionate propriety,
as if she has some sort of natural right to Pete and that his
welfare is her concern, imposing this claim on Julia just as she
had earlier imposed her presence, somehow making herself
the centre of attention – and Tiggy glances quickly at Julia,
already defensive on her behalf. Julia is still standing, her
head slightly bent, smoking her cigarette with her right elbow
cupped in her left hand.

'Oh, yes,' she answers. 'I've had letters. And he sends the
children postcards. They've been on exercise off Île d'Or and
then they went to Naples. They're finishing with a run ashore
in Athens. They're having a great time.'

'I can believe that.'

Angela sounds amused: the implication being that she
knows exactly what kind of good time Pete might be capable
of, and that she thoroughly approves. There is a little silence.
Liv, sensitive to atmosphere, lifts her head and, quick as

lightning, Cat thrusts out her tongue at her before cramming three fingers of her hand into her mouth and gripping her mother with renewed energy. Liv looks affronted; she stares indignantly at Julia, hoping that she's noticed, and Tiggy intervenes again.

'It's time for *Play School*,' she says. 'Come on. I'll switch the television on for you. Coming, Andy?' Courtesy makes her smile at Cat. 'Would you like to watch *Play School*?' she asks.

The child stares at her: the close-set squint of the eyes and the mouth stretched wide by having most of her hand thrust into it combine to give her a grotesque look that repels Tiggy. Surprised, and shocked at her depth of dislike, she gives a little smiling shrug and turns away with the twins.

'Wouldn't you like to go, sweetie?' Angela is asking persuasively when Tiggy returns. 'You like Big Ted and Jemima, don't you?'

Cat shakes her head, burrowing deeper, as if determined to resist any offer of anything pleasant, yet Tiggy notices that now the twins have gone she relaxes her grip and begins to look around her.

'So how long are you staying?' asks Angela. She crushes her cigarette carefully into the ashtray and picks up her coffee. 'Nice for Julia to have some company.'

'It's wonderful,' agrees Julia before Tiggy can reply. 'She's staying for some time yet. No plans.'

Angela raises her eyebrows. 'How nice to be so free of responsibility.'

'I'm between jobs,' Tiggy says – though she can hear the lack of conviction in her voice and she is conscious of the mesmeric quality of the narrow dark eyes studying her. It is an effort of will to remain calm, staring back at Angela so as not to lose face or to give herself away.

'Very lucky for me,' Julia is saying. 'The children can be exhausting and they adore Tiggy.'

Angela begins to talk about the difficulties of raising children with a husband away at sea for so much of the time but somehow Tiggy can't concentrate. She is aware of the need to protect Julia from something, although she doesn't know what, and she frowns and drinks some coffee. Cat slips down from her mother's lap and is making her way around the table, her eyes fixed unwaveringly on Tiggy's face. Tiggy forces herself to smile but the unresponsive stare repulses her and she turns to Charlie, who is beginning to grizzle again. She lifts him out of his high chair and joggles him a little, picking up a toy to distract him, carrying him through to the sitting-room where Big Ted and Little Ted are singing a song. Tiggy sings too, dancing Charlie up and down while the twins laugh, yet all the while the sense of uneasiness persists and she goes back into the kitchen.

With a shock she sees that Cat has got hold of the little Merlin. Somehow she has managed to reach him down from the dresser though her hands are barely big enough or strong enough to hold the little bronze and she is examining him closely. Tiggy's reaction is instinctive and immediate.

'Give me that,' she cries. 'Give it to me at once.'

Cat stares at her with a bright, almost malicious look, and deliberately drops the Merlin. Julia and Angela rise to their feet as if on strings, both speaking at once, and the twins come running in from the sitting-room. Charlie begins to cry, frightened by the shouting, and Cat sets up a prolonged whistling scream over which nobody could hear anything else. Presently Angela and Cat leave; Cat still screaming and Angela looking amused as if the whole business is rather pathetic and utterly beyond her comprehension.

The Merlin is retrieved, made much of by the twins and

placed on a high shelf safely out of reach of any of the children. Shaken by her own reaction to the episode – and to Angela and Cat – Tiggy keeps apologizing to Julia.

'I'm sorry,' she says wretchedly. 'I can't think what came over me. Honestly. I'm so sorry . . . I can't think why I felt like that, especially about a child. I just instinctively disliked them both on sight.'

'I thought it was just me,' says Julia. 'Angela will go on about Pete with that smug smile all over her face, but I feel guilty about disliking Cat too. The trouble is that every time I make a real effort to be nice to her she does something really horrid. Look, let's have a drink,' and she opens a bottle of wine and they sit together at the kitchen table until their spirits begin to rise a little.

Charlie has fallen asleep on the sofa under the window, with the Turk curled beside him, and the twins go upstairs to act out their own version of *Play School* with Andy's teddy and Liv's rag doll. It is much later when they are all set to walk down to the post office in the village that, after much searching, they find the twins' pictures for their father. The two sheets have been torn again and again, screwed into tiny pieces and left in a pile beneath the table.

CHAPTER FIVE

2004

A few weeks later, early one evening, Julia telephoned Liv.

'Someone phoned last night trying to track you down,' she said. 'A man called Matt Greenaway. Does the name ring a bell?'

'Yes,' said Liv. She had an instant mental image of a tall man with fair hair so pale it was almost silver and cut very short: a bony, pleasant face and a very disconcerting gaze. 'Yes, it does. He runs a very successful little hotel in Truro and he owns a couple of restaurants upcountry. Actually, I know his one-time partner better. I was at school with her. What does Matt want?'

'I've no idea. I thought it best not to ask and I didn't know whether you'd want me to give him your number. He's left his number here. Got a pencil?'

'Yes. No. Hang on. I might come over a bit later and make the call from there, Mum. Is that OK?'

'Perfectly OK. Would you like some supper?'

'That'd be great. See you later.'

'She's coming over for supper,' Julia reported to Pete. 'She's asked if she can make the call from here. He sounded rather nice. I wonder what he wants.'

'He probably wants a receptionist or a chambermaid or a cook,' said Pete irritably, filling two glasses with wine. 'Liv spends her life getting people out of problems with their staff.'

'Well, please don't nag her about it,' pleaded Julia. 'At least it might move her on from Penharrow.'

'I never nag,' said Pete indignantly.

Frobisher opened an anxious eye. He was acutely aware of tension. Raised voices distressed him, and now he wagged his tail in an effort to distract attention. Julia bent to pat him.

'It's OK,' she told him soothingly. 'We're not arguing.'

Pete rolled his eyes impatiently. 'Chance would be a fine thing. Ever since that wretched animal arrived I haven't been allowed to speak above a whisper. I just don't know why we can't have normal dogs, like other people do.'

'Zack was saying much the same thing last time he was home on leave,' said Julia. 'Frobes is fine. He's very good for us. Anyway, this Matt might be nothing to do with work. He might be making a social call.'

'Well, I have no doubt that you'll wheedle it out of her.'

'I never wheedle,' protested Julia. 'I'm very tactful.'

Pete snorted. '*Tactful?* Are you serious? It's all right, Frobes. Nothing's wrong. Good grief! This dog should apply for a job with Relate.'

'It's just that he can't cope with any kind of tension. He's settling in very well.'

'Why do we always have such thick animals?' asked Pete. 'We seem to finish up with other people's rejects.'

This was certainly true about Frobes, thought Julia rather

guiltily. Kept as a stud dog by his breeder, he'd proved hopeless when he'd grown old enough for action to be demanded
of him: bitches in season provoked nothing more in him than
horrified alarm.

'He's useless,' said his despairing owner. 'He utterly hates
it. Look, Julia, I know you've been thinking of having another
dog . . .'

'Honestly, Mum,' Liv had said. 'You're such a sucker. First
there was Bella, a field spaniel who threw a fit if anything went
bang, and then we had Baggins, a sheepdog who fainted with
terror at the sight of a lamb. But never mind, I think Frobes
is an absolute poppet. And, after all, why should he have to
perform to order, poor old doggle? Perhaps he's gay.'

Julia sat down on the sofa beneath the window and Frobisher
climbed up beside her.

'Liv thinks Frobes is gay,' she said, smoothing his soft flank
and dropping a kiss on his noble brow. 'If so, I couldn't
approve more. He's the least troublesome dog we've ever
had . . .'

'As long as nobody ever raises his voice above a whisper or
makes an unexpected noise,' finished Pete. 'He's not gay. He's
a wimp.'

'But he's so handsome,' said Julia. 'He has a kind of regal
look, doesn't he?'

'Oh, yes,' agreed Pete bitterly. 'Frobes is a true aristocrat:
beautiful, elegant, and thick as two short planks.'

'Is that a car?' asked Julia, suddenly alert. 'Is it Liv?'

Pete looked out of the window. 'Yes, it is.'

He strolled out to greet his daughter and they came in
together, Liv's arm linked in Pete's. Julia's heart lifted just at
the sight of her, and Frobisher's tail beat a welcome. Liv bent to
kiss Julia's cheek and stretched a hand to Frobisher.

'Hi, Mum,' she said. 'Hello, old doggle.'

Julia smiled at her, determined not to be betrayed into questioning Liv, though she longed to know who Matt Greenaway was and what he might want.

'How are Val and Chris?' she asked. 'Goodness, Penharrow must be such a change from London. Do they wonder what's hit them? You must bring them over for supper one evening, Liv. Are you hungry?'

'Well, I'd rather get the phone call over first, if that's OK,' Liv said. 'Then we can relax.'

'The number's on the pad on the dresser there,' Julia said. 'See it? It's a Truro exchange.'

'Got it,' said Liv. 'Thanks. Shan't be long.'

She picked up the telephone and went out, closing the door behind her. Pete grinned at Julia's expression as she watched her daughter disappear into the hall.

'"Everything comes to he who waits",' he quoted softly.

'Matt Greenaway?' Liv was querying. 'Oh, hi. It's Liv Bodrugan here. You spoke to my mother and gave her this number.'

'Liv.' He sounded pleased. 'Yes. How are you? It's ages since we saw each other.'

'I'm fine. And you're doing well, from what I hear.'

He laughed. 'It's nice to hear it confirmed. And so are you. I can't tell you how many people have told me that you're just the person I need for a new project.'

'Really?' Liv felt a little flutter of pleasure.

'Mm. Actually, I was hoping we might have this conversation face to face but I'd like to get your reaction to my plans. I think you know the wine bar in Truro called The Place, up by the cathedral?'

'Yes. Yes, I know The Place. I haven't been in for a while, though.'

'Well, it's up for sale.'

'*Is* it?' Liv was surprised. 'But it was doing so well. Liam, isn't it, the chap who runs it? He seemed so, well, so good at it. It was terrifically popular.'

'Did you know his marriage broke up?'

'Yes, I heard about that. I don't think anyone was surprised, were they? His reputation was pretty well known. But that was a couple of years ago, wasn't it?'

'Yes, it was. The latest gossip is that he's been playing around with someone's wife. Her husband took it badly and made a few public scenes. It got a bit tricky. Some of the staff have left and the magic's a bit tarnished, if you understand what I mean.'

'I can see that,' said Liv thoughtfully. 'A great deal of its charm was Liam himself. What a pity. What was the other fellow called? The chap who did all the hard work. Jim?'

'Joe, and he's prepared to stay on as bar manager, which is good news.'

'He'll be very valuable, I have no doubt. Why are you telling me about it?'

'I've got plans for The Place,' said Matt. 'The building's on three floors, though the top floors have only been used as storerooms and offices and lavatories. My idea is to turn the first floor into a kind of club. Open it up and use it for exhibitions, literary events, that kind of thing. Have a big open fire at one end, comfortable sofas. I want someone fronting it so that everyone who comes in has a great welcome. Sorry, I'm just talking off the top of my head at the moment but you get the idea. I want to create the atmosphere of going into someone's home, whether it's to look at paintings or listen to a poetry reading or have a party. I think you'd be great at creating that feeling, Liv, and so do a dozen other people who should know.' A pause. 'Am I pressing any of the right buttons?'

'I don't quite know. It sounds great but it's something I'd

need to think about.' Liv was flustered. 'You know I'm tied up at the moment?'

'Yes, I've gathered that. But it's not a permanent post, is it?'

'I thought I'd probably stay until the autumn.'

'Well, that's not a problem. It's very early days. There's a long way to go yet but I wanted to sound you out. This would be quite a commitment.'

Liv thought about Chris and Penharrow. 'Look, I need to think about it.'

'Of course you do,' said Matt easily. 'I wondered whether you might like to come down and see The Place again. Refresh your memory and let me buy you lunch. We can have a look at it properly and discuss options. What d'you think?'

'I'd like that,' she agreed. 'But I'll need to check my diary. Shall I phone you? Will tomorrow be OK?'

'That'll be great. I'll give you my mobile number, shall I?'

She wrote it down. 'Thanks. And thanks for thinking of me.'

'Your reputation goes before you,' he said. 'I need you, Liv.'

She laughed. 'We'll see. I'll phone you.'

'Great. And, Liv, don't mention this to anyone just yet, will you? Like I said, it's very early days.'

'Course not,' she answered. 'See you.'

Julia glanced up at her as she came back into the kitchen.

'Everything OK?' she asked brightly. She saw Pete's grin and bit her lip. 'Pour Liv a drink,' she said. 'And I'll get supper.'

'Thanks, Dad. Not too full; I'm driving, remember. Well.' Liv took a deep breath. 'Matt's got a new project and he'd like my help but it's a big secret at the moment so my lips are sealed.'

'Fine,' said Julia with determined cheerfulness. 'Did I tell you that we're planning a trip to Hampshire? We're wondering whether to take Frobes with us this time. What do you think?'

Behind Liv's unsuspecting head Pete silently applauded Julia's restraint. Grinning broadly, he picked up his glass and toasted her. She burst out laughing and Liv raised her eyebrows.

'What's the joke?' she asked.

'Nothing,' replied Julia. 'Just your father being a twit. We were remembering when Zack was younger and he used to call us Dumb and Mad just to annoy. We can hardly believe he's about to become dad himself.'

'Time is an illusion,' said Pete. 'Have a drink, Liv, and tell us about the latest goings-on in the Penharrow soap opera. But don't raise your voice. Frobes is feeling particularly sensitive this evening.'

1976

Spring comes to the peninsula once, twice, three times: each time, just when it seems that the winter is over at last, the warm sunshine and soft winds retreat before cold wet weather that races in from the west. The obliterating silvery-grey curtain can be seen approaching from a great distance, blotting out hills and valleys and familiar landmarks, swallowing up sunny sweeps of moorland and little fields, until, with an ominous rattle of the windows and the vicious spatter of rain against the window, the storm is upon them, sending Julia dashing out to bring in the washing, Tiggy to gather up Charlie and the dogs, whilst the twins collect their toys and carry them indoors.

Then, between one day and the next, spring finally arrives. Deep drifts of bluebells scent the woods on the road to St Tudy, blackthorn hedges in full bridal blossom bank the small scrubby fields and, up on the moors where Tiggy walks, skylarks fly up from the wet grass before her feet and the clear air is filled with their song. High on Alex Tor, watching the dogs racing in and out of the rocks in their eternal quest for rabbits, Tiggy mentally composes and recomposes a letter to her grandmother. They speak from time to time on the telephone but, though she always likes to hear about Julia and the children, she refuses to accept Tiggy's thanks for the very generous presents of money that she sends regularly to her granddaughter.

'I haven't anything else to give,' she says shortly, 'and I don't need it. At least it's something I can give you. Just take care of yourself, darling, and give my love to dear Julia.'

Each time, Tiggy screws herself up to the point when she might tell her grandmother the truth but each time her courage deserts her.

'She thinks I'm here because you need help with the children and that I needed a change after Tom,' she tells Julia. 'She lives so much out of the world that I don't imagine she thought about what would have actually been involved if I'd really just chucked up my job mid-term. She hasn't a clue, really. After all, she's in her eighties and she lives a very secluded life. Everything changed when Grandfather died, you see. He left the whole estate to my father and, since his marriage to Giselle, Grandmother rarely sees him. Grandmother simply doesn't get on with Giselle. She can't see why my father had to get married again, especially to a foreigner. And she tells me that Jean-Paul is a horrid little boy and she can't stand him, either. It's a disaster, really. My father can't turn her out but she feels she's there on sufferance and she hates it.'

'Couldn't she find a little place of her own?' Julia asks. 'I know she's rather fierce, and one of the old school and all that, but I rather like your old gran. It must be horrid for her.'

'She has very little money of her own,' explains Tiggy. 'Not enough to buy a house, however small, and she seems bent on giving most of her allowance to me, which is very nice for me, and with my savings it means that I can pay my way here and keep a bit put by, but I worry about her. I just can't think how she'll react when I tell her about the baby.'

Now, as she walks amongst the rocks in the late afternoon sunshine, with the sea dazzling away to the west, her grandmother is very vivid with her, and she determines that she will go straight back and write the letter.

Julia meets her at the door, her face serious. 'Oh, Tiggy, I've got some bad news. I've just had a call from your grandmother's housekeeper. Mrs Hartley, isn't it? Your grandmother's had a stroke.'

Tiggy stares at her blankly and Julia takes her by the arm, leading her into the kitchen, away from the sitting-room where the twins are watching *Roobarb*, and pushes her down on to a chair.

'They've decided not to take her into hospital but Mrs Hartley and a nurse are with her.' Julia sits down beside her, turning sideways to look at her. 'Mrs Hartley said that she'll be listening out for the phone. Would you like to call her?'

Tiggy nods vaguely, because she knows that she should, yet she is unable to react properly. The first great wave of panic and horror has receded, leaving her incapable of action, and she struggles to brace herself.

'Wait,' says Julia suddenly. 'Just wait a minute. It's such a shock, isn't it? We'll have a cup of tea first. Give yourself a chance to recover.'

Andy appears, demanding juice, and Julia fills two tumblers and carries them away to the sitting-room, with Andy in close attendance. She reappears with Charlie, who beams at Tiggy and gives her his Episcopalian salute. Despite her misery she smiles and holds out her arms to him. Julia puts him on her lap and Tiggy hugs him, her cheek resting on the top of his head, whilst he thumps on the table with his fist and talks his scribble-talk.

Julia pushes a mug of hot tea across the table, her pretty face so troubled that Tiggy's eyes fill with tears. It is beyond her greatest expectation, this love the little family has given her: it is quite outside her experience. She remembers her own lonely life as a child – her parents' rages and silences, her mother's death and her father's destructive behaviour – and she hides her face for a moment in Charlie's soft neck. He twists his head, trying to see her face, puzzled, and she smiles and kisses him.

'After all,' she says sadly to Julia, sipping the tea and putting the mug down well out of Charlie's reach, 'Grandmother is well over eighty. It's not so terribly surprising, is it? The fact is, we never think about the people close to us being ill. Probably because we don't want to. Because we need them we want to think that they are indestructible.'

She drinks some more tea and tries to smile reassuringly at Julia. 'I'm fine now,' she says. 'Honestly. I think I'll phone Mrs Hartley.'

The housekeeper's soft Welsh voice is calm: no, nothing can be done at present, no point in setting out so late in the day on so long a journey, better to wait until the doctor has seen her grandmother in the morning. Yes, she will give her Tiggy's love when she regains consciousness.

They talk for a little longer and then Tiggy hangs up.

'It doesn't sound very good,' she tells Julia. 'Grandmother is paralysed all down her right side and she can't speak; she's not properly conscious. The doctor isn't very hopeful. They've been in touch with my father and he's on his way. Mrs Hartley clearly thinks that there's not much use my being there. Oh, she didn't put it into so many words but that's what she implied.'

Julia bites her lip. 'I could drive you up,' she says suddenly. 'If you'd like that? Aunt Em would come over and baby-sit. It's too far for you to go in the van on your own . . .'

They stare at each other: now, nearly six months' pregnant, Tiggy will find it difficult to disguise her condition. She thinks about her father, imagines his expression when he realizes the truth; she remembers the strong, determined, invasive hands, the terrible, silent struggle and the blow that knocked her to the floor. She thinks about her baby and remembers her dream: supposing she were to have a little girl – Claerwen, Clare for short?

'I don't want to see my father,' she says strongly. 'I don't want him to know about my baby. Not ever. Promise me, Julia, that you'll never say a word to anyone about who my father is. I know Pete and your mum know, but nobody else. Promise?'

'OK,' agrees Julia quickly. 'I promise. I can understand that, given the way he behaved. And it's not as if he stays in touch, is it?'

'I haven't heard directly from him for years. Not since I left school. I expect he wouldn't want me to meet Giselle again in case I told her a few unpalatable truths.'

'But it'll be difficult, won't it? I expect you'd like to see your grandmother to . . . well, to say goodbye.'

Tiggy is silent, recalling their last meeting; her grandmother so anxious for her to take the little Merlin, the unexpectedly warm embrace.

'I think we've already said goodbye,' says Tiggy slowly. 'I didn't realize at the time. I was taken aback by her giving me the Merlin. She was so keen for me to have it as a keepsake, really keen. It wasn't like her at all. Maybe it was Grandfather's and she wanted me to have something by which to remember them both and my holidays with them. I think she knew.'

'When you get to that age I suppose you're used to imagining that something could happen at any moment. But does that mean you just won't go?'

'I'll think about it. Perhaps in the morning I might have a different perspective.'

But in the morning Mrs Hartley telephones to tell Tiggy that her grandmother has died in the night and that her father and his wife and child have arrived and are planning the funeral.

'Has he mentioned me at all?' she asks hesitantly. 'You know? Whether I should come up or anything?'

'No, Miss Tegan. He seems much more interested in your grandmother's will and what he plans to do with the house and its contents.' A pause. 'It might be sensible if I were to pack up some of your own things, Miss Tegan. Just for the present. The young boy, Jean-Paul, seems to think that everything up in the old nursery belongs to him, you see. All the old toys and the books, if you follow me . . .'

'Well, so they do, Mrs Hartley,' says Tiggy sadly. 'Anything that was my father's or his father's naturally goes to Jean-Paul.'

'But there are some things, Miss Tegan,' insists the soft voice. 'Things your grandmother bought for *you*.'

Tiggy chuckles unexpectedly. 'You're quite right. I can't see Jean-Paul wanting my Lorna Hill books. Or my collection of Georgette Heyers.'

'I could pack them up, you see. Just quietly without any fuss. Along with a few things she had put by for you. She was always angry that your father disposed of your mother's things and you had nothing. She talked it over with me because she knew that matters might be tricky at the end . . .'

The soft voice trails away and Tiggy stands clasping the receiver, thinking.

'I wouldn't want you to get into any kind of legal trouble, Mrs Hartley. My father is . . . you know, not stupid.'

'No, no, Miss Tegan. I shan't underestimate him, you can be very sure of that. These things aren't part of the estate. They belonged to your grandmother's family. Only a few little pieces of jewellery. They're already tucked away. She was prepared.'

Tiggy's eyes fill with tears. Why hadn't she known that she would never see her grandmother again? She would have hugged her more tightly, told her she loved her.

'She was content, Miss Tegan, if you understand me. And she hoped that it would be just like this at the end. Quick and very little suffering. She liked to think that you were with Miss Julia. She said that to me, after you'd gone.'

Tiggy swallows her tears with difficulty. 'What about the funeral?'

Another hesitation. 'Do you know, Miss Tegan, I wouldn't be too anxious about that. Listening to the way your father is making preparations I think it would be just as well if you stayed put.'

'Not come?'

'It's to be a very small affair. Your father says that those of her friends who haven't already passed on are too frail to attend. He sees no point in inviting them. You have to ask yourself what she would have wanted, things being as they are. That's what you need to think about. Apart from the lawyer, Mr Glynn, it'll just be your father and your stepmother by the sounds of it.'

'She's not my stepmother, Mrs Hartley. The word "stepmother" implies some involvement in the child's life. My mother died and I have no need of a replacement. Giselle is my father's second wife.'

'That's quite true. I'll go and pack up those things now, Miss Tegan. I'll telephone again later on and tell you what's happening.'

*   *   *

'So what will you do?' asks Julia when Tiggy had repeated the conversation.

Tiggy shrugs helplessly. 'It seems terrible not to go to my grandmother's funeral but I can't help imagining what it will be like.'

'I think Mrs Hartley is right,' says Julia. 'It won't work. I know that funerals are supposed to be part of the mourning process but how can it be in these circumstances? All that antagonism between you and your father. And you won't be able to pretend about the baby. I think you should take Mrs Hartley's advice. It's probably how your grandmother would want it anyway.'

'It just seems disrespectful,' says Tiggy sadly. 'Ungrateful and uncaring.'

'But *we* know it isn't, and nobody else matters,' says Julia firmly.

The box arrives so promptly that the girls believe that Tiggy's grandmother and Mrs Hartley had been well prepared. Apart from the books and some toys, the small parcel of jewellery is packed separately and with it is a letter. Tiggy takes it away to read.

My dear Tegan,

These things are mine so you have no need to feel anxious. They are not particularly valuable – the best pieces were given to me by your grandfather and must remain with the estate – but I hope you will take pleasure in them and think of me when you wear them. Perhaps one day you will have a daughter who might like them.

I have never been very good at showing my emotions but I hope you know how very much I love you. When you were born it was I who suggested your name. Tegan

means 'beautiful' and 'blessed'. I know you are the first.
I can only hope with all my heart that, in the life ahead
of you, you will be the second.

God bless you, my darling,
Your loving Grandmother

Sitting on her bed, Tiggy weeps. She opens the parcel and gently touches the string of pearls and the little silver locket. She threads the pretty garnet necklace through her fingers over and over again, as if some essence of her grandmother might be drawn from it, and weeps even more bitterly. It occurs to her that she has no family of her own left now; nobody to whom she might turn and nowhere that she can go for sanctuary. She sees her future, bleak and hedged on all sides with difficulty, and she is filled with despair. Sitting there, her fingers clenched on the necklace, her glance falls on the little Merlin. He stands on her bedside table, his chin up, hurrying towards the future, unafraid.

Was this the reason that her grandmother chose him as a farewell present? Tiggy picks up the bronze; smoothing the silky light-reflecting metal, remembering her grandmother's insistence that she should take it. The boy Merlin is both symbol and mascot: he stares bravely into the future, yet he is the future. Tiggy realizes that her own child could be seen in two ways: either as a dragging weight, causing her to be fearful and despairing, or as a reason for hope and the means of her own survival. The baby could either ruin her life or give it an exciting new purpose: only she can choose. She replaces the little Merlin on the table.

'I choose the future.' She speaks aloud, though she isn't quite certain whether she is reassuring herself or her grandmother. As if some kind of action is required to reinforce the vow, she gets up from the bed and puts the pieces of jewellery away. She folds the letter, places it inside her copy of *The Hollow Hills* and goes downstairs.

In the kitchen, chaos reigns: Bella has been copiously sick and the twins are holding on to a struggling Charlie whilst Julia is trying to clean up the floor and fend off an interested Turk. Tiggy turfs both dogs into the garden, picks Charlie up and passes Julia some more newspaper.

'I was thinking that it's a good day for the beach,' she says. 'We could make a picnic lunch and go to Rock.'

The twins cheer and hop about with delighted anticipation; Julia looks up, pushing her hair back with her forearm, her face bright with pleased surprise.

'Shall we?' she asks. 'I must admit that it sounds great. But are you . . . you know . . . are you OK now?'

'I'm fine,' Tiggy says, twirling round so as to make Charlie chuckle. 'Aren't I, Charlie?' She begins to sing her own version of Mud's 'Tiger Feet' with growly noises that make him chuckle even louder. 'Go on,' she says to Liv and Andy, whilst Julia dumps the newspaper in the rubbish bin and pours hot water and disinfectant into a pail. 'Go and find the buckets and spades and your warm jerseys, and I'll make some sandwiches.'

As Julia mops the floor, watched by Charlie from his high chair, Tiggy cuts sandwiches, puts some Munchmallows in a tin, and makes up a flask of Ribena. Her courage is renewed but she can see how crucial it is to cling to what is positive and how easy to embrace despair. From very early in her life she learned that life is neither fair nor straightforward, but since Tom's death it has become even more difficult to keep focused on her determination to be hopeful: the battle to maintain a balance is a moment-to-moment affair. It doesn't do to look too far ahead or to postpone simple pleasures; happiness is ephemeral and must be seized.

She thinks: We'll probably never be happier than we are now. One day we'll look back and remember the way we were today, young and strong and planning an afternoon on the beach with the children. I wonder what it will be like in twenty years' time when the twins will be nearly as old as we are now. Where shall we all be then?

Julia comes in from emptying the pail. 'Bella's been sick again in the back porch,' she says, resigned. 'The Turk seems to have eaten most of it, but is there any more newspaper?'

'I've been thinking,' Tiggy says later that afternoon. They lie stretched out in the sunshine, propped on their elbows, Charlie asleep on the rug between them and the twins building an enormous fort on the sand nearby. 'Pete will be home in a few weeks and I think it'll be a good idea if I take myself off for a while.'

'Oh,' says Julia, flustered. 'Well . . .' She flushes brightly, rolling over and sitting up, staring across the water to Padstow whilst she lights a cigarette. 'I'd hate you to think you were in the way or anything. Pete's looking forward to seeing you.'

'Come on,' grins Tiggy. 'You don't think I want to play gooseberry for a fortnight, do you? He's been away for nearly three months, after all.'

Julia smiles, still a little embarrassed. 'To tell you the truth, I've been thinking about it too. In fact, I wrote to Pete and we had an idea. We wondered if you'd look after the dogs and the house for us while we do a trip upcountry. We haven't seen the parents for ages and we thought we'd visit them and then go on for a week somewhere with the kids. It would be great fun if you don't mind having Bella. Pete's mother finds three children and the dog a bit much these days. My parents aren't bothered but they're younger. Thank God they all live in Hampshire. It makes life much easier. Could you cope?'

'Of course I could cope. If that's the way you and Pete want it then it's great. The Turk and I can take off when you get back, if you like.'

Julia shakes her head. 'Pete will be going into the dockyard every day so I shouldn't worry. To be honest, I wasn't sure whether to ask you about the holiday once we'd heard about your grandmother. I'm not certain if you should be on your own too much at the moment.'

'I shall be fine. Honestly. Aunt Em will keep an eye on me.'

Julia makes a little face. 'And I'm sure Angela and Cat would be only too happy to drop in.'

'No, thanks,' says Tiggy. 'I can manage without Angela and Cat.' She frowns. 'I wish I knew why I dislike that child so much. It makes me feel so guilty.'

CHAPTER SIX

2004

Zack stared at himself in the glass, turning his head very slightly so as to examine a slight discoloration on his jaw; nothing really. He ran long brown fingers through short dark hair, still wet from the shower, and stared into the light grey eyes. It was a habit he'd got into as a small child; peering at himself, trying to see who he was. Zack Bodrugan: but he wasn't, was he? That was the point. Zack picked up the towel and rubbed his hair vigorously. He knew that it was the prospect of fatherhood that had resurrected these negative emotions; raised doubts and questions. It wasn't insecurity as such; not fear of being unloved or unwanted, or doubt in his abilities – his family had supplied love and encouragement in full measure. It was to do with having no point of reference as to his understanding of himself: no ancestral map from which to chart his own development; no known parents or grandparents, no siblings or aunts and uncles that were truly of his own blood, to whom he could point in recognition and from whom he could claim his genetic inheritance: his determination and a passion for high, lonely places; an ability for lateral thinking and his oddball sense of humour.

Zack hung the towel on the rail above the heater and combed his hair, still staring at his reflection.

'I met Tom several times,' Mum had told him once. 'You're very like him.'

Of course that was much later; long after he'd discovered that he was adopted. He was convinced that it was the way he'd been told that even now had the power to upset him and to lend a terrible resonance to the word. As he'd grown older he'd been able to understand the dilemma; what is the right age to explain to a child that he is adopted? Too young and he can't grasp it; too old and he feels he's been lied to. Zack shrugged. He could imagine the temptation to postpone the moment of truth, especially in his own situation. It might be a little easier to explain the facts to a child who has been specially chosen by a couple who are unable to have children of their own, or to those children claimed by other members of their own families because of some tragedy. His own case was rather different: taken by friends into their already complete family because his parents were dead and had no families.

'I blame myself,' Mum had said, much later. 'But, you see, we couldn't say right from the beginning that it was simply that we'd picked you out because you were special. It was much more crucial than that. Dad and I believed that it was import-ant that you knew about Tiggy and Tom and that meant that you had to be told that they were dead. Explaining death to a small child is very difficult, especially the death of its parents, and we kept waiting for the right moment. It was stupid of us, of course, because there never is a right moment, though we knew we must do it before you went to school. Liv and Andy were old enough to understand and they promised they would never tell, and Charlie was too young to understand. But it should have been I who told you. I shall never forgive myself for that.'

It was inevitable, once the truth was told, that he should imagine himself to be the odd one out. Dispassionately studying his reflection in the glass, it was clear that his tall, muscular frame and dark hair could not be in any way linked genetically to the shorter, slighter build and fair colouring of the Bodrugans. At eleven or twelve he'd begun to look like the cuckoo in the nest, and many well-meaning, tactless strangers had commented on his dissimilarity to his siblings.

By that age he'd accustomed himself to the truth, found his own way of dealing with it so as to protect himself. Slowly, very slowly, he'd been able to assuage the pain of his abrupt loss of family identity with a new pride and growing sense of identification with Tiggy and Tom. That's how he thought of them: Tiggy and Tom, as though they were older siblings or a very young aunt and uncle. Once the truth was out, the whole family had been very ready to share their memories of them. He'd been given some photographs, not many but enough to make a connection. A romantic, adventurous, tragic couple they were: Tom with a group of fellow climbers, and Bwych y Moch making a magnificent backdrop, staring at the camera with a half-smile; Tiggy posing by the camper van, dressed in a cheesecloth shirt and denim jeans, laughing in the sunshine. Both of them orphans with no families of their own, he was the result of their union and he'd been determined to knit this fact into the strong fabric of his own family life so that the two pieces of his existence should become an indestructible whole.

Most of the time it worked, though there were particular moments of anxiety when it was necessary to explain it again to new friends: changing schools, starting university, contemplating marriage. He had a horror of the truth being told by someone else, pre-empting his own telling of it, yet at certain times he'd dreaded the need of explanation.

'I don't want to tell Caroline,' he'd said to Liv, very casual, a bit offhand. 'You know, about being adopted.'

Her quick look, a mixture of anxiety, sympathy, shock, told him what he'd already known.

'I shall, of course,' he'd said at once. 'It's just . . . you know.'

'It won't make any difference to Caroline,' Liv had said vehemently. 'Why should it? You're Zack. She loves you. You're special to her. To all of us. Why should it matter?'

'Because so far she only knows me in the context of our family,' he'd answered irritably. Sometimes the insistence on his specialness factor was tiresome; OK, he was special, so what? Everyone was special, let's not get wound up about it. Surely Liv could understand the reality here. 'She knows Mum and Dad, you and the boys. And I'm part of all that,' he'd said. 'She's bound to have taken a view, even if it's a subconscious one, of my character based on what she knows about all of us.'

'I see what you mean,' Liv had said after a minute. 'But it's down to nature and nurture. We've all had the same nurture, so we're all alike as far as that goes, and I expect our genetics are as much of an unknown mix as yours. And Tiggy and Tom were both teachers, weren't they? So that means they related to the young, so that's a positive start. But OK, I take your point. You're still going to have to tell her before somebody else does.'

The terror of that prospect had driven him to it. Clumsily – because, after all, how do you bring the subject up naturally? – he'd told Caroline about Tiggy and Tom. And he was right; there had been a few seconds when she'd stared at him blankly and, behind her eyes, he could see that she was re-evaluating, making new assessments. Luckily she'd been impressed by the tragic little story; moved by Tiggy's journey to the west after Tom's death, determined to keep her child.

'That was really brave back then,' Caroline had said. 'She must have been quite a girl,' and everything had been fine.

It was only in the last few weeks, with a new posting from Faslane to a submarine based in Devonport and a fortnight's leave, the old fears had resurrected: would he be a good father? Would some unknown trait suddenly appear and take him off guard? Whenever he had these rare periods of depression he wondered just how much his unhappiness was due to the way in which he'd discovered the truth. It had certainly been a baptism of fire. Time and love had dulled the shock but he could never forget the occasion: a birthday party given by one of their naval friends. It was odd that remembering the event always took on a dreamlike quality. Perhaps it was a subconscious form of self-protection but it seemed to Zack as if the action were happening to somebody else; a small innocent boy with whom he identified but could not protect. He could only watch the scene replay, waiting for the blow to be struck.

1980

Zack is wildly excited. He is four years old and it is his first real party with children older than he is. Because the twins and Charlie have all been invited, and it seems unfair to leave him out, he is to be allowed to accompany them although, he will be much the youngest child at the party.

'You must be a good boy and do as Liv tells you,' says Mummy.

He nods, almost sick with excitement. Charlie has told him all about it. There is to be a conjuror, then games in the garden with prizes, followed by a birthday tea.

'I hope he won't cry if he doesn't win anything,' says eight-year-old Andy loftily. He thinks that Zack is too young to be invited and might disgrace himself, thereby embarrassing Andy. 'He's too little, really, for this kind of party.'

'Of course he won't cry,' says Mummy firmly.

And he doesn't cry, not even when the terrible thing happens because it's not the sort of thing to cry about: it's much too big for tears.

To begin with, the party is everything he has imagined it will be. He knows most of the children already because they are Liv and Andy's friends, and the conjuror does wonderful magic that keeps Zack gasping with amazement as he sits cross-legged in the circle of boys and girls. When the games begin, he doesn't really mind that the bigger children can run faster or jump higher than he can – as the youngest of four he is used to being outdone – but he finds some sweets in the treasure hunt and feels very happy.

The birthday tea is delicious and it is only when the cake has been cut and shared round and everyone has sung 'Happy Birthday to You' that he becomes aware of a girl watching him across the table. At first he doesn't like the look of her; her eyes are close together and very dark, so that she seems to be squinting, but suddenly she smiles at him and her smile makes him feel quite differently; pleased and rather proud that she has noticed him. After all, she's much older than he is; about the same age as the twins. Presently, as the children disperse, she comes round the table and squeezes in beside his chair. He quickly finishes his last mouthful of cake – he always lags behind the others at mealtimes – and smiles back at her.

'You must be Zack,' she says, almost as a grown-up might, and he is flattered that she knows his name.

'How do you do?' he says politely, as Andy and Liv have been taught when they are introduced to grown-ups. She laughs and then glances quickly around the room. Liv is in the middle of a group of friends, Charlie is at the other end of the table and Andy has gone back into the garden.

She looks at Zack again. 'You don't remember me, do you?' she asks playfully, almost teasingly.

He shakes his head regretfully. He would like to remember her, if only to please her, but he knows he could never have forgotten her; close up like this she has a sparkly stare that fascinates him.

'What's your name?' he asks rather shyly.

She hesitates, just for a moment, as if debating how to introduce herself. 'It's Catriona,' she says, still watching him with those strange, dark, close-set eyes.

'It's a nice name,' he says – and she laughs again. It's as if she is waiting for something, willing him to do something, though he cannot think what it is. It's rather like a game but he doesn't know the rules. He frowns, for he would like to please her. 'Do you know all these people?' he asks.

'Well,' she appears to be thinking about it, her glance straying across the table, 'I know the girl over there with the long fair hair and that boy at the end of the table.'

'That's Liv and Charlie,' says Zack, greatly pleased. 'They're my brother and sister.'

Her eyes flash back to him so sharply, so triumphantly, that he feels anxious; at the same time he has the impression that this is what she's been waiting for.

'Brother and sister?' she repeats, keeping her voice low. 'But they're not really, are they?'

He is puzzled. 'Yes, they are. And Andy's my brother too. Andy and Liv are twins. They're eight and Charlie is nearly six. I'm the youngest. I'm four.'

'But they're not really your brothers and sister,' she says

insistently. 'Everyone knows that. You're adopted. Hasn't any-one told you?'

'No,' he says fearfully. 'What's adopted?'

'It means you haven't got your own mother and father.'

'But I have,' he cries with relief. 'I've got a mother and father.'

She glances swiftly round again. Her voice is even lower but just as insistent. 'They aren't your real mother and father. Yours are dead. That's why you're adopted.'

Dead. Adopted. The sinister words toll, bell-like, in his head; his stomach churns.

'No,' he says. 'No,' but she is suddenly distracted. Liv is coming towards them and Catriona slips away without another word, avoiding Liv, disappearing from the room.

Zack catches hold of Liv, frightened and confused, unable to think of the right words to frame his question properly.

'Mummy's here,' she says. 'Come on. It's time to go home.'

He slips obediently from his chair, following her out, looking around for Catriona but she is nowhere to be seen. Squashed in the back of the car with Andy and Charlie (it's Liv's turn to ride in the front) Zack perches on the edge of the seat, waiting for his chance to speak.

'The beastly Cat was there,' Liv is telling Mummy. 'They've moved back to Cornwall.'

Zack can't remember seeing a cat but he is too determined to have his say to wonder much about what Liv is saying.

'Mummy,' he says, clutching the back of her seat, speaking loudly over the boys' squabbling, 'there was a girl at the party called Catriona. She says I'm adopted.' He stands up so as to be able to speak right into her ear. 'She says you aren't my mother. She says my mother is dead.'

Liv twists round in the front seat, her face shocked – but it is not the shock of indignation at a lie; it is the shock of pity and fear. Even the boys stop arguing, frozen into watchfulness. In the terrible silence that follows Zack is filled with terror. He knows at once that it is true: he is adopted.

2004

Caroline came into the bedroom as Zack was pulling on his sweatshirt. Her bump was noticeable now, even under her loose shirt, and he was stirred with a mixture of love and anxiety for her. He had to try hard lately not to brood about Tiggy dying when he was born. After all, he told himself, it had been such a one-off situation; a car accident followed by a long walk in a thunderstorm. Even so, it was not always easy to hide his fear for Caroline. He looked at her critically; pregnancy suited her, no doubt about that. Her conker-brown hair shone with health and her honey-brown eyes were clear and happy.

'Liv's just phoned,' she said. 'She's suggested we go down and have some lunch with them. Would you like it? You haven't seen Penharrow since they officially opened. I went down for May Day and we went to Padstow to see the old 'Obby 'Oss. It was such fun. Even Val enjoyed it. The Teaser was hopping round, prodding the old 'Oss with his stick, and the 'Oss was snapping his jaws and then suddenly he grabbed Val and pulled her in under his capes. Well, you know what that's supposed to mean, the fertility rite and all that, and when poor old Val shot out again she was looking all flustered and embarrassed, but laughing too. Liv was in great form as usual. Anyway, she sends her love and says come to lunch.'

Zack sat down on the bed to put on his shoes. 'Would you like to go?'

'Well, I would. Liv's always such fun and we could have a walk on the cliffs.'

'OK, then,' he said. 'Why not?'

She sat down beside him and pulled his arm around her shoulder. 'It's nice here, isn't it, Zack? It's good to have you back.'

He held her gently, his cheek resting on her head, inhaling the scent of her hair. Love for her rendered him momentarily speechless, and fear for her and the child turned his guts to water. He is aware of a new and growing respect for Tiggy: she must have known a similar fear. How had she managed? Caroline leaned against him and the weight of her, and the warmth of her body, gradually restored him; giving him new strength, new courage.

1976

With her grandmother's death, Tiggy casts off any further dissembling: she no longer tries to hide herself away when Julia's friends turn up, nor does she avoid going into the village. She lets it be known that she and Tom were to have been married at Easter but he'd died before the wedding could take place. His baby must take his name, she decides, and so will she. She will no longer be Stamper but Dacre; nobody will care and, had Tom lived, her name would now be Dacre.

'It's odd,' she tells Julia, 'but now that Grandmother's dead it doesn't seem to matter any more. I admit that I would have hated to tell her about the baby – I was going to be cowardly and do it by letter – but now everyone might as well know the truth. Actually, it's a relief. Well,' she adds ruefully, 'most of the time it is.'

Julia nods. 'There will always be some people who will suck their teeth and roll their eyes and whisper – but who cares? The ones who really know you won't give a damn.'

'Angela doesn't belong to either of those categories,' says Tiggy thoughtfully.

'I'll tell her if you like,' offers Julia.

'Oh, no,' answers Tiggy cheerfully. 'To tell you the truth, I'm rather looking forward to it.'

'Poor you,' says Angela, blowing her cigarette smoke sideways, eyes narrowed with malicious amusement. 'Rotten timing. However will you manage?'

Tiggy shrugs. 'Impossible to say.'

'I expect your family will come round in the end,' suggests Angela, 'once they're over the shock.'

'I don't have any family,' says Tiggy bleakly. 'Now that my grandmother is dead I have nobody.'

'And you wouldn't consider adoption?'

'No.'

Angela raises her eyebrows, draws down the corners of her lips. 'Well, good for you. I'm full of admiration.'

Odd, thinks Tiggy, how this smiling commendation has the power to send a trickle of cold terror into her gut. Safe in her own strong fort of marriage and security, Angela regards her across the table; the narrow gaze penetrates Tiggy's brave exterior and probes the tender parts of vulnerability beneath.

'So will you stay here? In Cornwall?'

'Probably. I shall have to find a job, of course.'

'You make it sound so easy. But who will look after the baby?'

'I shall,' says Julia, intervening at last. 'Tiggy's part of our family now. One more baby won't make any difference to my mob.'

Angela's disbelieving, patronizing little smile is insufferable. 'When's Pete back?' she asks.

'Soon,' says Julia, after a moment. 'A couple of weeks.'

Angela makes big eyes at her. 'What fun,' she says suggestively, knowingly. 'I can't wait to see him.'

'You might have to,' answers Julia. 'We're going upcountry for his leave.'

'I expect I shall see him around. You'll have to come to dinner when you get back.' She glances at her watch. 'I must go and fetch Cat from playschool.'

Julia goes out with her; when she returns the girls stare at each other in silence.

'What *is* it about her?' asks Tiggy at last. 'I have this longing to be really rude to her. And all this hinting about Pete. Why do you let her get away with it?'

Julia shakes her head. 'It's like being with someone who plays by completely different rules from yours. You think you know the moves of the game but you can't be certain, and you hesitate and wait and meanwhile she gets right in there and hits below the belt.'

'But why?' demands Tiggy. 'I mean, why don't you just respond in kind? Be rude. Throw her out.'

'Because I'm afraid of her,' says Julia.

CHAPTER SEVEN

2004

'Val's in a bate,' Liv said, sitting on the sofa, legs curled under her, clasping a mug of coffee. She pushed a scarlet cushion behind her back. 'It's getting to be a permanent state so Chris is on a bit of a short fuse.'

Caroline sat down at the opposite end and looked around Liv's small living space. The sofa, at the opposite end from the kitchen, was built in beneath the huge window so that you could sit sideways and look across Port Isaac bay. At one end of the sofa, the portable television lived on a small trolley, which Liv wheeled out when she wanted to watch; at the other, the gate-leg table stood against the wall. One leaf was extended holding a laptop, several books and a jar of wild flowers. The atmosphere was one of comfortable, busy warmth, the bright spots of colour – a rack of splashily hand-painted plates, a framed photograph of sunflowers, the blue-glazed jar on the table – picked out by the sunlight that shone in through the kitchen window, which faced into the courtyard.

Sipping her coffee, Caroline watched Liv with affection. How did she manage it; to sit so light to things? To remain unaffected by bad atmosphere and people's moods? Her own non-confrontational character made it difficult for her to remain indifferent to unpleasantness.

'It must be worse for you with Chris and Val being married,' she said, 'than, say, being in an office. More personal. Doesn't it get you down?'

'Sometimes. Quite often, actually. It could be so much fun but just lately she's making it a real drag. The problem is that she needs for us to see how hard it is for her. If we jolly her along she thinks it's because we can't *feel her pain*,' Liv accentuated the words, made a dramatic face, 'and then she gets stroppy.'

Caroline chuckled. 'Sounds a bit wearing.'

'Oh, it is. Chris and I take turns for time off. He goes and stares at the sea while he drags on a ciggie, and I chat with Myra and Debs. That pisses her off too. It's odd, isn't it? You don't know anyone properly until you see them under stress. I think it's been a bit of an epiphany for Chris.'

'Seriously? That could be a bit worrying, couldn't it?'

Liv shrugged. 'It could but it's a bit late in the day for her to start throwing hissy fits. They're committed financially to making Penharrow work and that means all of us doing our bit. The trouble is that our Val is a bit of a control freak. Well, we all knew that but we didn't realize how much of one she is until now. Never mind all that. How are you? You look great.'

'I feel great. All the morning sickness bit is over and I feel really well. I'm loving it, actually. And it's great to have Zack home.'

Caroline paused, drank some more coffee and wondered how to phrase her anxiety about Zack. From the first meeting with Liv she'd felt she'd made a friend; she was so direct and easy. Gradually she'd become Caroline's confidante.

'But . . . ?' Liv was saying now, watching her quizzically. 'Why do I think there's a "but" coming next?'

'Probably because there is. Zack's having a bit of a downer. Not much of one but he's a bit low and I think it's to do with the baby.'

'I thought that might happen,' said Liv, resigned but unfazed – as if it were perfectly reasonable – and Caroline felt an instant lightening of heart. 'It's always been the same. Whenever he's facing something new he loses confidence, wonders if he'll be able to cope. He told me once that it's because he's afraid that there might be some negative gene he's inherited that will suddenly manifest itself. It's crazy, really; after all, that could be the same for any of us, couldn't it? But that's Zack for you. He's probably panicking about what sort of father he'll be. He's got nothing to go on, has he? He doesn't know what kind of fist Tiggy and Tom would have made of being parents.'

'It's odd the way he talks about Tom and Tiggy,' Caroline said. 'As if they were friends or something. Did Tiggy want him to be called Zack?'

'Family myth has it that Tiggy was quite sure she was going to have a daughter and that she'd decided to call her Claerwen, Clare for short. I think it means "clear white", or something like that. It was her grandmother's name and Tiggy loved her grandmother. They were very close; the only family Tiggy had, apparently. Anyway, as you know, she had a little boy instead but she didn't live long enough to give him a name, poor Tiggy. Mum decided to call him after Dad's grandfather. It has a Celtic flavour and goes well with Bodrugan.'

'They're all unusual names, aren't they? Tiggy, Claerwen and Zack.'

'Tiggy was just a nickname for Tegan, which means

"beautiful". Celtic too, probably.' Liv stood her mug on the floor. 'I'm sorry Zack's a bit low. He gets over it but it's part of the package, I'm afraid.'

'I just wonder sometimes if he's a bit daunted by the prospect and wishes we hadn't done it,' explained Caroline anxiously. 'I'm so happy about the baby and I want him to feel the same.'

'He's thrilled about it,' said Liv firmly. 'But there's bound to be the odd wobble, isn't there? I expect you have the odd moment of blind panic. It's pretty awe-inspiring, isn't it? A brand-new person to be responsible for; pretty scary.'

Caroline nodded. 'Well, sometimes,' she admitted. 'I don't let Zack see when I have those moments. It seems a bit mean to let him see me panicking when he has to go away so much.'

'Oh, I think you should share it,' Liv said at once. 'Much better for both of you than being brave and suffering in silence. It'll make him feel better about his own fears. Then you can take it in turns. Panic by numbers. Oh, here they are.'

Chris and Zack came in together. Caroline saw that Zack was looking relaxed, amused by some remark that Chris had made, and she felt a further lightening of spirits. Liv was right: his moodiness was a perfectly natural reaction. She got up and went over to him and he smiled down at her, putting an arm around her.

'Hungry?' he asked. 'What do you and the sprog fancy today? Fried squid? Raw pig's cheek?'

'Not in Debs' kitchen they don't,' declared Liv. 'Home-cooking plain and simple is the watchword here. Come on. Let's eat.'

From her window Val watched them leave the annexe and cross the yard to the café; she felt quite stiff with irritation.

'Can't we manage a bit of lunch for them?' Chris had asked

when he'd heard that Caroline and Zack were coming to see Liv. 'Something simple. I could go over and get some food from the kitchen, if it's easier.'

'I haven't got the time to sit around having lunch, even if you and Liv have,' she'd snapped. 'I've got to go to the cash-and-carry, and there's a pile of laundry to wash and iron. I shall grab a sandwich.'

He'd simply looked bleak and turned away. Val had wanted to scream at him. If only he'd recognize how hard it was for her; it wasn't that she wanted to nag all the time but, if she didn't, he seemed to think that it was all so easy. It was only by continually prompting him to action, correcting things he was doing the wrong way, reminding him of things to be organized, that chores got done properly. It was exhausting, making sure that he stayed on top of things, but even then he sometimes simply walked away from it. Like now, for instance.

Val stood at the window, rigid with annoyance, watching Liv and Zack sharing a joke before going into the café. She'd been certain that he'd come back when the others went to have lunch, but not a bit of it.

And what about me? she asked herself silently, angrily. I suppose I just have to sit here on my own.

For a moment, a very brief moment, she imagined herself joining them: laying down the burden of control and strolling into the café, quite casually, saying, 'I've got a spare half-hour after all so I thought I'd come and have some lunch.'

The promise of such relief, relaxation from her rigid need to control, briefly tempted her. Yet it would give off the wrong signals: Chris and Liv would merely assume that she'd given in, backed down. Val's jaw tightened. Of course, Chris would be relieved. His pleasure at her change of heart would manifest itself in attentive gestures: getting an extra chair, passing her the menu, hovering about asking what she'd like to drink. There would be a secret triumph in having him dance attention: it would soothe that itch of desire to see him under control; publicly putting her first. As for Liv – Val shrugged impatiently. Well, Liv would be as relaxed as always. Part of her, Val's, growing annoyance was due to Liv's imperviousness. She was only just beginning to see how thick-skinned Liv really was; indifferent to sharp remarks, unmoved by disapproval. She'd simply accept Val's presence as a perfectly normal procedure, unaware of any generosity on Val's part. No, there would be no satisfaction to be had there; no sign that Liv was grateful for this reprieve from censure. Caroline and Zack wouldn't care whether she was there or not: they'd come to see Liv, after all. Nevertheless, there would be some pleasure in slewing the centre of attention away from Liv.

Val tried to relax her shoulders; she was getting another headache. She turned away from the window and went to find her painkillers.

Before Zack and Caroline left, when Chris had gone back to the office and Caroline disappeared to the loo, Liv had a few moments alone with her brother.

'We're going for a walk along the coastal path before we go home,' said Zack. 'Thanks for lunch. You've done a great job here, Liv. Val seems a bit uptight, I thought. Stressed out. It's going well, isn't it?'

'It's going great; she's worrying quite unnecessarily, but that's our Val. By the way, have you heard from Andy lately?'

Zack shook his head. 'You're the one for keeping in touch. Why?'

Liv frowned. 'He's being evasive. Not answering emails, and when he does it's very brief. To use one of Dad's naval expressions, I think he's "trapping".'

'Well, why not? He's not seriously involved with anyone at the moment, is he?'

'No, but you know Andy. Usually, if there's a new woman in his life he just so wants to tell you how gorgeous and fantastic she is and how he's been selected from a cast of thousands. He likes to talk about the parties and the clubbing and all that. He's being very cagey.'

Zack shook his head; he'd always been slightly shocked by the way Liv and Andy exchanged the details of their private lives. 'Perhaps he's growing up at last. Just because you're twins doesn't mean he has to tell you everything.'

'True.' Liv grinned at him. 'I'm still curious.'

'You're still hopeless.' But he smiled.

Caroline appeared and asked if he'd told Liv about the party. 'It's a house-warming general jolly, Friday next week,' she said. 'I hope you can come, and stay the night, of course. Would Chris and Val enjoy it? The trouble is, we couldn't put them up too and it's a bit of a hike back afterwards or they could stay somewhere in the town. I thought I'd check with you first before I ask them. Things seem a tad fraught.'

Liv debated. 'I think it's better to leave it,' she said at last. 'I'm not sure Val's in party mood and then it might cause more arguments. I'd love it.'

She went out with them to the car, kissed them both, watched them drive away and then went over to the house, banged on the door and went into the hall.

'Hi,' she shouted. 'It's me. Anyone around?' She was always careful never to walk into any of the rooms without an acknowledging shout in return.

'Kitchen.' Val's call was brief.

Liv crossed the hall and put her head round the door. 'Just seeing if there's anything special to be done,' she said cheerfully. 'Have you been to the cash-and-carry?'

Val, sitting at the table with a pad and pencil in front of her, shook her head. Her face was drawn, jaw set. Liv noted all the familiar signs and sighed inwardly.

'Another headache?' she asked sympathetically. 'Poor you. Why didn't you come and have some lunch?' When Val didn't answer, Liv sat down opposite and looked into the tight, set face. 'Val,' she said gently. 'Val, you've got to stop this. You're letting yourself get into a downward spiral of anger and depression and you don't have to go there; you can choose not to. Everything is ticking along, the bookings are flowing in. Why do you want to be deliberately pessimistic? Chris and I both know that things might go wrong; we know we're not out of the wood, and we shouldn't count our chickens and all that stuff. We're not stupid. But neither of us thinks that we have to go round wound up like clocks simply to show that we know that there are possible problems. Just because we try to enjoy the good bits doesn't mean we're blindly optimistic, Val. Stop trying to force us to be worried and miserable because you choose to be.'

Val's eyes flicked up briefly, then down again, and Liv saw that she was close to tears. She'd already noted the glass of water, the strip of tablets, and now she leaned over and took the pad, tore off the shopping list.

'I'll do the cash-and-carry,' she said. 'I'll take the Subaru. Go out and walk in the sunshine, or just sit in the sun out of the wind. Switch off for a moment, Val, or you'll crack into pieces.'

She didn't wait for an answer, she simply put the list in her shirt pocket and went out. In the silence that followed Val put her head down on her forearms; she felt that if she were to start crying she might never stop. Chris, coming in unexpectedly, caught her by surprise. His first reaction was the, by now, familiar frustration but as she raised her head, startled, he saw her expression and felt a pang of remorse.

'I've run out of milk in the office,' he said. No point in asking what was wrong; he knew the answer to that one. 'But since you're here I'll have my coffee with you. I thought you'd probably gone to the cash-and-carry.'

'Liv's gone,' she said. 'Well, she enjoys it. Anything to be off in the car.'

Her voice lacked its usual bitterness, however, and he decided not to defend Liv this time. He was beginning to be seriously worried about the reignition of his affection for Liv; it had seemed so right at lunchtime in the café to be there with her, joking and at ease, as if they belonged together. Just lately he was convinced that Liv felt the same way. A tiny but insistent voice in his head told him that they were doing no harm; that they needed to support each other. The same voice was beginning to hint that he deserved all the help and love he could get from Liv, and that Val was asking for it. He longed to believe the voice but, each time he worked himself into a self-pitying mood of agreement with it, his conscience disturbed from its heavy sleep and reared up to tell him with finger-wagging righteousness that he'd be a cheating bastard. Chris, cursing beneath his breath, suddenly remembered Liv's silly chant – pee po piddle bum – and had to choke down an unexpected spurt of laughter.

'Tea?' he asked abruptly. Val nodded, and, as the kettle boiled, he cast about in his mind for some topic that would reconnect him with her.

'Zack was very impressed,' he told her. 'Of course, he hasn't seen Penharrow since we've been up and running properly so it was good to have his reaction. He really liked the way Liv designed the café and the shop.'

She didn't respond directly but accepted her mug of tea,

looking thoughtful. 'Caroline was looking well,' she said.

Chris sat down opposite. 'Mmm.' He took a sip. 'I suppose she was.' Val looked at him; her wide-eyed unsmiling gaze unnerved him. 'What?' he asked defensively, as if she'd accused him of failing in some observation or duty.

'Perhaps we should be thinking about it,' she answered. 'Having a baby, I mean.'

He was shocked by his instinctive negative emotional response. A baby: the final commitment, the big one.

'Well, that's a conversation stopper.' He pretended to laugh it off, hoping she hadn't noticed his initial reaction. 'I'm a bit surprised that you think you could cope, to be honest, love. You're finding it such hard going as it is, aren't you? Surely a baby on top of running Penharrow would be the last straw. How would you manage?'

She gave a kind of facial shrug. 'It was something Liv said just now made me think about it,' – and Chris felt a tiny jolt of pain, as if Liv had somehow betrayed him – 'about pulling myself out of this downward spiral. Seeing Caroline looking so well and happy made me wonder if perhaps we should try it.'

He bit back the retort that Prozac might be a cheaper, easier option, and pretended to consider her suggestion. 'A bit drastic?' he offered tentatively. 'Of course, it's up to you.'

'Is it?' She gave him that same unsmiling stare. 'You mean you don't get to have a say in whether we start a family?'

Chris thought: Probably not, if you've already made up your mind – and was taken aback by the depth of his anger at his helplessness. He didn't answer.

'But if I could cope,' she argued after a few moments, 'if it, you know, would get me back on track, how would you feel about it?'

'I'm not against having a family,' he answered defensively; 'it's just the timing. We don't *know* that being pregnant would help you to be less fearful and anxious, do we? It might even make you worse. It's a big chance to take. Wouldn't it be more sensible to give this another six months? See how it goes before we start having kids?'

Her face fell into dispirited lines and his heart sank.

'Look, it's up to you,' he said. 'Honestly. If you really think you could manage and that it would help . . .'

His voice trailed away and they continued to sit in silence, each of them trying to gauge the other's thoughts.

Driving back from Wadebridge, Liv decided to make a detour up to Trescairn; it was a good afternoon to have a walk up on the Tor. Driving between wild, high hedges, streaked and splashed with paint-bright colours of the celandine and campion and buttercups, she pondered on her earlier reaction to Val. Liv realized that by talking to her in such a way she'd done her own cause no good. Instead of standing aside to give Val plenty of space to self-destruct, she'd offered her a lifeline back to normality – and to Chris. It would be so easy – and so tempting – to let Val dig her own deep pit and then topple into it, requiring barely a nudge from anyone else.

So why had she felt the need to stretch out a hand to her? Had it been the pitiful sight of that tense, immobile figure, shut off from the happy little group in the café, that had roused her compassion? Whatever had been the cause of her pity she'd felt the need to respond to it.

'More fool you,' Liv told herself crossly – but she couldn't quite regret it. If Val insisted on alienating Chris then she needed to see the extent of the damage that might follow; that was only fair. She, Liv, had no intention of letting him topple into the pit with Val.

It had been such fun at lunchtime; sitting with Chris, opposite Zack and Caroline. Not only was there the fizz of excitement at being so close to him but also a nice, comfortable quality too. After all, they'd done this before. They'd sat in cafés with friends, walked through the streets of Durham and over the Northumberland moors; laughed, fought, made love.

Driving through a small hamlet of granite cottages, where the clematis, charming 'Nelly Moser', scrambled up the walls and across the roof of a small stone hut, and laburnum trees dripped golden pendent blossom over garden walls, Liv tried to remember exactly how their love affair had ended. There had been no dreary deterioration, none of the painful disillusion that Chris and Val were suffering now; it had been an amicable parting of the ways. Chris had been offered a very good job in the financial department of a huge pharmaceutical company, whilst she'd been determined to travel. She'd had no such tempting job offer to make her weigh up the advantages of going with Chris to London and, anyway, she'd always wanted to see the world. Another student friend had invited her to go to Australia with her; she had relatives there, she'd said, and they'd be able to pick up work as they went along. Liv had been unable to resist. The parting had been hard, they'd promised to stay in touch – and there had been several moments when she'd seriously considered giving it all up and coming home to him – but in the end they'd drifted apart. Distance had not made the heart grow fonder.

Which must surely mean, Liv told herself now as she approached Trescairn, that it wasn't meant to be; our love simply wasn't strong enough to survive.

She turned up the drive, parked outside the house and climbed out. The car wasn't in its usual place and the back door was locked. She had a key but she didn't go inside; instead she passed round the end of the house and through the little gate that led directly on to the moor. Climbing the track amidst the scattered granite rocks she breathed great gasps of the cold fresh air that poured over the high uplands and sang amongst the stones. Larks flew upwards ahead of her, their song falling in a showering of liquid notes all around her, and she paused to glance back at the shimmering rim of sea at the land's edge. Vapour trails crisscrossed at sharp angles: delicate rafters in the sky's roof. Out of the west a small black speck appeared in the sky, grew larger; the jet plane screamed overhead and dwindled away to nothing.

Just for a moment she allowed herself to wonder what it might be like to run Penharrow with Chris: just the two of them together. It was such an idyllic prospect that she deliberately blotted it out. Her conversation with Matt slid into her mind; their lunch date had had to be postponed, rearranged for next week, but she was very interested in his idea for The Place.

'It would be quite a commitment,' he'd said. Instinctively she shied away at such a thought – she liked to sit loose to things – but a tiny part of her was attracted by his ideas. She'd decided to wait until she saw Matt again before she gave the project too much thought; she knew that the chemistry between them would be crucial for such an undertaking.

A blast from a horn echoed up from the valley and she saw a dazzle of sun on a windscreen. A Land Rover bumped slowly across the lower slopes, herding sheep before it, whilst a rangy collie sped to and fro like a shadow at the outer edges of the flock. Liv stood looking down on Trescairn's chimneys and beyond to the stand of trees where the new pale green twiggy fingers of the larch contrasted sharply with the black pines: so many childhood memories. She stuck her hands in her pockets and began to climb higher, leaping and jumping amongst the granite slabs and bony ridges of the Tor.

1976

As the day of Pete's return approaches the twins grow more and more excited. Tiggy helps them to make a banner with the words 'WELCOME HOME DADDY' painted across it, which is to be strung outside the front door on the great day. They assemble paintings, things they've made at playschool or at home, and vie to outdo each other in amazing him with their prowess. Charlie, meanwhile, has taken his few first unsteady steps and the twins are rehearsing him for his great entrance. The plan is simple: the moment Pete opens the front door Charlie will be released from the kitchen to walk unaided into his father's arms.

They practise it over and over again; Julia has to be Pete noisily opening the door so as to give the alarm and then, once inside, crying: 'Golly! Goodness me! Can this be Charlie? Walking? Oh, how wonderful!' Tiggy has to hold Charlie in position with the twins whispering encouragement. 'Wait! Not yet, Charlie. Wait. Listen for the door. Now!' Then Tiggy releases him, pushing him gently towards Julia, while they watch breathlessly until he's achieved the full length of the hall, when they all cheer loudly. It takes many rehearsals before Charlie fully grasps what is expected of him but at last he connects the start of his marathon across the hall with the opening of the front door and he staggers forward, his eyes wide with amazement at his own cleverness, beaming delightedly and eagerly waiting for the round of applause from the anxious trio at the kitchen door as he falls into Julia's waiting arms.

'The problem will be that the boat will dock at midnight and it'll be too late for Charlie to be up, or he'll be so surprised to see Pete that he'll be struck all of a heap and sit down on the floor,' Julia prophesies. 'I shall have to rehearse Pete on the way back from the dockyard.'

'It'll be fun.' Tiggy grins, remembering the latest rehearsal. 'Charlie positively vibrates, you know, when I'm hanging on to him, waiting for him to go. He's like the Turk trying to get down a badger sett.'

'Let's simply pray that the boat gets in at a reasonable hour. I'm glad you've given up the silly idea of not being here when Pete gets home. It's not as if we're newlyweds, not with three kids.'

'It would have looked a bit obvious,' agrees Tiggy, 'and with you all going off on holiday so quickly it's not quite the same as us all sitting around staring at each other for two weeks.'

'Actually, we both tend to feel a bit shy to begin with,' admits Julia. 'It sounds silly but it takes a little while to get back to normality after a long separation. I told you, Pete's often very wound up when he gets back from sea. You being there will make it easier.'

'If you say so. I know it sounds crazy but I'm looking forward to it just as much as the rest of you. I've never done anything like this before. It's wonderful to be a part of a family. I've missed so much, I can see that now. You'll never know how much I used to envy you, when we were young and I used to stay with you sometimes in the holidays. It was an utterly different world.'

'It was a madhouse, if that's what you mean,' says Julia, but she's pleased.

Pete makes the whole thing very easy: the homecoming exceeds every expectation. The boat docks at two o'clock in the afternoon, the welcome party is ready and Charlie performs wonderfully: the sight of his father seems to spur him to even greater heights and he propels himself into Pete's arms shouting with excitement. Tiggy suspects that Julia has done more than rehearse Pete for the big welcome home scene; she's also explained Tiggy's reluctance to be present and her fears that she'll be *de trop*. She slips away as soon as the twins have rushed out into the hall, only reappearing when the family has had plenty of time to be reunited.

As soon as she comes into the sitting-room, Pete holds out his arms to her. 'Tiggy! Great to see you.' He hugs her warmly and she feels all the usual gratitude and relief at being so genuinely welcomed by someone on whom she has no claim. Before she can speak, however, the twins burst in upon the greeting, clamouring for his attention to look at some new piece of work. Pete winks at her. With his fine, curly fair hair and fresh, slightly freckled complexion, he looks like an older version of Andy. Tiggy smiles at him with affection.

'I can't get over all this industry,' he says. 'And old Charlie walking out like that. You know, I think that all this effort deserves some reward. Now where did I put those presents?'

There is an instant silence: the twins' eyes follow his movements attentively and only Charlie, who can't remember previous returns from sea, continues to make his own particular Charlie-noises. Julia smiles at the twins' strained expressions of expectation. Pete crouches down and opens his grip, pushing some items of clothing to one side.

'Ah,' he says. 'Here we are. First one for Mummy. Could you give it to her, Liv? Be careful, it's heavy. And this is for Charlie. Here we are, old chap. Now *this* one,' he hefts it in his hand, 'yes, this one is for Andy. And here's yours, Liv.' The children settle down at once to tear away the wrapping paper and Pete takes out one last parcel and hands it to Tiggy with a little grimace. 'Hope I've got the colour right,' he says.

She is truly surprised and deeply touched that he should have thought of her. The tissue paper falls away to reveal a long scarf in a dark, brilliant crimson silk threaded with silver and gold. She glances up with involuntary delight but he is looking at Julia, moving towards her, kissing her, as she holds her own present – a huge bottle of scent – in both hands and smiles back at him. Tiggy swallows down an odd constriction in her throat, winds the scarf about her neck and goes out into the kitchen to put the finishing touches to the welcome-home tea-party.

CHAPTER EIGHT

2004

Despite the sunshine it was too cold to sit outside. The wind whirled in the courtyard, whipping up fallen petals, and the air was chill. A fire burned in Em's tiny drawing-room that looked northwards over the delightful village green. The pale apple-green walls and glossy white-painted wood reflected the stretch of grass that lay smooth and flat as water beyond the sash window.

Em took the spray of azaleas, the yellow *luteum*, that Liv had picked in the garden at Trescairn, and bent her head to inhale its heady scent. She was assailed by a memory, fleeting and poignant, but was too busy welcoming Liv to pursue it.

'I love your house, Aunt Em,' Liv said, waiting for her tea to be poured. 'It's very couth, isn't it?'

Em chuckled at the word. 'Is it?'

'Oh, yes. You've avoided the old-world cottagey bit and retained its proper house-like qualities even though the rooms

130

are small. It's very elegant, though Uncle Archie always seemed rather too big for it.'

'Poor Archie.' Em was seized with compunction. 'If I hadn't nagged he'd have probably stayed on at Trescairn.'

'Well, I love Trescairn too. It was a fantastic place to grow up in.'

'To be honest, Archie was getting rather weary of carrying logs and coke, and the grounds needed quite a lot of work. They still do. It's nice for Julia that Pete is retired now and can take on some of the load. And it was very sensible to convert the Rayburn to oil and put in central heating. It's much easier to run now than it was back in the seventies. Archie had permanent backache at Trescairn.'

'I remember how he used to lie along this sofa.' Liv smiled at the recollection. 'Feet up on one arm, his head on the other. He was so tall. Actually, your ceilings are higher than Trescairn's so he was better off here from that point of view. He always had to duck at home.'

'Trescairn is a group of cottages converted into one big house.' Em passed Liv her tea, offered a plate of fruit scones. 'This is a little Georgian house. Quite different. He liked to stretch out along the sofa and listen to the Third Programme, though he couldn't bear anything composed after eighteen fifty.' She laughed. 'He was such a dinosaur. He always said that there were three phrases he never wanted to hear when he tuned in to listen to a concert: "The composer is with us in the studio", "This next work has been specially commissioned" and "World premiere". He'd switch off at once.'

She fell silent, and Liv glanced at her.

'You must miss him terribly,' she said. 'Poor Aunt Em. Isn't it beastly?'

'Well, it is,' said Em. 'I've grown accustomed to certain aspects of being alone but we were married for forty years, he was retired for twenty-five of them, and there are certain things I never quite get used to. It's mostly not having him around to talk to any more. I miss the way he'd read something aloud from an article, or call out clues from the crossword puzzle when I was making breakfast. It's the companionship, of course. You have to learn to live without it.'

'I can't really imagine it,' admitted Liv. 'Not forty years of it. Of course, Chris and I lived together during the last year at Durham but that's not quite the same.'

Another pause.

'And how is he?' asked Em warily. 'Chris, I mean. And Val too, of course.'

Liv finished her tea, accepted another scone. 'They're OK. They get a bit wound up now and again. You know what it's like with a new venture; bound to be a few problems. We'll get over it. I've enjoyed the challenge actually. I wish I owned Penharrow but I think I'll have to lower my sights a bit.'

As she poured more tea, Em studied Liv covertly: she seemed less effervescent today, more thoughtful. Oddly this was just as worrying, though Em wasn't quite sure why.

'Come and see us,' Liv said when she got up to go. 'You haven't been over for ages and they'd all love to see you again.'

'What about Thursday next week? Is that a good day? What sort of time?'

'Come and have lunch. Debs will be thrilled to see you because you're always so complimentary about her cooking. If you come about one o'clock I can have some legitimate time off with you for a change.'

Em waved her off, went back inside and began to clear the tea things. The scent of the *luteum* drifted through the house and Em paused, holding plates in one hand and the teapot in the other, remembering.

1976

The rhododendrons that encircle the lawn and edge the drive are now at the height of their beauty: every colour from creamy white to rich crimson. Tiggy carries twigs of the azalea's fragrant yellow blossoms *luteum* into the kitchen and arranges them in a blue jug.

Aunt Em telephones. 'I'm probably speaking out of turn,' she says, 'but I've had a thought. A friend of ours is thinking of letting her holiday cottage in Padstow on a long-term let. She's fed up with summer visitors and the weekly changeover and she wants to try having a tenant. It's very small and I couldn't help wondering if it might suit you once you've had the baby.'

Tiggy's first reaction is terror and then a faint excitement. 'I still can't quite take in,' she says, 'that the moment will ever arrive when it'll be me and the baby. I simply can't imagine it. I don't know about the cottage. It sounds . . . possible.'

'Poor Tiggy. Don't let me push you into anything. Archie says I'm interfering.'

'No,' says Tiggy quickly. 'Oh, no, it's not that. It's pure cowardice on my part. And, anyway, I've got to make some plans soon.'

'Well, there's no rush. She can't let it until the middle of September because she's already booked up for the summer but she's willing for you to see it. Since you're a friend of mine, and I've said you'd be a reliable and trustworthy tenant, she's prepared to keep the rent reasonable. I can't see that it would do any harm just to look and, after all, you might hate it. I'll come and pick you up after lunch and we'll go and have a poke round this afternoon.'

Tiggy is filled with gratitude and affection. 'You are so kind. I'd love that.'

*   *   *

Aunt Em opens the front door and goes in, calling out to Tiggy. The dogs come rushing to meet her and she stops to talk to them, bending to stroke Bella's head and giving the Turk a pat, before making her way to the kitchen. She breathes in the scent with delight, seeing the *luteum* in a blue jug on the kitchen table.

'Heavenly, isn't it?' she says to Tiggy, who comes quickly in, and stands for a moment in the doorway. Em holds out her arms for a hug: she knows that Tiggy will be feeling nervous about the proposed visit to the cottage in Padstow and Em, too, is filled with anxiety.

'Do you think it might be the answer?' she says earlier to Archie, who rustles his newspaper uneasily.

'I'm not sure that you should interfere,' he says at last. 'I can't see why it shouldn't work but you mustn't interfere.'

'I'm not interfering,' she says, hurt. 'I'm trying to help.'

'Ah,' says Archie wisely. 'It's a very fine line between helping and interfering.'

'I know that,' she answers crossly. 'It's also easier to do nothing but it doesn't get us very far.'

He smiles then. 'It's worth investigating,' he admits. 'It could be just the thing. But we must let Tiggy decide for herself.'

'Naturally,' says Em, still nettled at being accused of interfering.

'We all want to see her settled, obviously.' He shakes his head, folding the paper and putting it aside. 'Though how on earth she'll manage I can't imagine. Poor kid.'

Em is softened by his sympathy. 'Between us we'll cope somehow,' she says.

Now, looking at Tiggy's anxious face, Em smiles encouragingly. 'There's no need to feel pressured,' she tells her. 'It's just a faint possibility. Anyway, it's a lovely day for a drive to Padstow.'

Her eye falls on a little bronze model of a young boy: the swirl of the tunic, the set of his shoulders, the chin thrusting forward – the whole design is one of movement. Em stretches out her hand towards him.

'How beautiful,' she says. 'It reminds me of something. Is it yours?'

Tiggy nods. 'It's Merlin as a little boy,' she says, picking him up, offering him to Em. 'I was polishing him up a bit. He belonged to my grandfather. He was a great collector and he was fascinated by the myths of Arthur and Merlin.'

'It's the most perfect thing,' says Em, turning it round, examining the detail. 'And even the signature carved here at the base: "Vischer". That reminds me of something but I can't think what. This little fellow is really delightful.'

'My grandmother gave him to me when I came west,' Tiggy says. 'She didn't think my father would miss it. He's got a gallery full of things like this as well as his own private collection . . .'

She falls suddenly silent and Em remembers that Julia has told her that Tiggy has no family apart from her grandmother, and that it's a painful subject better avoided. In Em's conversations with Tiggy about family, she has never mentioned her father, and Em has assumed that both her parents are dead. The silence is an uncomfortable one.

'Beautiful.' Em briskly hands the little Merlin back and smiles at Tiggy. 'So. Are you ready? I'll get the dogs into the car, shall I?'

Tiggy stands the Merlin high on the dresser shelf and reaches for her bag. 'I'm ready,' she says.

The cottage is painted a cheerful pink and seems to be in danger of being crushed between the two more imposing houses on either side. The front door opens straight off the narrow cobbled street and leads into a hallway with a cloakroom behind it and stairs twisting upwards, out of sight.

'Room for the pram,' says Aunt Em. 'And for coats and boots and a wet dog. Let's go upstairs.'

The living-room and the galley kitchen are open-plan, which gives a sense of space; one window looks into the cobbled street at the cottage opposite, the other shows an irregular but rather charming roofscape, and more stairs lead up to the bedroom, the bathroom and a tiny boxroom.

'She's letting it furnished,' says Aunt Em, peering from the bedroom window. 'Look, you can just see a glimpse of the harbour between those chimneys. So at least you wouldn't have to worry about buying anything apart from things for the baby. There's room for a cot in the other little room.'

'It's odd but rather sweet.' Tiggy is trying to get used to the change from the big rooms and rural setting of Trescairn. 'It's a bit cramped but I suppose it won't matter with just me and the baby.' She feels suddenly fearful at the prospect of being alone with her baby with nobody else at hand: how will she manage? 'I shall be close to shops,' she says, trying to be positive, 'and if I could get some sort of job in Padstow it would be good. But then who will look after the baby?'

She sits down suddenly on the edge of the bed, daunted, and Aunt Em sits beside her and puts an arm around her.

'It's difficult,' she admits. 'Between us all we shall manage somehow. This might not be the right place for you to live but I thought you ought to have the chance to think about it. From what you told me I hoped you could afford the rent and have a bit over.' She gives her a hug, rocking her slightly. 'Don't be downhearted. This is just a start. It might be better for you to be out in the country, nearer to Julia. You need to be able to compare things, see how things might work for you.'

Tiggy takes a deep breath. 'You're right. I've got to face it and make a decision. This would be a place to start. With the allowance I shall get for the baby I might be able to scrape by with some part-time work to begin with.'

'I can help out with the baby.' Aunt Em continues to hold her. 'Archie and I aren't far away. It'll be fun. You're not alone, Tiggy.'

'I feel such a fool, you see. And now I'm causing trouble for my friends.'

'But isn't that what friendship is about? It's like faith, isn't it? It only has meaning when the chips are down. If it isn't tested then it has no value. And how do you know that you're causing trouble? You might be offering me an opportunity to be useful, to share in your life and the life of your baby. Can you imagine how wonderful that would be for me?'

Tiggy puts both her arms around Aunt Em and hugs her tightly. 'Thanks,' she says. 'I don't know how to answer that.'

'You don't have to. Let's go back and have some tea. You need time to think but at least you know you've got somewhere to go if you want it.'

'So what did you think of it?' asks Uncle Archie.

He towers in the small kitchen, courteous and genuinely interested, whilst Aunt Em makes tea. Tiggy feels a wave of affection and gratitude: it is incumbent upon her to be positive.

'I liked it,' she says. 'I think it might work.'

'Splendid.' Archie picks up the tea-tray and carries it out into the courtyard. Em follows with the teapot.

'This is so different from Trescairn.' Tiggy sits down on a little wrought-iron chair and looks around her. Brightly coloured flowers tumble and trail from terracotta pots and valerian clings to niches in the surrounding wall. It is hot and sheltered here, the flagstones warm beneath their feet. 'Don't you miss the space after Trescairn?'

'No,' says Aunt Em firmly. 'I do not. Nor do I miss the end-less wind, the mists, the draughts and the dispiriting fact that hardly anything would grow in such inhospitable conditions.'

Uncle Archie grins at Tiggy. 'Does that answer your ques-tion?'

'Very definitely.' Tiggy grins too. 'What about you?'

'Well, I'm rather fond of the old place but I could see Em's point. When my tenant here died we thought it was an excellent moment to make a change. And Pete and Julia were looking for something bigger. Worked out splendidly, hasn't it, Em?'

'Splendidly,' agrees Em rather drily. 'Though I had no idea how busy village life could be.'

Archie takes his tea from her and winks at Tiggy. 'I neglect her,' he says. 'It's terrible.'

'That's why he hopes you like the cottage,' says Em, passing Tiggy her cup. 'He thinks you'll distract me and I'll be too busy to keep on nagging him to stay at home more.'

Tiggy remembers what Aunt Em said earlier, about sharing in her life, and smiles.

'Well, he could be right,' she says.

2004

Em put the tea-things on the draining board. It was odd that she should remember the little incident; strange that scent could be so powerfully evocative.

But after all, she reminded herself, it was hardly surprising that she should be thinking about Tiggy just now, when Caroline was expecting Zack's baby: Tiggy's grandchild, incredible though that was to believe. It seemed an impossible idea simply because Tiggy had not remained to grow old like the rest of them. Em knew that in her mind's eye Tiggy would always be young, hardly more than a child herself, just as she'd been on that May morning twenty-eight years before in the kitchen at Trescairn.

The scent of the *luteum* was all around her and Em, once again, saw Tiggy's anxious expression and the delightful figure of the little Merlin. Now, stacking the plates on the draining board, emptying the teapot, putting the remaining scones into a tin, Em racked her memory. There had been something familiar about the bronze – and whose signature was it that had been carved into its base?

The raucous ring of the telephone sliced across the tenuous link with the past and Em put the incident out of her mind, wiped her hands, and went to answer it.

CHAPTER NINE

2004

Back at Penharrow, Liv helped Debs to pack away the shopping and then went into the office. Chris sat at his desk, looking preoccupied. She murmured 'Hi', and sat down at her own computer, not wanting to distract him. She had some new photographs to add to the website but she checked emails first: two new bookings and a nice message from a recent visitor who wanted to return in the autumn. Liv checked the diary, made notes, answered the emails. She wondered if Val had managed the laundry and done the ironing, and glanced across at Chris to see if she might ask him.

He was watching her with an expression that jolted her heart and sent the blood racing into her cheeks. Immediately he dropped his gaze to the computer screen, pretending to be absorbed, whilst Liv regained her composure.

'Do you know if Val got the ironing done?' she asked. Her voice sounded normal; that was good. 'Don't want to interrupt you or anything but I can get on with it now if she didn't.'

He pursed his lips, shook his head, keeping his eyes on his screen. 'I really don't know. She had a headache at teatime but I've been here ever since then.'

Liv got up. 'I'll go and see.' She went out into the yard, her heart still beating unevenly, but she didn't go into the house; she couldn't face Val just yet. Instead she went across to the laundry-room. It was clear that Val had been busy although there was still some ironing to be done. Almost thankfully, Liv switched on the iron and set to work. She felt confused and frightened; as if some mighty machine had been put in motion that could easily get out of control.

She remembered her mother's words: 'It can be dangerous', and her own confident assertion that there was nothing to worry about, that she would never do anything to hurt Val. But what if Val insisted on hurting herself, damaging her relationship with Chris because of her obsessive need to control? The question was: how much effect was her, Liv's, presence having on the situation between Val and Chris? Did Chris depend too much on her support and approval when Val was being tiresome?

Liv banged the iron to and fro over the sheets and pillowcases, defending herself against the charge of taking sides. It was precisely because she hadn't wanted an unequal fight that she'd spoken to Val earlier, pointing out the dangers of her behaviour. Presently, piling the laundry into the big airing cupboard, slamming the doors, Liv decided to call it a day.

She went into the annexe, poured a glass of wine and sat down at her laptop. Andy's email was such a shock that she quite forgot Chris and Val and simply stared at the screen, re-reading his message.

To: Liv
From: Andy
OK I might as well tell you before someone else does.
Cat has come back into my life. I know! I know! But it's
rather different now than when we were all kids. Anyway, she's fun and she sends her love. Says she'll look
you up when she's down in Cornwall! Can we be adult
about this? Please!

Liv was filled with a mixture of anger and dread. It was
absolutely out of order that Andy should allow family loyalty
to be elbowed aside for the beastly Cat and she wrote at once
to tell him so.

To: Andy
From: Liv
I simply can't believe I'm reading this stuff. Right up to
sixth form you utterly loathed her. We all did. She was
always mean and spiteful and loved getting people into
trouble at school. And remember what she did to Zack.
You can't be that desperate, surely!

She took her glass and went to curl up on the sofa, feeling confused and miserable, yet a small part of her remained secretly
elated by Chris's expression. As usual the panoramic view
calmed her: the great curve of stormy green-black sea filled
the whole of the horizon, its long curling breakers racing in-
shore to smash themselves into arcs of flying spray against the
stony, unyielding cliffs. In the face of such elemental force, her
problems and anxieties seemed puny.

Nevertheless, she went eagerly back to her laptop several
times during the evening to check her emails but there was no
other message from Andy.

1976

The thing that is the most difficult to get used to, once they've gone, is the silence in the house. There is no sound of the twins arguing over the Lego, Charlie's scribble-talk or Julia humming to her favourite Carly Simon album while she does the ironing; no plans made over breakfast; no voices singing along with Big Ted or the Wombles; no bedtime nursery rhymes.

The dogs follow Tiggy around, puzzled by the empty rooms but pleased by the extra walks they are getting.

'It's something to do,' Tiggy tells Aunt Em when she comes for lunch one day. 'I miss them all dreadfully.'

'Julia was worried about you being alone so soon after your grandmother's death. She feared that you'd have too much time to think.'

'She's right. I'm not quite as good at being alone as I thought I'd be.'

'There are an awful lot of hours to be got through,' says Em. 'I found from four in the afternoon till seven were the longest when Archie was at sea. But of course I had no children to keep me busy, though I sometimes worked part-time. I refused to do anything that might interfere with being at home when he was on leave. It restricted me but I did quite a lot of voluntary work.'

'I miss teaching,' Tiggy says. 'I've begun to see that having some kind of structure to the day is important. Children give you that. So do dogs, up to a point.'

'When I was young,' says Em, 'I looked after one of my elderly aunts. In those days, just after the war, it was perfectly reasonable to expect a younger member of the family to care for an older one and, anyway, I was constantly reminded that I was very lucky that they'd been prepared to look after me and that now it was my turn to repay the debt. Being at the beck and call of a self-willed, cantankerous old woman might have been exhausting but at least I never had to worry about how long the day was.'

Tiggy laughs. 'It sounds awful.'

'I spent my time daydreaming. I was physically busy but the inside of my head was mine. I used to make up long dramas that went on for weeks at a time. I was the heroine, of course, and some brave but weary fighter pilot or sailor back from the war would take a major role. It was all very romantic stuff, of course.'

'Oh, I know exactly what you mean,' says Tiggy eagerly. 'I was the same. I used to spend most of the holidays with my grandmother and I'd read and read – Georgette Heyer especially – and I used to make up stories about how one of those tough, strong-jawed types would find me and carry me off.' She shakes her head. 'It sounds a bit pathetic, doesn't it? But it worked for you, Aunt Em.'

'Yes, it worked for me. One day I met Archie at someone's bridge party and everything changed. Poor Archie. I sometimes wonder if he knew what hit him.'

'How do you mean?'

'Well, it was so fantastic, you see; my dream actually coming true at last. I threw twenty-eight years of frustrated and unrequited love at him. In some ways I can see now that I needed him to be everything I hadn't had: mother, father, siblings, lover, husband. A lesser man might easily have crumpled beneath the weight. Archie managed to handle it, probably because he had time off when he went to sea. Luckily he's a very generous man and I've learned to be more rational. Not always, though: I still get resentful sometimes when he's busy and his time is taken up for some cause when we could be together. I feel I'm still trying to catch up on everything I missed. I suppose the sad fact is that however hard you try you can never replace a happy, balanced childhood.'

'Tom used to talk about that. His parents were killed when he was very young and he spent most of his childhood away at school, including the holidays. He told me that he was always looking for someone that he could attach himself to, whether it was other boys and their families, one of the matrons or a master. He was very lucky when he went to his second school at thirteen to have a chaplain who understood how desperate he was and what he was feeling, and this man and his family really straightened him out. He told Tom never to use his lack of family as a hook to hang his failures on. It would become a habit, he said; an excuse.'

'That's interesting,' says Aunt Em thoughtfully. 'I think I see what he means. It's fatally easy to excuse a negative aspect of one's own behaviour by thinking that it's a result of not having had a normal childhood. I do it myself.'

'Well, this chaplain said that simply being part of a family didn't necessarily guarantee a stable, happy future and that Tom must learn to see himself clearly and honestly.'

'Not that easy,' murmurs Aunt Em.

'Tom talked about it often. Obviously he was trying to help me come to terms with certain things, too, but it had made a very deep impression on him.'

'The drawback with seeing oneself clearly and honestly is that it's such a devastating experience.' Aunt Em grins ruefully. 'Rather shattering to the self-esteem.'

'Ah, but the thing is that you have to be generous too. Tom made a point of that. The chaplain told him to look at yourself honestly, not with self-pity, but be able to forgive yourself – something like that, anyway. I wish I'd known him. I suppose one never knows how much is due to nature or nurture when it comes to character. Tom was great fun but he drove himself physically. He told me that he'd longed to have a family who would've come to school to see him play rugby or cricket and cheer him on like the other boys' families did. That's what drew Tom and me together: the lack of a family. By the time we met he was much more self-confident than I was. Having been at school and university for most of his life he was very self-contained too. But we sort of recognized each other.' She looks rather shyly at Aunt Em. 'I had that feeling when I met you.'

Aunt Em smiles. 'So did I. Odd, isn't it?'

'Yes. And rather nice. Of course, Julia's family were wonderful to me. I can't tell you how I loved being with them. It's difficult to explain to Julia because it was natural for her but, though there were arguments and noise and all the hurly-burly of family life, there was none of those terrible undercurrents and tensions of my own life. It was so *normal* and utter heaven. And now she's rescued me again. They'll never know, any of them, what they've done for me. The trouble is, in some way it just adds to my own sense of inadequacy. One doesn't want to have to go through life being rescued.'

'It wasn't your fault that Tom died,' says Em. 'That kind of tragedy can happen to anybody. At least you have his child.'

'But can't you see that in some ways that makes it much worse? Oh, I want my baby, of course I do, but I feel that I've already set the pattern for her – or his – life and it won't be the one I always dreamed of: no father, no happy normal family. The headmistress where I taught showed me exactly how it's going to be for the future. I'm hardening myself to it a bit but you can see the reaction in people's faces, and it's not just the older ones. With some people it's simply embarrassment rather than disapproval. They can't just enthuse in the way they would if there were a father on the scene. It's like when Tom died. Nobody quite knows what to say to you so they avoid you if they can. It's very isolating.'

'I'm so sorry,' says Em gently. 'You're quite right. I'm taking a very narrow view because I longed so much to have Archie's child. You get to the point when you think it would be worth anything to have a child: it becomes an obsession. All you see are pregnant women or mothers with small children and you'd sacrifice anything to be one of their number. I take your point. If there's anything we can do to help in any way you must ask.'

Tiggy smiles. 'I might take you up on that. I spend hours wondering how I shall be able to earn a living for us both. Julia, bless her, says that she'll look after the baby while I'm working, but I'm not sure I could ask her to take on such a responsibility. Anyway, she probably only said it because the ghastly Angela was being nosy.'

Em's expression changes: her smile fades and she looks serious. 'Angela? She's a bad girl,' she says.

Tiggy stares at her in surprise. 'How do you mean, bad? Julia said that she had a bit of a fling with Pete before they got to-gether and she likes to rub it in.'

'I don't trust her,' says Em. 'Angela's not the kind of woman who likes being dropped – well, nobody does, of course – and she's still trying to hurt Julia.'

'I think Julia's afraid of her,' says Tiggy anxiously, after a pause.

'With good cause,' says Em grimly.

The next day Tiggy drives herself to Tintagel, parks near the church and walks out across Glebe Cliff with the dogs. The castle has ceased to be the object of her interest; instead she is drawn to the cliffs and to the sea, though she looks back from time to time towards Tintagel Island and the dark entrance to Merlin's Cave. On this hot May day the water is clear green and dark purple, colours that remind her of a jockey's silks. Making her cautious way out between the bright-flowered gorse bushes to a little patch of smooth granite at the edge of the cliff, she finds she can look down, far down, to where the waves cream against the sheer rock face. Mesmerized, she stares downwards, inexplicably drawn to the clear aquamarine depths, feeling a little dizzy, almost light-headed: how welcoming the sea looks, how calm. It would be so simple to take that one last step into its infinite embrace.

A bird flies up, almost into her face, and she screams, moving back on to the grass, her feet slipping so that she sits down for safety and almost overbalances. She cries out again in fright, clutching at the coarse tufted grass, and the dogs bark frantically, their paws scrabbling amongst the loose stones on the slope above her. She inches back carefully, mocking herself for a fool, until she reaches safer ground where the dogs lick her face and she hugs them, trembling a little and giving herself time to recover.

Later, after a long walk along the cliffs with her eyes fixed towards the west, beyond Port Isaac Bay to The Mouls, she sits drinking coffee with the van door open to the sunshine and the dogs curled at her feet. A large black bird with red legs drifts upwards into view at the cliff's edge and she wonders if it might be a chough: perhaps it is the bird that brought her to her senses.

Tiggy shivers. Presently she turns to look across at the Norman church, with its strong square tower, and suddenly is moved to inspect it more closely. Its dramatic setting in the huge churchyard high on the cliff has already made a great impact upon her but now she decides to go inside. She shuts the dogs in the van with plenty of water and the windows partly open, and crosses to the lich-gate. There is no thatched roof to protect the coffin-bearers from the rain but she pauses for a moment with her hand on the long coffin stone and then walks slowly up to the porch.

Inside, she is instantly aware of the powerful, soul-moving atmosphere created by more than a thousand years of worship and prayer, and shaken by the sense of light and peace. Her glance takes in the massive stone font, upheld at each of its four corners by curving serpents, and at the crude heads carved between them; the figure of St Christopher with the Holy Child on his shoulder, set in a niche opposite the door; the sweep of the high arched beams above her. She makes her way up the aisle and sits down in a pew, staring at the rood screen, but taking nothing in except the need to sit for a moment and be silent.

Here, the conviction she's felt on the moors and out on the cliffs comes to her even more strongly: it seems that the deaths of Tom and her grandmother have given eternity the opportunity to break through the earthly barriers between life and death, bringing them close to her and offering courage and hope. She tries to pray for them, and for herself and her child, but no words will come – and, in the end, it seems unimportant. She is held in a silent communion in which no words are needed and presently she lights two votive candles, one for Tom and one for her grandmother, and then goes back out into the sunlit, wind-raked spaces of cliff and sea and sky.

That night Tiggy dreams again, the same dream: once again she seems to be present in the dream whilst at the same time watching what is happening. Tom is there, and Julia, and the shadowy third person who holds out the baby and says: 'Her name is Claerwen, Clare for short.'

She wakes suddenly, just as she is stretching out her arms to take the baby, and lies huddled in the dark, trying to adjust to reality and feeling bereft. Knowing that she will not be able to go back to sleep for a while, she sits up and switches on the bedside light: nearly four o'clock. Tiggy groans, pulls on her dressing gown and pushes her feet into sheepskin moccasins. The Turk raises her head, watching Tiggy from the comfort of the bed, reluctant to stir unless it is absolutely necessary. Bella, sleeping in the old Lloyd Loom chair, stirs and stretches but makes no attempt to move.

Tiggy goes out on to the landing and down the stairs; before the kettle has boiled, both dogs arrive in the kitchen, slightly puzzled but expectant. She gives each of them a biscuit, makes tea and sits down at the table. Her gaze takes in the big, warm room, which is so similar to the kitchen in Julia's home in Hampshire and so central to family life: Charlie's high chair strung about with toys and teething rings, Andy's Fisher Price aeroplane, which has landed on the deep granite windowseat, Liv's *Milly-Molly-Mandy* books piled on the dresser. On the arm of the sofa lies Julia's discarded knitting: a jersey for Liv in chunky multicoloured wool, the several pieces rolled up and pierced by two thick wooden needles. On the wall by the fridge hangs a plastic notice board on which Julia jots her shopping list or special dates or things to be taken to playschool. A series of postcards tracing Pete's Mediterranean journey – Gibraltar, Toulon, Naples, Athens, Malta – are stuck round its edges. Across one corner he's written: 'I love my Mrs B.' At some point Julia has responded with: 'I love you too.'

Tiggy thinks: I wish Trescairn was my house. Mine and Tom's.

The thought triggers a memory. One evening, driving through the lanes from Blisland, she pulled the van close in against the hedge and stopped so as to allow a rider on a nervous horse to approach and pass. As she sat waiting, she glanced across the escallonia hedge into the cottage garden beyond. It was a pretty garden, somewhat overgrown and neglected, though it was clear that attempts were being made to tidy it up. Bedding plants, still in their pots, stood in a row beneath the open window beside a newly dug bed, and on the small patch of worn grass a young man was busy at work, rubbing down an old pine table. The front door was open to a cosy, cluttered interior and, as Tiggy watched, a girl appeared carrying two mugs. The young man straightened up, smiling with relief and pleasure at the interruption. He took his mug and, having kissed the girl with great tenderness, they both turned to look with tremendous pride at the table. As they leaned together in the doorway, Tiggy saw that the girl was expecting a child.

She was gripped with an agonizing sense of loss: she and Tom would never share such a happy, loving moment; never build a home together for their child. The pain was so intense that, even though the horse and its rider had passed, she was unable to put the van in gear and drive on; only when she saw that the young couple had become aware of the stationary vehicle and were staring curiously did she pull herself together and drive away.

Now, remembering, she finishes her tea and wonders if she should have a biscuit: anything to distract from the memory. Another memory rises in her mind's eye: a picture of them all sitting round the table in the middle of the night and Julia missing Pete and saying: 'Wouldn't it be wonderful if we could be four years old again and have all our problems solved by the prospect of a chocolate biscuit?'

For no particular reason, Tiggy thinks about Angela and what Aunt Em said.

'I'm afraid of her,' Julia admitted – and Aunt Em said, 'With good cause.'

Tiggy's stomach tenses with anxiety and she stares at the notice board for courage.

'I love my Mrs B.' 'I love you too.'

She recalls the expression on Pete's face when he gave Julia the bottle of scent, and other gestures she's witnessed since, and shakes her head: it is impossible that Pete should be unfaithful to Julia with Angela. To begin with, the two girls are so unalike. Angela is thin as a pin, always chic, with sleek black hair and eyes so dark brown they are almost black. Julia is too rushed to be smart; her thick fair hair thrust behind her ears, one of Pete's old shirts tucked into her jeans, which are always a bit tight because of finishing up the children's breakfast toast and teatime treats. There is a generous warmth about Julia that is completely missing from Angela's character.

Yet, Tiggy reminds herself, Pete fancied Angela once: they had a fling.

She is distracted from these thoughts by a subtle change: it is no longer dark and the lamp's light glows less cheerfully as the early-morning light filters in at the curtains' edge. The Turk uncurls herself and stretches, stiff-legged, and goes to the door, followed by Bella, whose tail wags hopefully. Tiggy gets up and lets them out into the porch. She opens the back door and stands quite still, listening in delight. Flights of larks are ascending, their song bubbling up and up; and then, away to the east, beyond the black scrawled outline of Rough Tor, the sun seems to burst out of the earth, filling the world with brilliance.

CHAPTER TEN

2004

In Tavistock, Caroline shut the door of the terraced house in Chapel Street and set off into the town. Wonderful though it was to have Zack home again, she liked these moments when she left him busy with some project and went shopping alone. Zack wasn't a shopper; he didn't care much for sitting in a café idly drinking coffee when he could be getting on at home. Probably this was because he had so little time at home but, whatever the reason, Caroline was happy on this warm, sunny morning. She paused in West Street to look at the pretty linen clothes in the window of Wandering Nomads and then strolled on past the church and crossed Bedford Square where the stalls of the farmers' market had been set up. Caroline lingered beside the mouth-watering displays of cheese and preserves and crisp fresh vegetables but shook her head smilingly at the vendors' banter; she'd buy one or two treats on the way back so that she didn't have to carry the bags too far.

'Are you sure you won't need help?' Zack had asked anxiously. 'Should you be carrying heavy things?'

She'd assured him that she'd be fine; she was warmed by his concern but looking forward to her foray to the shops. After all, she had no intention of weighing herself down with heavy groceries – they'd do the supermarket run together later with the car – and it was hardly any distance to walk back home. She knew how lucky they were to be renting the cottage in Chapel Street; the owners, another naval couple, had been posted to Washington and were only too pleased to let their house to Zack and Caroline, especially as Zack had offered to undertake some of the landscaping work for the garden in their absence. It would be even nicer if it were their own house, of course, but with prices as they were this was a dream yet to be achieved. Meanwhile it was such fun to wander out like this, while Zack was laying paving slabs in the garden. He'd be enjoying himself; at breakfast he'd been busy with sketches and measurements, working it out, quite content for her to leave him to it.

She'd learned early on that he liked to have some kind of project; something to work at when he was on leave. He had terrific vitality and needed to push himself physically, though he wasn't particularly social outside his own close circle of friends. Well, that was fine: so far she'd managed to maintain a fine balance between her own natural friendliness and his reticence, just as he prevented her from being too lazy. Of course, she missed her family in Edinburgh, and the gossip of the staff-room at school, but this move to Tavistock was an exciting new stage in her and Zack's lives together and it was a bonus to have Zack's family near at hand, especially Liv. Right from the beginning she and Liv had got on really well. She'd asked Liv once whether Zack had ever wanted to track down his ancestors; after all, these days it seemed to be a popular hobby. Liv had shaken her head.

'Zack's an odd fellow,' she'd said. 'He has these fits of worrying about his genetic inheritance but some instinct tells him that he doesn't want to probe into his past. I asked him about it once and he said he thought it might be divisive and painful, like opening Pandora's Box. He told me very firmly that we are his family, that he knows all he needs to know about Tiggy and his father, and that's that. He's able to compartmentalize it, I suppose.'

Caroline had been able to accept that: Zack was exactly the same with his job and his home life, keeping them very firmly in different boxes as much as he could. Occasionally he might have doubts regarding his abilities but everyone had those from time to time.

'Anyway,' she'd said to him after the trip to Penharrow, 'I know you're going to be a great dad. We know enough about Tiggy and Tom for you to be confident about that. Tiggy was your mum's best friend, she was Charlie's godmother and she loved children. And she loved your father. That's good enough for me.'

In Brook Street, Caroline stopped to buy a copy of the *Big Issue* and then went into Creber's to choose some marmalade and something delicious for lunch; perhaps a wedge of game pie or some pâté. She was trying to be careful with her diet, though she'd decided not to be too influenced by the shelves of books dedicated to the wellbeing of pregnant women; it was easy to become overwhelmed by so much information. She knew she was lucky to feel so well; being pregnant suited her and she was determined to enjoy every stage.

Outside again, she consulted her shopping list: a birthday card for her brother and moisturizing cream. She crossed the road to Boots the Chemist, where she pottered for some time; she postponed the buying of the card – she'd have a look in

Allan Dolan's on the way back to Chapel Street – and decided to take a little rest before walking home.

Splashed with sunshine, the tubs along the edge of the colonnade and the hanging baskets were full of bright flowers; sitting outside Duke's Café, drinking coffee and watching the shoppers passing in and out of the Pannier Market, Caroline sighed with contentment.

By Thursday, when Aunt Em arrived at Penharrow for lunch, Liv was incandescent with fury at Andy's recalcitrance. He stolidly refused to be cowed by her sisterly disapproval, insisting that Cat was a changed being now that she was a sexy, fun thirtysomething. His last email had a finality about it.

> To: Liv
>
> From: Andy
>
> We're not kids any more, Liv, and I'd certainly hate to be judged permanently on something I did when I was eight. I expect Zack's forgotten all about it, and anyway Mum always said it was her fault for not telling Zack earlier. Cat's doing brilliantly. She's in futures and earns a packet. We're going to Le Caprice tonight and she's managed to get tickets for *Chicago*. I can't remember when I had so much fun.

Liv had thumped the table with despair and tried to think of a suitable rejoinder. The trouble was that every response that occurred to her would be unreasonable in Andy's eyes: after all, it *was* unfair to judge someone on a childish misdemeanour.

'But it wasn't just what she did to Zack,' Liv told herself crossly. 'She was always a beastly child, otherwise we wouldn't have disliked her so much.'

Aunt Em's arrival coincided with two of the visitors leaving amidst cheerful farewells and promises to return. Liv waved a welcome as Aunt Em parked her car and Val came to greet her too, pleased at the visitors' wholehearted approval for all their hard work.

'It's nice when people are happy,' she said. 'And I like to think of them coming back again. Makes them seem more like friends than visitors.'

Behind Val, Liv raised her eyebrows and rolled her eyes at Aunt Em, surprised at such a positive reaction, wickedly inviting complicity; Aunt Em resolutely ignored her and smiled warmly at Val.

'I'm so pleased that it's going well,' she said. 'I'm sure it will be very rewarding once you've ironed out all the small starting-up problems. It's such a fabulous location. Of course people are going to love it. They'll come back year after year.'

'Well done, Aunt Em!' Liv said approvingly, as Val went back to the house. 'That's the stuff to give the troops. Of course, it'll only last until we get the next problem but it's good to see her smiling. You did well. Very convincing. I almost believed it myself.'

'You sound jaded,' complained Aunt Em. 'Almost cynical. I thought you said she needed encouraging.'

'Oh, she does,' said Liv. 'Lots of encouraging. I'm not really jaded, I'm just having a run-in with Andy and it's getting me down. Come and see Debs. She's made that Mediterranean vegetable lasagne you so enjoyed last time you were here so I hope you're feeling hungry.'

Debs was delighted to see Aunt Em; she was clearly touched that Aunt Em remembered the names of her children and their various histories, and bridled with pleasure at the reception the lasagne was given.

'Careful, Aunt Em,' Liv murmured, as Debs turned away

to serve two generous portions. 'If you carry on with all this goodwill you'll do yourself a mischief.'

'You're asking for a smack,' Aunt Em told her, as they took their plates to a table by the window. 'I recognize this mood of old. In a minute we'll have "pee po piddle bum" and toys all over the floor.'

Liv laughed. 'You are so right,' she agreed. 'I'd simply love to go into orbit and do the whole bit. Isn't it tiresome when you're supposed to be grown up and you can't just let it all rip?'

'Poor Liv.' Aunt Em was eating with relish. 'This is very good. But what has Andy done to incur your wrath?'

'It sounds silly, really,' admitted Liv. 'You'll think I'm crazy to get so upset just because he's met up again with the wretched Cat and seems to be falling for her. It is crazy, isn't it? Do you remember Cat, Aunt Em?'

'Oh, yes,' said Aunt Em. She seemed to have lost her appetite though she finished the last few forkfuls. 'I remember Cat very well.'

'Well, then.' Liv's tone implied that nothing more need be said. She finished her own lunch and glanced curiously at Aunt Em, who was sitting silently staring at nothing in particular. 'He says it's all such a long time ago that she was so beastly to Zack, and I take his point, but we never liked her. And Mum never liked Angela, did she?'

'No,' said Aunt Em. 'No, she didn't.'

'Well, then. I'm just so cross with him. It's disloyal, and now he's talking of her coming down to Cornwall and dropping in on us. He must be out of his mind. Anyway, that's why I'm in a bate. Oh, here's Chris.'

She brightened, moving her plate a little to the side, her volatile mood enhanced by his presence; she had the urge to be really outrageous just to make him laugh but reluctantly abandoned the idea. Aunt Em's unusually thoughtful expression dampened her spirits a little.

'I've just come to say hello,' he said, 'not to interrupt anything. Are you well, Mrs Bodrugan?'

'Very well, thanks.' Em smiled up at him. 'Penharrow seems to be going from strength to strength. You must be very proud. Are you having some lunch?'

'Val's getting us something.' He shifted, pushing his hands into his pockets, as if he were deciding whether to sit down beside Liv. 'Just a sandwich or some soup.' Still he hesitated. 'We've got a busy afternoon, actually, so I suppose I'd better get on.'

'You do that,' said Liv cordially. 'Hurry away. Mustn't keep Val waiting.'

He looked confused, even slightly irritated, smiled again at Aunt Em and went out. Liv drummed a little tune on the table top and pulled a face. Aunt Em watched her sympathetically.

'Shall we go for a walk along the cliffs?' she suggested. 'Then you can have a really good scream.'

Liv burst out laughing. 'I don't know what's wrong with me,' she said.

'Don't you?' asked Aunt Em drily.

Liv stared at her, the laughter dying out of her face. 'What do you mean?' she asked almost fearfully. 'I told you I'm all wound up about Andy.' She looked away from the older woman's direct gaze. 'It's Andy,' she repeated. 'Never mind. Let's have some pudding.'

Later, in Liv's flat, Em made up her mind. The mention of Cat's name at lunchtime had had a surprising effect upon her; a stomach-churning anxiety out of all proportion. This sense of unease, combined with Liv's behaviour, forced her to a resolution. Nervously she prepared herself, assembling her thoughts, formulating sentences in her head, waiting for the right moment.

'We'll have coffee at my place,' Liv had said. 'Debs is a terrific cook but the coffee isn't as good as mine.'

So now here they were, Liv putting the pot down beside her and pushing a pretty, fragile mug towards her. Em straightened her spine and took a steadying breath.

'I couldn't sympathize more with your reaction to Andy's news,' she began. 'I feel exactly the same myself about Cat. Odd, isn't it? Of course, I can't help being prejudiced against the child because of my dislike for her mother.'

'For Angela?' Liv looked alert. 'I know Mum never liked her. It seemed to be a family thing, didn't it? Was there a particular reason?'

'Oh, yes,' answered Em bravely, heart hammering. 'Angela tried to break up your parents' marriage.'

Liv sat down, holding her coffee, looking shocked. 'Did she? But how? Weren't they all old friends? I seem to remember Angela and Cat from the earliest time of my life.'

'Angela and your father were very old friends. They went out together before he met your mother.'

'Really?' Liv was very interested. 'I didn't know that. What, really seriously?'

'Seriously enough to make Angela pretty cross when Pete dropped her for Julia. She never forgave him and she never let him forget it either. She made your mother very unhappy. At one point I feared that Angela would succeed in driving your parents apart.'

'But when was that?' Liv looked almost frightened; her safe, secure vision of her family was being threatened. 'Dad never would have left Mum for Angela.'

Her voice was almost contemptuous but underneath Em could hear the tremor of anxiety.

'Angela was clever,' she answered. 'She knew that Pete felt guilty for dropping her and she played on it. Julia was jealous, insecure, and Angela played on that too. I feared her and disliked her. The odd thing is that I felt – feel – exactly the same about Cat, though I don't know why, except that she is her mother's child – and for the way she treated Zack, of course. But that was a long time ago.'

'That's what Andy says. And, anyway, Mum always says that she's to blame, really, for not telling Zack earlier.' Liv was silent for a moment. 'I didn't know that about Dad and Angela,' she said at last. 'Do you think I should tell Andy? Do you think it would put him off Cat?'

'No, I don't,' said Em at once. 'Andy might tell her the story and I think that would be wrong.' She frowned. 'I said that quite instinctively,' she said. 'Why should I think it might be dangerous to tell Andy?'

'Maybe you think it would give Cat extra ammunition?' suggested Liv.

'I think that Andy's sympathies are going to be biased towards Cat,' said Em thoughtfully. 'If he's falling in love with her then he will want to exonerate her – and Angela – from any suggestion of bad behaviour. There must be no excuses for them to feel like star-crossed lovers. That's so dangerous. Cat will simply use everything he tells her as a weapon if she can. Oh dear.' She shook her head. 'How vindictive that makes me sound. Why should we think that Cat has any axe to grind? Perhaps I shouldn't have told you either, Liv. I just felt that forewarned is forearmed – or something like that. You must keep it as a confidence. Promise?'

Liv nodded. 'Promise. I'm glad you're on my side, though. Shall I say anything to Mum about Andy and Cat?'

'Perhaps not just yet. It might so easily be a flash in the pan, mightn't it? Perhaps give it a week or so and see what happens.'

'OK. Of course, he might tell Mum himself if it gets serious. I'll wait a bit, I think. It's different now I know about Angela.'

Em glanced at her watch. 'I think I should let you get back to work, don't you? I shan't be so welcome next time if I take advantage.'

She drove away, aware of Liv's preoccupation, still anxious; had she had the right to tell Liv about Angela and Pete? She realized that her message had become confused and she suspected that Liv was far more concerned with the involvement between her father and Angela than with the warning that Em had intended.

'I've been interfering,' she murmured remorsefully to Archie, whose shade she felt might be hovering accusingly. 'You were always warning me about interfering. It's not that I think I know best. It's just such utter hell watching the young walking blindly into trouble.'

Chris was already at his desk when Liv arrived in the office. He looked at her warily. He recognized the brittle mood she'd been in all day and guessed that something was worrying her. His own feelings for her – tenderness, affection, mingled now with an odd sense of guilt – made it difficult for him to be natural with her. Liv, unwittingly, came to his rescue.

'I'm fed up,' she said, sitting down at her desk and putting her elbows on it. 'I'm furious with Andy.'

Chris was ludicrously relieved; at least it was nothing to do with him or Val. 'What's Andy up to?' he asked cheerfully. The relationship between Liv and Andy had always amused him. They were fiercely loyal to each other but competitive, too; each reserving the right to criticize the other's life yet very open about their own affairs.

'Does Andy have to know everything about us?' he'd asked Liv once, way back in the early stages of their relationship.

'Oh, I don't tell him everything,' she'd answered airily. 'Only the bits that I think will interest him.'

'I'm not sure that I find that particularly comforting,' he'd murmured.

'It's nothing really,' Liv said moodily now. 'It's just that I hate the beastly girl he's taken up with. The whole family hates her. And her mother. He's being stupid and disloyal.'

Chris couldn't help smiling. 'How old is he?' he asked. 'Thirty-one? Thirty-two? Isn't he old enough to choose his own girlfriends?'

'Age has got nothing to do with it. She's just very bad news. Aunt Em feels the same about her.'

'Does she?' He was surprised. Liv's Aunt Em gave him the impression of being a very well-balanced woman. 'What's wrong with this girl?'

'It's family history,' Liv said reluctantly. 'Private stuff.'

He could see that she was longing to confide and he wondered if he should push it a bit, tell her she could trust him, but before he could speak the door opened and Val came in. He could see that she was still on a high, though he knew that it wasn't simply because of the praise she'd received earlier from the visitors. It was much more than that: she'd overborne his caution and they'd embarked on a new and exciting journey.

'Don't tell Liv we're trying for a baby,' she'd cautioned him. 'I don't want anybody to know yet.'

He hadn't needed the warning; he had no desire to tell Liv the news. He had the oddest feeling that he was somehow betraying her, though the idea was ridiculous. He knew, looking at Val, that this shiny bright mood was all to do with winning and being in a new position of power. She was already displaying 'I am a pregnant woman' symptoms, which he felt touching and irritating by turns, depending on how much of a power struggle was involved at the time.

'I was just thinking about Saturday,' Val was saying. 'I'd forgotten that you're going to see Zack and Caroline tomorrow evening, aren't you, Liv, and staying the night? We've got two changeovers the morning after, and I suddenly wondered how we'll cope.'

Chris felt a tug of irritation. This was so typical of Val: an attempt at manipulation, a private hinting to him that she might already be in a delicate condition and that the extra work shouldn't fall to her. What did she want him to do: forbid Liv to go out?

'It's fine,' Liv was saying, not at all put out. 'I'd already thought of that. Myra's sister is coming up to help. No problems.'

'Oh.' Val looked disconcerted. 'Oh, well then.' She gave a short, rather artificial laugh. 'As long as we can afford the extra labour.'

Chris was angry now. 'I doubt that paying Myra's sister for a few hours will break the bank,' he said coolly. He picked up his telephone rather pointedly, pulled a file towards him, and Val shrugged and went out.

Liv was still sitting, elbows on desk, chin in hands, and he smiled at her awkwardly, apologetically. She smiled back at him, understanding, and he was seized with a deep, simple and overwhelming affection for her.

1976

The family return from their holiday, and Tiggy and the dogs are delighted to see them. The twins and Charlie are glad to be home and settle happily into their routines, Pete goes daily to the dockyard where a new captain is about to join the submarine, and a new pattern emerges that is very similar to the old one but with small significant differences. Tiggy makes an effort to be alert to Pete's presence, and tactful when he and Julia have time together and the children are in bed, but their natural acceptance of her makes it very simple and she begins to feel as if she might be a sibling, truly one of the family, and relaxes a little.

She takes Julia to see the cottage, whilst Aunt Em minds Charlie and the twins, and they quietly discuss its merits and its disadvantages.

'It really all depends on where I can find a job,' says Tiggy, sitting on the long, orange-covered G Plan sofa. 'If I can get one in the town then this is a good place to be. I might be able to work the lunchtime shift in one of the pubs. Uncle Archie's got his ear to the ground. The size I am now, nobody takes me seriously when I go in and ask for a job.'

'I can believe that,' agrees Julia, poking around in the small but well set-up kitchen behind the Formica breakfast bar, 'but I hoped you might be a bit nearer to us.'

'So did I. I phoned the local pubs but they don't need anybody and I can't find any cottages for rent around St Breward or Blisland.'

'Does it have to be a pub?'

'The hours are more flexible and my brief experience shows me that they don't ask so many questions. Of course, a bit later I hope to get back into teaching – but who knows?'

'How long before you have to say yes or no?'

'Oh, a few weeks yet. Aunt Em says that there will be loads of people after it if I don't want it so there's no great pressure.'

'In that case we'll have a really good scour around nearer to home,' Julia says.

Pete comes home one hot June evening in a very grumpy mood.

'The new captain has decided that he wants a work-up,' he

says, pouring himself a gin and tonic. 'Give us all a chance to shake down together, he says. That means a month in Scottish waters. Everyone's really fed up.'

'Oh, no.' Julia lights a cigarette. 'Oh, darling, what a bore.'

He glances irritably at her cigarette, as if he is looking for an excuse for a quarrel. 'I thought you'd given up,' he says tetchily. 'You said you would.'

'I nearly have,' says Julia. 'Except at moments like these. The kids will be really upset.'

'Then don't mention it just yet,' says Pete. 'I can't hack them giving me grief about it. Oh, by the way, I saw Martin in *Drake* today. He and Angela have invited us to dinner.'

There is a little silence. Tiggy, glancing at Julia, sees that her cheeks are brightly flushed and that she draws very deliberately on her cigarette before she answers.

'What did you say?' she asks abruptly.

Pete shrugs. He seems ill at ease and his tone is truculent when he answers. 'I said I didn't see why not but that I'd check with you. It's next Saturday and we haven't got anything planned as far as I know. It's Martin's birthday so it's going to be a really big thrash. I assumed that Tiggy wouldn't mind baby-sitting.'

He glances at her and she assumes a willing but non-committal expression, not wishing to upset Julia who still stares at the tip of her cigarette.

'I suppose we shall have to go,' she says at last.

'Well, don't sound so thrilled.' Pete finishes his drink. 'I'm going to have a bath.'

He goes out of the kitchen, through the hall and into the sitting-room, and Tiggy and Julia hear the children greeting him with cries of welcome.

'I suppose she can't be too awful at a party,' Tiggy ventures at last.

Julia looks as if she might burst into angry tears. 'Angela can be awful anywhere,' she says.

On the night of the party, Tiggy goes to bed before Julia and Pete arrive home and rises early next morning so as to make sure the children don't bother them. Julia looks preoccupied and tired when she appears in the kitchen seeking coffee; Pete stays in bed very late and, when he eventually gets up, he goes off with the dogs, not inviting anyone to go with him and thus incurring the wrath of Liv and Andy.

They chant 'Pee po piddle bum' and begin one of their tiresome duets: '*Why* is Daddy so mean . . . ?' 'Yes, but *why* is he . . . ?' until Julia shouts at them, silencing the twins and making Charlie cry.

'Sorry,' she says wretchedly. 'Sorry, darlings. That's what happens when mummies go to bed too late. It's OK, Charlie. Do shut up, there's a good boy.'

She smiles at Tiggy, who is looking as anxious as the twins. 'It's nothing. But . . . well, you know how she is.'

'Who?' asks Liv curiously. 'Who are you talking about?'

'Nobody,' says Julia. 'Nothing. Who wants to help me make pastry for lunch?'

Pete returns and makes a great effort to entertain the children: he helps them to erect a tent on the lawn and creates some rough but adequate furniture out of old tea-chests. A camp bed is set up and covered with a tartan blanket and some cushions, the little Merlin is placed on the table for an ornament, and Bella allows her basket to be carried out and put by the door flap so as to lend an authentic homely note. Tea is to be eaten in the tent; even Charlie is welcomed in. Tiggy, coming into the kitchen to fetch some Ribena for the twins, finds Pete with his arm about an unyielding Julia with whom he seems to be pleading. Tiggy backs out hastily and hovers around near the front door until presently Pete comes out of the kitchen and goes upstairs. When she ventures back into the kitchen, Julia is standing quite still, staring out into the garden. Tiggy slips her hand under Julia's arm and Julia presses it against her side with her elbow.

'It's OK,' she says, in answer to Tiggy's unspoken query. 'Honestly. I'm just being silly.'

She takes a deep breath, as if making some resolution, and when Pete comes in she speaks to him quite naturally. Tiggy hides her relief, pretending that she notices nothing amiss, which seems to enable Pete and Julia to relax even more. Tea has to be eaten in relays, first Julia, then Pete, then Tiggy, being invited into the tent, and by the time it is over good humour has been restored.

The next morning, Pete comes back to give Julia an extra kiss before driving away.

'Angela was awful,' Julia says to Tiggy as they clear up the breakfast things and the twins rush out to the tent. 'She was all over him. Martin makes a joke about it, says that he and I should get together and things like that. I make a joke of it too, of course, but I hate it. And I hate Pete because he makes no effort to resist her. He drinks too much and then it makes me look like I'm a prig. And I'm not. I like to drink and enjoy myself.'

Tiggy wants to hug her. 'He probably feels he'd look a fool if he slapped her down. As if he were paying it too much importance.'

Julia shrugs. 'Probably. I wouldn't mind if it were anyone else. Everyone gets a bit silly at parties; I do. But there's something different with Angela. I can just feel it.'

Tiggy remembers Aunt Em's words and feels sick in her stomach. 'It's just a macho thing,' she says. 'And Angela's just one of those cows who likes to upset other women. Don't give her the satisfaction of seeing that you think she has any power.'

'I try not to,' says Julia gloomily, drying her hands and reaching for her cigarettes. 'But then I remember that they had this thing together and I wonder if he regrets giving her up.'

'Did he give her up?'

'That's what he says. He says the usual things: "If I'd loved her we'd still be together", and "I married you, didn't I?", and stuff like that. I know it's silly of me to mind but I can't help myself and then I feel guilty afterwards.'

Just after lunch, a Radio Rental van comes slowly down the drive.

'Brought you a new television, love,' the driver says. 'Your husband phoned and said it was time you had a change. Wait till you see it.'

He carries the set into the sitting-room and installs it, and presently the children are staring transfixed at the inhabitants of Camberwick Green – and the firemen, Pugh, Pugh, Barney McGrew, Cuthbert, Dibble and Grub – in brilliant blues and reds and greens. Even Charlie is mesmerized by the glory of it.

'So what do you think?' asks Pete later. He looks rather shamefaced but pleased with himself.

Julia smiles. 'You only did it so that you could watch *The Magic Roundabout* in colour.'

He puts his arms round her, winking at Tiggy over her head. 'Actually I was thinking more about *Star Trek*,' he says.

CHAPTER ELEVEN

2004

On the morning of the day of Caroline and Zack's house-warming party, Liv was in Truro. Having parked behind the cathedral she made her way amongst dawdling holiday-makers, through the narrow streets to The Place and went in. Looking around her she saw that nothing had changed since her last visit: the black and white tiled floor, whitewashed rough-stone walls and the large gilt-framed mirrors. The long bar stretched the length of one wall and, as she closed the door behind her, Matt got up from one of the bar stools and came to meet her. She'd forgotten how tall he was but the short silvery-gold hair and the straight glance were just as she'd remembered.

'Liv,' he said. 'It's so good to see you again. D'you remember Joe?'

'Of course I do.' She smiled at the man behind the bar. 'How's it going?'

Someone called to him as she spoke and he turned away,

casting a quick apologetic smile back at Liv over his shoulder.
She grimaced at Matt.

'That was a bit tactless, I suppose,' she said. 'He's hardly
likely to be thrilled with all this, is he?'

'Joe's OK,' said Matt. 'He'll be glad to get it sorted. Liam's
sold his house and moved upcountry so Joe's been left holding
the baby. He's suggested we go and look around upstairs first
so we can talk about it over lunch. He's keeping the table in
the snug for us so we can have a bit of privacy. Would you like
a drink?'

'I'll leave it until we eat.' Liv grinned at him. 'I have this feeling that you can hardly wait to get up there.'

Matt laughed. 'Is my enthusiasm showing? Sorry. I'm really
looking forward to having your reaction. I will admit that I've
got a very good hunch about all this.'

Liv found that she was responding to his personality, enjoying being part of his excitement.

'Go on then,' she said. 'Let's have a look at The Place Upstairs
or whatever you're going to call it.'

He led the way up the narrow staircase to the first floor;
talking as they went along, he threw open doors, going into
the office and the storerooms, outlining his ideas.

'We'd need to gut all this,' he said. 'Open it right up and have
one huge area. Reinstate the fireplace at that end, sofas here
and here. What d'you think? Make it more elegant than the
bistro atmosphere downstairs. A bar, of course . . .'

She asked a few questions, examined the rooms carefully,
and then he showed her the two big attic rooms on the second
floor.

'These could be converted into a nice little flat,' he told her.
'You could do what you liked with the conversion if you're
drawn to the idea of living over the shop. It would be up
to you.' He saw her wary expression and held up his hands

171

placatingly. 'I know you haven't made up your mind yet, and I'm not trying to rush you, but I wanted you to know that this could be part of the package.'

Liv looked out of the dormer window at the cathedral spire; the sun slanted through at an oblique angle on to the dusty floor and she was seized with a sudden sense of optimism. Matt was watching her with that disconcerting gaze; hands in pockets, head slightly lowered.

She thought: How attractive he is – and gave a little involuntary shiver.

'You've thought about where you'll rehouse the things that are upstairs?' she asked, playing it cool. 'The office and storerooms? The lavatories?'

'There's plenty of wasted space out beyond the kitchens,' he told her. 'Though we might need to keep the loos where they are, I think. Can't send the punters through the kitchens, though we might be able to use part of the cellars and put in a new staircase. Lots to talk about, anyway. What d'you think so far?'

'I think it's very exciting,' she answered – and smiled at the mixture of relief and hope that flared over his bony attractive face.

'Great,' he said. 'That's all I need to begin with. Let's go and have some lunch and throw some ideas around.'

She followed him back downstairs and settled in the little snug whilst he went to fetch drinks from the bar. Examining her feelings, Liv realized that she was enjoying being with a sexy man who had no emotional commitments: it was a delightful change. The Place was filling up, and people were laughing and talking; comfortable and at ease in the basket-weave chairs at the round, black-stained beech tables. There was a cheerful, lively buzz and Liv sat back in the corner of the snug, relaxed and happy.

*   *   *

By the time she arrived in Chapel Street that evening, Caroline and Zack were already partying. The barbecue was smouldering satisfactorily, and chairs and several tables were set out ready for supper under the pergola at the bottom of the garden. Caroline led Liv down the garden ('Thank goodness the path set in time to be walked on!') and Zack, who was sitting with his feet propped on a chair, put down his glass and got up to give his sister a hug.

'It's thirsty work getting all this ready,' he said, grinning.

'Sure it is,' said Liv. 'Yes, please. Red for me. So this is the great new construction work, is it?'

Caroline watched them affectionately as they inspected the path and Zack explained his plans; she was looking forward to her party and to meeting up with old naval friends. Zack seemed to have recovered from his mood of self-doubt and was in good form.

'After all,' she'd said to him, remembering what Liv had told her, 'both Tom and Tiggy were teachers, weren't they? I know that Tom taught at university level, but even so they must both have been good with young people. I know from my own experience that you really have to love kids to want to spend most of your life with them. I think that says something important about Tiggy and Tom.'

She'd seen that he'd been encouraged by her observation; taking it on board, thinking about it. Ever since, he'd been in high spirits; getting on with unpacking the last of the tea-chests, which she'd begun to find so tiring. He'd rearranged the smallest bedroom, pushing the divan against a wall so that there was room for the cot and the nursing chair, and was planning to make a shelf on which she could change the baby comfortably. There was already a chest of drawers in situ. They were both superstitious about buying too much in advance, though she knew that Zack wanted to do as much as he could before he went back to sea so that she wouldn't be left totally unprepared if the baby were to arrive early.

Sitting in the dapple of the pergola, Caroline tried to imagine life with a baby: it was impossible. In less than three months their lives, hers and Zack's, would be turned upside down and nothing would ever be the same again.

'Rather you than me,' Liv had said. 'I'm beginning to think that I'm not mother material. I'm a natural aunt. All the fun and none of the responsibility.'

Watching her with Zack, laughing and pretending to cuff his ear, Caroline didn't believe it for a minute. They came back towards her and she was seized with love for Zack; he looked so sexy and strong that she had to restrain herself from getting up and going to put her arms round him.

The doorbell's peal echoed across the garden. Zack said, 'Here we go,' and went up the garden and into the house to greet the first of the guests.

1976

It is hot; very hot. It's been weeks now since there has been any rain and the ground is dry and parched. At the end of July the submarine sails and, with Pete gone, the household resumes a more languid routine. They are glad of the cool, slate-floored rooms, and of the shade of the tall rhododendron bushes that encircle the lawn. Even the tent is too stuffy for comfort. Occasionally great bruise-coloured clouds hang on the horizon, and thunder growls and complains in the distance, but no rain falls.

Walking is no longer a pleasure. The open moorland offers no shade and the dogs pant along unwillingly; even on the cliffs the sluggish breeze is hot, bringing no refreshment, and the sea dazzles blindingly beneath the relentless sun. Sheep lie in the shadow of the dry-stone walls and wild ponies crowd beneath sparse thorn trees whose leaves brown and wither in the scorching air.

The children are fretful. Tiggy drives them to Daymer Bay and Trebarwith Strand, and to Truro. They go to Liskeard, where she and Julia buy wrap-around skirts in Indian cotton and cheesecloth shirts in the market, and to Rock where they swim in the warm sea and, afterwards, eat their picnic with damp towels draped tent-like over their heads to prevent their skins from burning; but as the heat intensifies even the van loses its charm and the children grow lethargic and drained of energy.

Nearly a week after Pete has gone, Julia comes downstairs one morning looking so happy that Tiggy stops putting out bowls and spoons and looks at her curiously. Julia grins back at her.

'Guess what?' she says – and when Tiggy shakes her head, bemused, she says, 'I'm pregnant.'

'Oh, Julia!' Tiggy runs round the table to embrace her. 'Oh, that's fantastic. Are you certain?'

'Well, I've missed two months and you know how regular I am. It's crazy really, I suppose, but we decided we'd like another little girl.'

'It's wonderful,' says Tiggy warmly. 'A friend for Claerwen.'

Julia laughs. 'It'll probably be another boy. Don't say anything to anyone yet.'

'Of course I shan't. Do you feel sick or anything?'

'I feel wonderful,' Julia says firmly.

A few days later, Angela drops in unannounced on her way to Rock. ('If only she'd let us know that she was coming,' fumes Julia. 'But that's the whole point,' answers Tiggy. 'To catch us unawares.') The twins with unfeigned reluctance take Cat out to see the tent whilst Angela sits down at the kitchen table, accepts coffee, lights a cigarette and offers the packet to Julia.

'You're looking very well,' she says, looking at her critically.

'Am I?' asks Julia casually – but she can't prevent the flush that stains her cheeks as she refuses the cigarette. 'Thanks, but not just now,' she says.

Angela raises her eyebrows; her narrow, sharp eyes amused. 'Don't tell me you're in pig,' she says lightly. She laughs at Julia's vexed expression. 'Don't worry,' she says. 'I shan't tell. Goodness, Pete is *such* a baby-maker, isn't he?'

It is a coincidence that Cat should come in at that moment, sidling under her mother's arm, so that Angela's gaze should fall upon the child's head as the remark hangs in the air between them all. In the strained silence they can hear Charlie crying in the garden and Julia gets up without a word and goes out.

Cat removes her fingers from her mouth. 'Charlie's a cry-baby,' she says, staring at Tiggy with her cross-eyed, inimical look.

Tiggy experiences the familiar sense of dislike and even fear, as if the child is some kind of threat, and her baby moves suddenly within her as if warning her of danger. Instinctively, she places her hands over her bump and Angela glances at her.

'Poor you,' she says. 'You look as if you might pop at any minute. Gosh, you must feel vulnerable. Just between you and me, I know this dit you're putting around, but your baby isn't Pete's too, is it? People are beginning to wonder. You know; the three of you all so cosy here together.'

Tiggy shoves back her chair so sharply that the Turk growls but neither Angela nor Cat flinch: they simply stare at her, coolly calculating what she might do next.

She swallows down her anger, catches at her temper. 'You're wasting your time, you know,' she says as calmly as she can, and follows Julia into the garden.

Presently Angela comes out with Cat and waves her car keys.

'Must get on,' she calls, 'or we'll be late,' and they drive away, leaving Julia still kneeling, comforting the sobbing Charlie whilst the twins keep up their furious duet.

'She pushed him over . . .' 'She pushed him *really* hard, Mummy . . .' 'We hate her, don't we, Liv?' 'Yes, we really hate her . . . Don't cry, Charlie . . .'

Julia looks up at Tiggy: all her happiness has fled and her face looks pinched and drawn.

'It's not true,' Tiggy says urgently but quietly, so that the twins won't hear. 'It's simply not true. She's just suggested the same thing about me. That my baby is Pete's. She's crazy.'

'She actually said that?' Julia stares up at her, distracted briefly from her own terrible suspicions.

'She hates you. And me, for some reason. She's mad. You simply mustn't take any notice of her.'

The twins barge round, talking to Charlie, telling their story again, and Julia stands up with Charlie in her arms. His knees are scraped and bleeding a little and he has earth on his cheek; his mouth turns down at the corners and his eyes look puzzled at the world's unexpected treachery; his innocence smudged for the first time with fear. Julia holds him close and kisses him, and they all go together into the house.

CHAPTER TWELVE

2004

On the afternoon that Pete and Julia were due home from their week in Hampshire, Em drove up to Trescairn, taking with her a cold chicken and a strawberry trifle. She stopped at the Stores in St Breward for milk and bread, butter and cheese and a lettuce, and then drove out of the village, over the moor. It was a cool day with soft grey clouds drifting from the west, the sharp-edged tors smudged with clinging shreds of mist. Even the bright flowers of the rhododendrons crowding the lawn were dimmed and subdued in the vaporous, shifting air.

Em parked the car, got out and passed a critical eye over the garden. She unlocked the front door and carried the bags through the house and into the kitchen. It looked as if Liv had already been in: Em saw that there were flowers in a vase on the kitchen table and a piece of card with the words 'Welcome home' printed on it.

A faint, very faint, fragrance lingered in the air, and Em saw a twig of the yellow azalea – the very last of the *luteum*

– amongst the blooms in the vase on the table. She was reminded again of the scene with Tiggy, here on this very spot,
and she instinctively glanced up at the dresser, wondering if
she might see the little bronze still standing where Tiggy had
placed him twenty-eight years before. Of course, he wasn't
there: Em smiled at her foolishness.

She passed through the house, opening windows to the cool,
fresh air, straightening an ornament, shaking out a curtain. As
she wandered from room to room, she saw that Trescairn was
remarkably unchanged and she could easily recall those years
in which she'd lived here with Archie, before Pete and Julia had
taken it over. The sitting-room looked just as comfortable with
its big sofas and swept hearth, logs piled each side of the huge
grate in the granite inglenook. The dining-room, which had
doubled as a playroom when the children were growing up,
was very tidy, very smart, the pretty chairs set around the long
rosewood table; the elegant silver candlesticks hazily reflected
in its richly polished surface.

Upstairs, the twins' room was now the guest room, and
Charlie and Zack's room had become a study with a sofa-bed
and had one whole wall dedicated to overflowing bookshelves.
Tiggy's room, which had been Liv's when she'd grown too old
to share with Andy, was a nursery with a cot and a small bed
where Charlie's children now slept when they came to stay.

Em paused for a moment in each of the rooms, her thoughts
vivid with scenes from the past. Suddenly she heard the hoot-
ing of a horn and she hurried to the window: Pete's car stood
on the gravel below and Julia was already out and at the tailgate, releasing Frobisher. Em gave a little cry of delight; she
rapped on the window and waved, and then went hurrying
downstairs to meet them.

*   *   *

Val set the dishwasher going and glanced at her watch. By now Liv would already be over in the café doing her morning shift and Chris had gone to Wadebridge to get his hair cut. Val felt an unusual contentment; a sense of pleasure that everything was going smoothly and that each piece of the whole enterprise was under control. Even the irritation she'd begun to feel for Liv had disappeared. The old affection had resurfaced and with it a rather pleasant feeling of superiority. Liv had been such a mover and shaker in getting Penharrow on its feet that there had been a kind of obligation to be grateful to her that had become irksome.

Now, with the secret about the baby, she could almost feel sorry for Liv: she had no man, no home, and her job depended on Penharrow doing well. There might soon come a time when Liv would not be needed and the annexe required for extra accommodation for visitors. Of course, Chris had been upset when she'd mentioned this prospect but then he always stood up for Liv. It might be different when the baby arrived: his priorities would change.

It was funny how certain she felt that she was pregnant. Lots of women said they knew at once – some deep maternal instinct, perhaps – and she knew now what they meant. This relaxed feeling of wellbeing was exhilarating.

'Don't get your hopes too high,' Chris had warned her.

'But I feel so different,' she'd argued. 'It must be to do with some physical change. I feel great.'

'Perhaps it's all the extra sex,' he'd said, almost bitterly.

She'd been hurt and even slightly angry. 'What do you mean?'

'Well, you've been too tired for it for the last few months, or you've had a migraine, but now we've decided we want a baby and suddenly we're at it like rabbits. It seems a bit mechanical, that's all.'

She'd laughed then. 'Wounded pride,' she said. 'Typical male. Just be grateful for it.'

Just for a moment he'd stared at her as if he disliked her.

Remembering, Val shrugged. He'd be the first to be doing the proud father bit when the time came. She had a satisfying little vision: she was holding the shawled and sleeping baby, looking down at it, and Chris was standing beside her, watching both of them with a tender, proud expression. She was pierced with a desperate longing. She could hardly wait; she wanted this baby more than she'd ever wanted anything. She simply longed to go into the café and tell them all that she was pregnant . . . but supposing she wasn't?

Val drew in a sharp breath. Chris was right, she mustn't get too complacent, but there was a lot to think about, to plan for and organize. She went upstairs to make the bed and to look again at the small bedroom in its beguiling new light as a nursery.

Liv was preoccupied: thinking about Matt and The Place. She'd just had a good session with the girl whose pretty silver jewellery they had for sale, and had put in a new order; she'd completely rearranged the display of silk scarves and had made a note of how many cards were selling and which of the local scenes were the most popular. The café was busy this morning but she'd managed to grab a cup of coffee in between helping Debs in the kitchen and serving out front.

'Going great, isn't it?' Debs had said. 'Even Val looks happy these days but Chris was a bit grumpy yesterday. Can you get the scones out of the oven? Thanks. Was that the bell?'

As she went to and fro, Liv was distracted from her thoughts of Matt and brooded instead on Debs' remark: she'd noticed it herself. As Val's spirits soared so Chris's seemed to descend. It was clear that there was something on his mind but when she'd asked him if he had a problem he'd shaken his head, said he was fine. She couldn't help worrying about him; just recently they'd lost that sense of intimacy, of being in the same boat, of acknowledging the need to encourage Val and keep things going. She'd found that she couldn't get him out of her mind and the moment that she had nothing to do she'd be back on the same mental track, wondering what was wrong. It was during one of these periods of reflection that she'd remembered what Aunt Em had said about the danger of early relationships.

At the time she hadn't connected: she'd been too shocked by the story about Angela and Dad, too shaken by the thought that her own secure childhood had come so close to being threatened. It was much later that she saw the connection: that Aunt Em was implying that she might well be a threat to Val because of her closeness to Chris.

'It can be dangerous.' Those had been her mother's words – and now she, Liv, could understand why she'd said them: she'd been thinking about Angela. If Val and Chris had serious problems they might never be resolved if he always had someone else to whom he might turn for consolation. Had she and Chris, in the easy familiarity of their old intimacy, been edging Val out into the cold? Liv consoled herself that it certainly didn't look like that at present: on the contrary, Val was on top form and it was Chris who now seemed rather depressed.

It had been bizarre, going to Trescairn a few days ago, and seeing her parents in the light of Aunt Em's story. It was impossible to think that they'd ever suffered the pangs of jealousy or guilt; that Dad had once been attracted to Angela or that Mum had ever considered leaving him. They'd been full of the visit to Charlie and Jo and the rest of the family, and with messages they'd brought back for her. They'd joked about Dad going off in a few weeks, sailing in the Med with an old naval chum, and all the while Liv had been thinking about Angela and the harm she might have done.

She'd got over it, of course, pulled herself together – but the idea was there now, fixed at the back of her mind. Not that she and Chris were remotely involved – of course they weren't – but it would be untruthful to say that either of them was totally unaware of the other. She remembered how she'd stood up on the Tor and allowed herself the brief enchanting vision of running Penharrow with Chris: how tempting, how desirable a prospect it had been. She'd pushed it to one side and imagined no harm was done but she understood a little better now. She'd laughed at the idea, pretended that she and Chris were proof against the danger; now she wasn't quite so confident – and she had Matt's offer to consider. Perhaps she'd got it wrong when she'd said to Aunt Em that she was providing a comfort zone for Chris and Val; perhaps it was the other way round. Did she dare to accept the challenge of Matt's proposals?

Myra had come in, ready for the afternoon shift, and Liv left her to it and went out into the yard. Chris was there, talking to a young woman who'd just got out of an open-topped sports car. She was laughing, frowning against the sun, and he turned, gesticulating towards the annexe; but as soon as he saw Liv his face changed, he beckoned to her, and he turned back to say something to the woman, who now slammed the car door and came towards her.

With a jolt beneath her diaphragm Liv saw that it was Cat; thin as a pin, shiny black hair curving across her cheeks, chic in linen trousers and a black shirt. Her skin was the colour of treacle. Slim though she knew herself to be, Liv felt clumsy and dowdy, and furious at being caught off guard in an old T-shirt and jeans, with her hair dragged back.

She saw that Cat was smiling, a sly secret smile: how odd it was that the slant-eyed look that had been so ugly in the child should be so attractive in the woman.

'Liv,' she was saying, thoroughly enjoying Liv's discomfiture. 'Hi. What a fab place. Andy told me all about it and I couldn't wait to see it.' She made as if to embrace Liv who instinctively stepped back, folding her arms across her breast. Cat looked amused at this childish gesture of rejection and glanced at Chris as if to make certain that he'd noticed it. 'We're old friends,' she told him, her smile widening, black eyes glinting. 'Aren't we, Liv? Andy sends his love.'

Liv felt wrong-footed, helpless, and it was Chris who came to her rescue. She realized with relief that he'd remembered their conversation in the office, made the connection, and now he moved closer to her, as if to protect her.

'I'm glad you like Penharrow,' he said pleasantly. 'I'm Chris Todd. My wife and I own it but we have Liv to thank for its success.'

Cat raised her eyebrows and her glance slid between them. 'How very nice,' she drawled. 'I remember now. Weren't you two an item once? Andy said something about it.' She held out her hand to him. 'I'm Cat Lisburne.' They shook hands 'I'm staying with friends in Rock but perhaps we could catch up on old times while I'm down, Liv? We could have some coffee one morning, if Chris can spare you. Andy says you have a café here.'

She was looking round, taking it all in. Chris caught Liv's eye, gave a tiny shrug.

'Yes, of course,' said Liv flatly. 'Why not?'

Cat laughed; it was as if she'd scored a point. 'Great. I'll be back soon. Must dash.'

She got back into her car, drove away with a flourish of her hand, whilst Liv stood staring after her, her arms still crossed over her breast.

'So that's the beastly girl the family hates,' said Chris. 'She's a bit scary, isn't she?'

Liv was silent; she felt threatened but she couldn't understand why. She gave a little shiver and Chris put an arm about her shoulder.

'Come on, love,' he said gently. 'She can't hurt you.'

Liv smiled gratefully – but she had an instinctive feeling that he was wrong.

Julia and Pete stood together on the drive, waving goodbye to Zack and Caroline. It had been such a happy day. The sun was so warm, the sky so cloudless, that they'd eaten lunch in the garden and afterwards they'd wandered up on the Tor with Frobisher; Zack and Pete strolling ahead talking about Zack's new posting as first lieutenant and Pete's sailing holiday in the Med with an old naval chum, whilst Caroline and Julia lagged behind, planning how Caroline might come to Trescairn for a few days when the submarine sailed.

Several times during the climb Zack glanced back, smiling with such caring concern at his wife that Julia's heart leaped with joy at the deep love between these two dear children.

'It's lovely to see them together,' she said now to Pete, slipping her arm in his. 'Caroline is such a darling and I'm so proud of Zack. Oh, Pete, supposing we hadn't adopted him! What a lot we'd have missed.'

'But was there any question of not adopting him?' he asked, as they walked back up the drive. 'It was a foregone conclusion as far as I remember. After all, we were his guardians and there was nobody else, was there?'

'No,' agreed Julia. 'But that didn't mean that *we* had to do it.'

'Oh, we couldn't have let him go,' protested Pete. 'Funny

little sprog that he was. After old Tiggy being here all that summer, they'd become family, hadn't they?'

Julia squeezed his arm. 'Lots of men wouldn't have felt like that.'

'Oh, well,' he said lightly. 'You know me. "All heart that isn't armpit", as they say in the navy.'

She laughed but shivered suddenly. 'How terrible it was,' she said, her face sombre.

'Come on, old love,' he said. 'It was a long time ago. All over now. I'm going to mow the lawns. A cup of tea would go down well if you felt like making one.'

He turned away, crossing to the barns, and Julia walked on slowly. She could hear the sound of a car approaching and stopped at the door, looking back to see if it were coming to Trescairn. Liv's little car appeared. She parked near the barn, waved to her father and came up to Julia; her face was anxious.

'You just missed Zack and Caroline,' Julia said. 'What a shame. Did you pass them on the road?'

Liv shook her head. 'There's something I want to tell you, Mum. I was going to mention it before but I thought it might worry you. But now . . .'

She hesitated and Julia watched her in alarm. 'What is it?' She drew Liv into the house. 'Is it to do with Chris?' she asked anxiously.

Liv frowned and shook her head. 'No, it's to do with Andy. He's been seeing Cat. He met her out of the blue and they've been going out together. I hoped it would simply be a flash in the pan but it isn't. She turned up just now at Penharrow.'

Julia gazed at her in disbelief. 'At Penharrow? But why?'

Liv shook her head. 'To make trouble,' she said bitterly. 'Why else? Oh, I don't know why. She's staying with friends at Rock. I'm furious with Andy, and I've told him so, but he simply doesn't care. I'm probably being silly but my hackles still rise at the thought of her. You should just see her now.'

'What's she like?' asked Julia almost fearfully.

'Very attractive. Odd, isn't it? She was always such an ugly child.'

'Does she look like Angela?'

'Yes,' said Liv after a moment. 'Yes, I suppose she does.' She glanced at her mother, distressed. 'Oh, Mum, I'm sorry, but I just thought you ought to be warned. You never know. She might turn up here. What can we do?'

'Nothing,' said Julia. 'Nothing at all. We can't prevent Andy from seeing whomever he likes. I'd just rather it wasn't Cat.' She made an effort to be cheerful. 'Come on. Let's go and make some tea for your father.' But her pleasure in the day was gone and she was filled with foreboding.

1976

The heat increases; the shimmering moor bakes gently, hardening and cracking into great fissures. Now, when Tiggy comes out of the house, she seems to walk into a wall of heat that makes her breathless, as if the sun has sucked the oxygen out of the air. She wades, heavy-limbed, through the heat, pinned down by it, and she looks back with astonishment and disbelief at the icy, wintry weather and the cool, misty days of spring. It seems impossible to imagine that she has ever been cold.

The washing, hanging motionless on the line, dries quickly. When she unpegs the clothes they are so hot, so crisp, that she expects them to crumble to cindery dust in her hands. Getting into the van or the car is like climbing into a furnace; so stifling and unbearable that they keep the windows permanently open and park the vehicles in the shade of the trees on the drive. There are rumours of birds dying in their thousands, reports of forest fires, warnings of standpipes.

'Thank goodness we have our own water,' says Julia. 'Uncle Archie says the spring has never failed yet.'

Even so, they are very sparing with it, rationing every drop, sharing the bath-water. Tiggy is so big now that she can hardly manage to get into the bath, and she keeps her overnight bag ready to hand; meanwhile they pray for rain. It comes at last on Bank Holiday Monday.

Tiggy rises unrefreshed after a restless night: pains in her lower back have prevented her from any kind of prolonged sleep, though she'd dozed heavily around sunrise. She sits on the edge of the bed, one hand pressed to the small of her back, willing down anxiety. The baby isn't due for another ten days and she has no wish to worry Julia, now nearly three months' pregnant, unnecessarily. Even so, she feels some kind of change in the rhythm of her body: supposing today is the day?

Mentally she reviews the plan which is quite simple: when labour starts, one of them will phone Aunt Em who is standing by to baby-sit whilst Julia drives Tiggy to Treliske Hospital.

'Aunt Em would take you,' Julia offered rather awkwardly, 'and I suppose that might be more sensible. But I'd rather be around if that's OK with you, though I'm not going to risk driving the van.'

Remembering, Tiggy smiles gratefully as she perches on the side of the bed.

'I'd like you to be with me,' she said. 'Having come this far it would be nice to see it through together, much as I love Aunt Em.'

'She'll be fine with the children,' Julia said confidently, 'and if it takes a bit of a time Uncle Archie can come out and join her here.'

'Don't worry,' Aunt Em promised when asked. 'I shan't go further than the local shop during the last week. Archie can cope with anything else. We'll be on twenty-four-hour call. No, of course we don't mind. We never want to do much in August anyway. Far too many holiday-makers around.'

Now, Tiggy pulls on the loose cotton smock that is the only garment that fits comfortably, and goes carefully downstairs. She thinks she can detect a difference in the atmosphere as well as in her own body, but she is reluctant to confide her fears just yet: she'd feel a fool if it were simply backache.

'I think the forecast for scattered showers might be right,' Julia says just before lunch. 'There are some rather black-looking clouds over the Camel estuary.'

'Good,' says Tiggy, but the word ends in a kind of involuntary groan and Julia looks at her anxiously.

'Are you OK? Oh God . . . is it the baby?'

'I don't know.' Tiggy tries to straighten her aching back. 'It's just that I've been having these pains. No, no. Not labour pains. In my back. And now I'm leaking a bit.'

'Oh God!' Julia says again. She hesitates for a few moments, then: 'I'm going to phone the doctor,' she says firmly. 'No, don't argue! Sit down and practise your breathing lessons.'

The doctor says that it's a bit early, that backache is fairly standard at this stage and the other might simply be incontinence, but that it is probably better to be safe than sorry. Julia phones the maternity ward at Treliske to warn the staff they are on their way, and then Aunt Em, who answers straight away.

Tiggy fetches her case while Julia explains to the twins that she is going to take Tiggy to collect her baby and that Aunt Em will be with them until they all get back home; they must be very good, she tells them, and help Aunt Em with Charlie. Impressed by Julia's gravity they stare solemnly at Tiggy, who smiles at them reassuringly, but they are distracted from the usual flow of questions by a sudden and unfamiliar tattoo; a hollow drumming on the roof of the back porch. For a moment they all stare at one another, puzzled, until Liv cries: 'It's raining. It's absolutely pouring,' and they all run outside to look.

It comes in torrents, sizzling and bouncing off the hard-baked earth so that soon the bare moorland looks as if it is covered in a low cloud of steam. It hammers on the roof and clatters on the leaves of the rhododendron bushes; it dislodges stones and washes the loose, dry topsoil away in rivulets of muddy water that pour down into the lanes.

Aunt Em drives in looking faintly alarmed and they hurry to greet her, drawing her into the house.

'Bad timing,' she says. 'This downpour is making driving very difficult. There's lots of bank holiday traffic about.'

Tiggy picks up her case and kisses the Turk on the nose.

'Look after her,' she says privately to Andy, and he nods, looking important and pleased at having such a responsibility entrusted to him. She kisses the children, hugs Aunt Em and goes out with Julia to the car. Panic is beginning to sweep over her in shuddering waves; she has the presentiment that something terrible is going to happen, something that has happened before is about to repeat itself, although she can't clearly remember what it was. Trembling, she climbs into the car, trying to control her formless terror but wanting to cry out that this is wrong; that they shouldn't be leaving the house.

Julia is talking, starting up the engine, edging round Aunt Em's car, trying to sound confident and reassuring. Out of the shelter of the rhododendrons, however, the car receives the full force of the storm and Julia is momentarily silenced by its violence. Tiggy can sense her anxiety as she grips the wheel and peers out through the streaming windscreen.

'Stop!' she wants to say. 'Stop, Julia,' but her mouth is dry, her muscles disabled with fear, and she crouches silently in her seat, her arms wrapped protectively around her body.

The narrow moorland road is greasy with rain, covered with liquid mud, and, as the car approaches the T-junction, Tiggy is struck by the remembrance of her arrival: her mounting terror of some disaster and the van sliding out of control. She cries out, a groan combined of anguish and pain, and Julia glances at her fearfully. It is a quick glance, lasting only a few seconds, but it is enough to distract her, so that, as the car begins unexpectedly to aquaplane, she turns back in a panic, braking a little too hard and sending it skidding across the lane at the junction and crashing into a huge lump of granite.

Tiggy is flung against the windscreen; both girls scream. Tiggy covers her eyes with her hands, unable to move, rendered powerless by fear; but Julia is out of the car in a moment, hurrying round to the nearside to see the damage. She comes back and leans into the car, half kneeling on the driver's seat, and Tiggy raises her head, biting her lips, to look at her. Julia's face is white and her hair, dark with rain, is plastered to her cheeks.

'It's no good,' she says, distressed. 'The wing's smashed in and the tyre's flat. We must go back to the house.' She hesitates for a moment, as if debating with herself the wisdom of this decision. 'I think we must. I can't just leave you here on your own. Aunt Em will have to take you to the hospital in her car, or we'll call an ambulance. Are you OK? God, I'm so *sorry*. Look, you'll have to get out this side.'

Tiggy manoeuvres her bulk into the driving seat and swings her legs out: shaking violently she stands up and immediately gives a cry of pain. Her head throbs and her left shoulder and arm feels badly bruised.

'Oh my God.' Julia puts her arm around her and Tiggy can feel that she is trembling too but making a great effort to control herself. 'Perhaps you should stay here. Get back in and I'll run and get the car.'

'No,' cries Tiggy desperately. The prospect of being left alone is too frightening to contemplate. 'I can manage. Really, I can.'

The rain streams down in torrents as they stumble slowly along the slippery, stone-strewed road. Tiggy, leaning on Julia who is half carrying her, can barely walk. She can feel warm water gushing down her legs and a savage pain is now beating, now receding, at regular intervals low in her back. She clings to Julia's warm hand, to her strength, whilst Julia's voice speaks in her ear, encouraging her, willing her forward: 'I can see the gate. Nearly there now. Not much further. Be brave,' until there are other voices, other hands, and she collapses at last into a blessed, senseless darkness.

PART TWO

CHAPTER THIRTEEN

August 2004

'TO THE WEST': Ringwood Bournemouth Poole. Driving along the A31 at the edge of the New Forest, Julia read the familiar signpost with mixed emotions. She was sad to be leaving Charlie and his little family yet those words – 'TO THE WEST' – had long been a symbol of the journey home to Trescairn. For thirty years she'd been driving this route between Cornwall and Hampshire: first as a young wife and mother visiting her family, and Pete's, and now travelling to see Charlie and Jo and their two small children.

'Take care, Mum,' Charlie had said, giving her a big hug. 'Give us a buzz when you're home. Love to Dad when you speak to him.'

'Whenever that might be,' Julia had answered, resigned. 'He's not given much to telephonic communication. A run ashore in Gib, yes. Checking out the Sliema Club in Malta, yes. Telephoning home, no.'

'These sailing holidays in the Med are getting to be a bit of a habit, aren't they?' Charlie grinned sympathetically. 'Still, if you don't mind . . .'

'Oh, I don't mind. He and Mike have been sailing together all their naval careers since they did their first tall ships race when they were at BRNC. Can't expect him to break the habits of a lifetime just because he's retired.'

Travelling between tall banks of gorse that edged the road through the Forest, Julia was aware of a faint but increasing sense of unease. Ever since breakfast, this feeling had hovered at the edges of her mind: yet she couldn't pin it down. She reviewed the morning's events but could think of nothing unsettling that had occurred either during the usual breakfast routine with Charlie and Jo and the children or afterwards, when she'd been packing up the car and saying goodbye.

Julia drove on, mentally picking away at fragments of conversation that might offer a clue to this uneasiness and, at the same time, aware of Frobisher, scrabbling behind her. She wondered if he'd mislaid his bone.

'You'll have to wait,' she told him, glancing with amusement in her rear-view mirror at his despondent expression. 'It's probably under your rug. Look about a bit. Don't be so helpless.'

He collapsed with a sigh and Julia shook her head: Frobes showed very little initiative. She remembered other journeys and other dogs: Bella and the Turk, then Baggins. The children would beg for the dogs to be allowed to sit with them. Liv and Andy would bicker, practising their own particular form of gamesmanship. First, before the journey had begun, there would be the contest as to whose turn it was to sit in the front; next, which one of them would be first to see the familiar landmarks along the way: the magnificent stone lion atop the lodge gate in the brick wall that surrounded Charborough

Park, then the great stag on Stag Gate, then the first glimpse of the sea.

Now, as she turned on to the A35 heading towards Dorchester, Julia hoped with all her heart that Liv would accept Matt Greenaway's offer. Once the sale was going ahead he'd agreed that she could talk about it with her parents and Liv had suggested that they should go down to Truro and have a look at The Place.

'You won't be able to go upstairs, of course,' she'd said, 'but I'd like to have your impression of it.'

They'd loved it. 'She'd be crazy not to have a crack at it,' Pete had said. 'It's exactly what she needs.'

Julia agreed with him; she remembered that there had been a text message on her mobile from Liv earlier that morning: 'B in 2 c u pm.' Well, that wasn't a problem although 'pm' was a bit vague. Julia chuckled. Liv could be the most irritating and infuriating person in the world but just the sight of her – blonde hair flying, wide smile, always with some little treat in her hand – dissolved any feeling except huge affection.

She stopped at Bridport for petrol and chocolate, then drove on until she reached the turning to Eype where she could use the public lavatory and let Frobisher out for a run. The parking bays were nearly full on this warm, sunny morning but she found a space and got out to release Frobisher. As she walked him from the car park towards the lane, an old orange VW camper van came trundling in and motored slowly round, its driver looking for a place to stop.

All in a moment Julia was transported back twenty-eight years: she could hear the twins bickering, Charlie shouting, and was aware of the shade of Tiggy at her shoulder, thrusting her hand under her arm and saying, 'Let's go and have a picnic.'

Instinctively, Julia pressed her elbow against her side,

remembering. She stood quite still, staring after the van until Frobisher tugged impatiently on his lead, and she moved forward automatically, feeling oddly shaken. After all, she'd never forgotten that summer – how could she? Losing Tiggy and her own child within hours of each other; how could she ever forget? Yet today, in the hot sunshine, the sight of the old orange van had the same unsettling effect that had begun to manifest itself earlier. Further up the lane, Julia unclipped the lead so that Frobisher could potter unhindered and as she wandered after him, head bent, arms crossed beneath her breast, she brooded on this strange sensation. She felt a very strong desire to be at home and she took out her mobile and sent a text to Liv: 'B home about 3. C u then.' Julia realized that the prospect of seeing Liv was very comforting indeed.

She walked back to the car peering for the van, which was now nowhere to be seen, and set off again. To the west: down into pretty, thatched Chideock, past Charmouth and Axminster, round Honiton and on to the M5. She could remember the days when they'd driven through the busy towns of Honiton and Exeter to reach the A30 but now the great roads sliced across the countryside and she drove at a steady speed, pulling off the new A30 on to the old road through Whiddon Down, and parking by the entrance to a public bridleway. She let Frobisher out and he disappeared into the tall grass of the bridleway whilst she sat sideways on the passenger seat with the door open, eating a sandwich and drinking coffee from the lid of the flask. The sun was hot and Julia sat quietly, eyes closed, trying to relax. In years past this had been a favourite stopping place on the way home, to let out the dogs and allow the children to stretch their legs. She finished her coffee, screwed the lid back on the flask and stood up. The northern flanks of Dartmoor shimmered with a powdery golden light in the afternoon heat and Julia was once again assailed by the sensation that Tiggy was somewhere near. So strong was this feeling that for a mad moment she seemed to see the Turk's low, strong, supple body, racing towards her, scimitar-shaped tail waving. Of course it was Frobisher who came panting up to her: his silky, feathery coat was black, not coarse and wheaten-grey; his deep-set eyes in the noble brow were pensive, not round and dark and intelligent like the Turk's.

Julia bent to stroke him, her hands trembling just a little. She was not given to flights of fancy, or an over-active imagination, and she was disturbed, even frightened.

'Not far now,' she said aloud, as much to comfort herself as to reassure Frobisher. 'We should be home in an hour and a half at the most.' She was filled with a great need to be at home, having tea with Liv, telling her about Charlie and Jo and the children. 'Come on,' she said to Frobisher. 'Let's get on our way.'

She drove on through Sticklepath and rejoined the A30: past Okehampton, over Dunheved Bridge with Launceston away to the right and its castle crouched on the hill. Julia remembered how the children had always cheered and clapped as they'd crossed the Tamar into Cornwall.

'Hooray!' they'd shout. 'Nearly home.'

As she drove, Julia was unusually conscious of the route of the old A30, now merging with, now departing from, the big dual carriageway that carved its way across Bodmin Moor. No longer did the heavy traffic pass through Five Lanes but, as she crossed Hendra Downs, she could see the old road snaking away to the left, up past Jamaica Inn at Bolventor; and here at last was the signpost to St Breward. She pulled into the middle of the road, waited for a break in the traffic and turned right, jolting over the cattle grid and on to the open moor.

If she'd expected to feel some relief from her uneasiness now that she was so close to home she was disappointed. She knew that it was going to be one of those bad moments when she approached the turning at the bottom of the lane, where all those years ago the car had aquaplaned into the great granite boulder.

'It wasn't your fault that Tiggy died,' Pete had said, over and over. 'The weather was appalling. You did the only thing you could have done. Oh, yes, I suppose you could have left her there while you went for help but she was in labour, dammit. Stop torturing yourself, love. We've simply got to put it behind us.'

Easy to say, thought Julia grimly now; almost impossible to do. The bad moments had occurred less often with the passing of the years but today the sense of horror and loss possessed her again and Julia knew that it would require all her willpower to overcome it. She drove into St Breward, parked outside the Stores and went in to buy milk and bread and a few other necessities, and then headed back out of the village to Trescairn. She turned down the drive, pulled up outside the house and groped in her bag for her keys. Frobisher was standing up now, his tail wagging at the prospect of freedom, and Julia climbed out and opened the tailgate.

'Safely home,' she said with relief. 'Let's go and make a cup of tea.'

Forty minutes later, Liv arrived; bundling in, her blonde hair slipping down from the casually twisted top-knot, carrying a paper bag.

'Hi,' she cried, giving Julia a hug. 'Are you OK? How are Charlie and Jo and the babes?' She flourished the paper bag. 'One of Debs' cakes. I know you're always a bit miz when you've left Charlie and Jo so I thought we'd need something special.'

'I'm fine,' said Julia, her heart lifting at the sight of her daughter. 'Everyone's fine. They send their love.'

'Hello, old doggle.' Liv embraced Frobisher. 'Have you had a lovely time? Did everyone spoil you rotten?' She continued to kneel, stroking Frobisher, but her eyes were on Julia, who was making a fresh pot of tea. 'You're looking worried,' she said. 'Are you sure they're all OK?'

'Quite sure. I'm tired, that's all. It's a long drive.' Julia put the pot on the table. A new thought occurred to her, bringing with it a darting stab of fear. 'I suppose Caroline's all right? Have you heard from her?'

'She phoned last night to say that Zack's due back at the weekend, just in time for the baby, if all goes well.' Liv took plates from the dresser, arranged the cake and sat down opposite her mother. 'She's torn between longing to get it over with and wanting Zack to be there.' She cut a piece of the coffee sponge and bit into it with relish. 'Poor old Caroline. It's a bit hot for being very pregnant.'

Julia took a slice of cake and stared at it: how hot it had been, that summer of '76. It was the first time she'd ever let the Rayburn go out; they'd heated things up on a small camping stove. She looked up to see Liv staring at her curiously.

'Do you remember Tiggy, Liv?' she asked. 'I mean, actually *remember* her, not just know about her because she's part of the family history.'

Liv frowned consideringly. She picked up her mug and sat holding it in both hands, her elbows on the table.

'Not really,' she said at last. 'Not if I'm honest. I remember the camper van and all that stuff but when I rack my memory Tiggy herself is a sort of shadowy figure. Good vibes, though. She's very real to me because you've often talked about her and described things we all did together, but actually remembering her? No. Why?'

'Nothing in particular. I saw a camper van just that same orange colour and since then she's been on my mind a bit. And there's something else that happened before that, when I was still at Charlie's, and I simply can't remember what it was. It's bugging me.'

'What kind of thing?'

'Oh, I don't know. Just something I heard or saw that triggered off a kind of anxious feeling.'

'Is that why you asked about Caroline?'

'Probably. I'm just being silly.'

'Caroline's fine,' said Liv firmly. 'But I know what you mean. It'll come to you at three o'clock in the morning. Don't fiddle about with that slice. Respect the cake.'

Julia laughed. 'You're right. It's very good cake. Thank you, darling. Sorry. Just having a senior moment.'

'You're missing Dad,' diagnosed Liv, 'and Charlie and everyone. I know you hate leaving them. Tell you what, I'll stay and make us some supper. What have you got in the freezer?'

Liv got up and went out to the back porch, rooting in the freezer, while Julia ate thoughtfully. There was something so capable about Liv, so strong and positive.

Julia thought: I wonder if that's how Tiggy saw me all those years ago. Was I like Liv, full of confidence and quite ready to take on other people's problems?

'There's some fish,' she called to Liv. 'Dover sole. It can go straight into the oven. I bought some brown bread and there's a lemon in the fridge. That will be plenty for me. I never want much when I've been travelling. Can you stay the night?'

'Sorry, Mum, I simply can't. There's far too much to do tomorrow. You know what it's like at this time of the year.'

'Yes, of course I do. It's sweet of you to come over when you're so busy. How are Val and Chris? Rushed off their feet? So much for the quiet life.' Julia laughed. 'I expect they wonder why they ever left London. Have some more tea and then we'll take Frobes for a walk.'

*   *   *

Driving back later that evening, Liv was grateful that Julia never pried into her private life. If her mother longed for her to settle down, like Charlie and Zack, she'd stopped mentioning it long since. She hadn't mentioned Matt either, although, now both she and Dad knew about the project at The Place, they were keen for her to accept Matt's offer. She'd seen him several times during the last few weeks and each time she was with him she felt the force of his personality and a growing confidence that her immediate future was with him at The Place. However, once she was alone again, out of his field of magnetism, she fell prey to doubts and, though he was making no attempt to press her, she knew she must come to a decision very soon. She was confident that she could meet the professional requirements of the job but she wondered if she had the temperament to make the long-term commitment that Matt needed.

As for Chris . . . Ever since Aunt Em had told her about Angela, she'd tried to keep a line between them that she was determined not to cross. Even now, with Val inexplicably plunged once more into bad temper and fits of gloom, Liv was managing to hold Chris at arm's length whilst still trying to support and encourage him.

He'd been so sweet that morning when Cat had arrived for coffee.

'Don't leave me alone with her,' Liv had pleaded with him. 'I know it sounds crazy but please stay with me.'

And he had. They'd come out of the office together when the little sports car pulled into the yard, and it had seemed quite natural for the three of them to stroll over to the café.

'We were just going to have a break,' Chris said. 'Nice timing.'

If Cat realized that she was being outwitted she didn't show it: she was amusing, complimentary, fun. Only when Val appeared, puzzled by the empty office and not recognizing the car, was Cat able to take revenge.

'So you're Val,' she'd said, as though she'd heard a great deal about her. 'Great to meet you. What a set-up you have here.' She'd laughed, making a little face. 'A fun threesome. I'm impressed that you don't mind that these two were an item. That's really cool. I'd be afraid that they were getting up to all sorts of things when I couldn't see them. Old flames can cause a lot of trouble. Isn't that so, Liv?'

There had been no appropriate answer, only confusion and embarrassment. Cat had been delighted.

'You're right,' Chris had said grimly to Liv much later, after she'd gone. 'She's bad news. Val's furious.'

Liv parked the car, glancing round the yard. From two of the cottages light streamed out but the other two were dark and two cars were missing: probably the visitors had gone out to supper. She'd just put her key in the latch when she heard footsteps behind her, caught the smell of Chris's cigarette.

'Hi,' he said. 'Nice evening?'

'I've been to welcome Mum back,' she said; her heart was beating just too fast for comfort but her smile was friendly, nothing more. 'It's a bit miz coming home to an empty place after a week with family so I stayed for supper.' She paused, door open now. 'Everything OK?' Then, very casually, 'Like some coffee?'

'I've got a message from Val.' He sounded rueful. 'Debbie's phoned. Can't get in until lunchtime tomorrow. Val says could you open the shop in the morning?'

'Sure. No problem.'

He hesitated and she waited. The silence stretching between them was far more eloquent than any words could have been.

'Better take a rain check on that coffee. But thanks, Liv.' His voice was regretful.

'See you in the morning, then.' Liv went inside and shut the door firmly.

CHAPTER FOURTEEN

2004

Julia woke early the next morning. She rolled on to her back and lay for some moments, staring at the ceiling, thinking through the events of the previous day. No revelation had been revealed to her at three o'clock, as Liv had foretold, but she felt too tired to pursue her anxiety: tired but not relaxed. Presently she got out of bed, pulled on a thin cotton dressing gown and went downstairs. Frobisher opened an eye and thumped his tail once or twice but showed no desire to rise. Julia pushed the kettle on to the hotplate, took a mug from the dresser and spooned in coffee and sugar. Yawning hugely, she unlocked the back door and looked out into the early summer morning.

No wind stirred the soft, warm air; the sun had already risen high above Rough Tor. Julia made her coffee and, pushing her bare feet into gumboots, stepped out into the garden. She crossed the grass to stand beside the wall where she could look over the moor towards St Breward and, far beyond, to the white china clay pyramids behind St Austell. It was eerily quiet;

no birds sang. On the slopes below Trescairn a group of skew-bald ponies cropped the bleached grass where stunted gorse flowered amongst the scattered rocks.

Drinking her coffee, Julia allowed the peace and beauty to soothe her troubled spirit. She stood the empty mug carefully on the uneven stone wall, pushing her thick hair behind her ears as she bent to look at a small root of heather growing in the crevice, touching the tiny purplish-pink bell-like blossoms. Frobisher came out to find her, sniffing along the base of the wall where, earlier, a fox had passed. He disappeared into the dense shadow of the rhododendrons, and Julia picked up her mug but remained leaning against the wall, unwilling to relinquish this moment of tranquillity, remembering.

1977

A baby is crying: a thin, high wail that pierces the fog of sleep and brings Julia fully awake. She lies for a moment, with eyes closed tightly against the coming day, curled into Pete's comfortingly warm but unyielding back. As the months have passed she's grown more adept at blocking the unhappy memories that assail her awakening and, anyway, the baby gives her little opportunity for self-indulgent grief, but she dreads the moment of rising. The wails grow more insistent and Pete stirs, drawing the quilt more closely round him, muttering irritably. A door opens; voices can be heard and steps approaching.

Reluctantly Julia abandons the warmth and comfort of the bed, reaches for her dressing gown and is at the door as Liv arrives, portentous and reproachful at her mother's tardiness.

'Zack's crying, Mummy,' she says reprovingly. 'And he's woken Charlie.'

'Yes, thank you, darling,' answers Julia wearily. 'I heard him.

Be a good girl and go and talk to Charlie while I get Zack's bottle, would you? Thanks, Liv. You're *such* a help to Mummy.'

Liv bustles away, glowing with pleasure at the prospect of all the good deeds to be accomplished, and Julia gives brief thanks that the twins aren't jealous of Zack but have accepted him in the same spirit of benign indifference with which they'd welcomed Charlie. They are too secure in their own relationship to feel threatened, though they are occasionally irritated or bored by the younger ones. Starting school has increased their self-importance and they've developed a tolerant, world-weary attitude towards Charlie and Zack that amuses Julia.

As she picks Zack up from the cot, speaks to him tenderly and cuddles him, she can hear Liv's voice, schoolmistress-like across the landing.

'Mummy will be here soon so stop fussing, Charlie. Shall I read you a story until she comes?'

Julia smiles. Zack lies in her arms, staring at her placidly, and her heart gives the little familiar tick of love and pain. Often she conducts unspoken conversations with Tiggy, as though the dead girl stands at her elbow, and in this way she tries to share her grief and guilt. The shock and horror of Tiggy's death are still vivid with her: postpartum haemorrhage. Everyone assures her that it need not have had anything to do with the accident and the agonizing walk back to Trescairn, or the long wait for the ambulance. Still, the guilt remains – and joy too. Zack is so sweet, especially now those early exhausting weeks of little more than a repetitive cycle of screaming, feeding and sleeping have given way to a slowly growing awareness: to these calm moments when he smiles at her or watches the other children; or simply lies on his back kicking and waving his fists. The Turk raises her head and is watching from her basket in the corner; she insists on sleeping there, just as she had when it had been Tiggy's room, and Julia hasn't the heart to forbid it. It is as if the Turk knows that this is Tiggy's child and that she is watching over him.

Andy appears, books beneath his arm and a hopeful expression on his face, but Julia shakes her head.

'Don't wake Daddy,' she warns him. 'Please don't, Andy. He's very tired this morning and he's going back to sea tomorrow. Take the books downstairs and we'll look at them while I feed Zack.'

Andy makes a face and disappears, and Julia follows him out and down the stairs, bracing herself for another busy day: breakfast first then the washing and dressing marathon followed by the school run. At least Zack makes certain that they don't oversleep – and for one more morning she can leave the two little ones and the dogs with Pete while she takes the twins to school. She knows she'll really miss Pete but a tiny part of her is looking forward to being alone, free from the strain of trying to be cheerful for his benefit. Immediately after Tiggy's death and her own miscarriage, he'd been a tremendous comfort to her; shocked at the news, he'd been sympathetic with her sudden attacks of low spirits and he'd shown himself to be a tower of strength with the children. But now he's grown a little impatient with her inability to come to terms with her grief.

Well, I *am* better, Julia tells herself as she drives the twins to school; but on this bone-chilling winter morning, with a drizzling mist obscuring anything more than ten feet beyond the windscreen, it is only too easy to allow the old horror to take control, especially as she approaches the place where she'd aquaplaned into the boulder. Resolutely Julia turns her eyes away from the slab of granite, wondering if she'll ever be able to drive this stretch of the road without the memories resurfacing.

'After all,' Pete said, 'with the benefit of hindsight we can all see what we ought to have done. You couldn't possibly have foreseen what effect that sudden downpour was likely to have on the roads after weeks of drought. It wasn't your fault, love. You did everything you could and stayed with her right up to the end. Nobody could have done more.'

He'd make a cup of tea for her, put her and the children and the dogs into the car and take them for a drive to the sea; later he'd pour her a drink and peel vegetables ready for supper or produce his one culinary dish – a curry. He is kind and thoughtful but he expects his kindness to show results.

'There,' he'd say cheerfully, putting her plate in front of her, refilling her glass. 'You're looking better, darling. The day out has done you good,' and, if she didn't respond with a positive assurance that she was cured, he'd look rather hurt, even annoyed, and a gloom would descend.

The trouble is, thinks Julia as she waves the children into the village school and gets back into the car, that it's all so complicated: a walk on the cliffs and a glass of wine simply don't compensate for the loss or do away with the guilt.

'It's not just Tiggy that I've lost,' she cried on one occasion when he chided her for being morbid. 'I lost my baby, Pete. Our baby. Can't you imagine how I feel about that?'

'Well, of course I can,' he said, half awkwardly compassionate, half resentful at the implication that he didn't care. 'But it was very early stages, wasn't it? Only a few months, after all. And we've got Zack. We have to think about him.'

'I do think about him,' she answered quietly. 'I don't have any choice but to think about him. But I think about my own baby, too. Babies aren't interchangeable, you know.'

He looked rather shocked and she felt fearful that this terrible thing might force a wedge between them. Her feelings alarm her: it is out of character for her to feel so heavy of heart and limb, so disabled by grief and guilt. However hard she tries to block it, that day last summer replays itself in her head whilst she finds herself working through a series of 'if only' alternatives: if only she'd insisted that Tiggy had waited in the car; or if only she'd called an ambulance straight away instead of attempting the drive in the first place.

As she goes into the Stores to pick up the newspaper and some groceries, she is seized by a different kind of guilt: poor Pete must be heartily sick of it all. It was she who invited Tiggy to stay and persuaded Pete to allow Tiggy – who could never have guessed how crucial it was to be – to name them as her child's guardians; and he has accepted her baby uncomplainingly into his family. In her remorse, Julia buys him a large bar of chocolate and then goes to the butchery department to select some fillet steak. Pete's last day at home shall be a good one.

He is stretched out on the sofa in the kitchen when she gets back. Zack lies peacefully across his chest whilst Charlie has dragged his Fisher Price garage close beside them on the floor and is running the little cars in and out with an accompaniment in his own particular Charlie-speak. Noses on paws, Bella and the Turk watch him, eyes flicking warily from side to side, as the brightly coloured cars come perilously near. He is enjoying himself enormously.

'Here comes Mrs Geen,' he shouts – he has difficulty with any r-sound – 'and here comes Mr Yed! Oh, dear! Oh, *no*! Bang!' Gleefully he crashes the two cars together; the two tiny occupants tumble to the flagstones, and the dogs wince and stir about anxiously.

Pete opens an eye and looks up at Julia. 'I hope he has better road sense when he grows up,' he observes. 'Hello, darling. This baby smells terrible.'

Julia dumps the shopping on the kitchen table and lifts Zack up, wrinkling her nose. 'I'll go and change him,' she says, 'and then if we're lucky he might have a little nap. Put the kettle on, Pete.'

When she gets back downstairs he's made coffee and they sit companionably together, listening to Charlie's running commentary.

'Uncle Archie phoned,' Pete says. 'He's offered to drive me into the dockyard tomorrow. I said almost definitely yes but that I'd check with you.'

'Oh.' Julia is both relieved and slightly disappointed. 'Well, it's sensible, of course, but I like to take you in when you're sailing.'

'I know you do, love, but it's a bit crazy, all of you and the dogs getting ready so early in the morning, isn't it? Harbour stations at nine thirty, remember. We'd have to be away at seven thirty at the latest.'

Julia shakes her head. 'We'd never make it. Although Aunt Em might come and hold the fort while I take you in. No, on second thoughts, it's all too much for her with school as well. It's probably best, if Uncle Archie really doesn't mind.'

Pete shrugs. 'He suggested it.'

'You don't regret it? Living this far out from the dockyard? It's madness really, I suppose.'

'It's getting a bit dire when the boat's alongside for any length of time but that's because of transport. It makes no difference when I'm on leave, of course. We're going to have to think of buying another vehicle, Julia. There's no way I can leave you out here without a car, and for you to be ferrying me to and fro twice a day will be impossible with the twins at school and now with Zack.'

Julia thinks carefully before she answers. The subject is a touchy one; last autumn it resulted in a row. Back then, with the boat alongside for six weeks and Zack only two months old, Julia found it difficult to combine successfully her roles of mother and chauffeur. It was the first time that transport became an issue. For the whole of the last spring and summer they had Tiggy's van at their disposal but, though Julia valiantly attempted to control her feelings and drive the van, the combination of its size in the narrow muddy lanes and the memories it invoked almost overwhelmed her.

At this point, Pete suggested that the van should be sold and that he should buy himself a little sports car: just the job, he said cheerfully, for dashing in and out. Once or twice he came home late, and there was a secretive air about him that aroused all Julia's old fears. Angela dropped in one morning and hinted at meetings and conversations with him, so that Julia, still raw with her own grief, rather unwisely asked Pete outright if he were having an affair with her. His outraged response neither confirmed nor denied but simply implied that Julia was the one who ought to be ashamed for harbouring such suspicions.

The next week the boat sailed on a six-week exercise and in November Martin and Angela, with Cat, moved to Faslane. Until now there has been an unspoken truce on both subjects but the problem of transport needs to be resolved.

'I don't see why not,' Julia answers now. 'To be honest, I don't see how we can manage with just one car. I think we were a bit starry-eyed when we first moved here, weren't we? It seemed so blissful after married quarters that we were ready to cope with anything.'

'Well, I don't regret it for a minute,' Pete says. 'And it's great for the kids. Andy and Liv are really happy at the village school, and old Charlie and Zack will be able to race around all over the moor in the summer.'

Suddenly Julia is overwhelmed with love and gratitude for him. How many men, she wonders, would so readily take on the child of a friend? She wants to reward him for his generosity, for not making her feel guilty about Tiggy and Zack.

'I think your idea of a little sports car is a good one,' she says. 'We don't want another estate car. Something nippy would be fun. We'll sell the van and when you're home again you'll have to look around.'

Pete's expression amuses her; he looks like Andy when he's been given an unexpected treat. 'Actually,' he says, 'David's talking of getting rid of his MGB now that they've just had the sprog. I might have a word with him.'

'You do that,' she says, pleased that he is happy, enjoying this moment of normality. 'You could phone him. Settle it before you go.'

Pete looks surprised at this enthusiasm. 'I might just do that,' he says.

The twins come out of school wildly excited: there are to be great celebrations for the Queen's Silver Jubilee. They stand behind Julia's seat as she drives them home, explaining in a rather confusing duet – one in each ear – their various roles.

'We're going to dress up and march to the old school and have lessons like they did a hundred years ago and you can come and watch us, Mummy.'

'And there's going to be a big tea in the schoolroom.'

'It sounds wonderful,' Julia says. 'Fantastic. You must tell Daddy all about it when we get in.'

In the west the setting sun plunges down between bars of crimson cloud towards the shining sea. Plashy, reed-ringed pools tremble with fiery colour as the wind shivers over the moor, and a single distant star hangs in the eastern sky high above Rough Tor. This afternoon, at the corner by the granite slabs, Julia feels no horror but, to her grateful relief, only an odd peacefulness; an acceptance. She's had this experience a few times; braced for the pain of remembrance, she experiences instead this unexpected sense of grace. It doesn't last but she takes it as a sign that one day she might recover.

'Are you listening, Mummy?' demands Liv. 'I need to learn to *knit*. Mrs Crosley says we're going to have a banner with a picture of St Branwalader.'

'Gosh!' says Julia faintly.

'And a raven,' says Andy, in her other ear, 'perched on Rough Tor. Because Branwalader,' he stumbles over the word, 'means a Raven Lord.'

Once she's put the car away and they've all hurried indoors they tell the news again to Pete, Charlie, Zack and the dogs. As they sit round the table, Julia and Pete drinking tea while the children eat boiled eggs and soldiers, Liv starts up again with her need to learn to knit, which Julia has been tactfully parrying.

'But *why* can't I, Mummy?'

'I think Mrs Crosley must mean the older girls,' begins Julia. 'Your hands are very small to do knitting, darling, but we can try.'

'They've got to knit Rough Tor,' says Andy casually, man to man, to Pete, who stretches his eyes and makes such a disbelieving face that Andy laughs inordinately. Showing off, he picks up a Munchmallow and bangs it on his head as though it is an egg. Carefully he unpeels the red and silver foil in case the broken chocolate shell should fall out and eats the pieces before biting into the delicious marshmallow.

'When you say "knit Rough Tor",' says Pete, refilling his cup, 'how d'you mean exactly? Rough Tor's how many feet high? Sounds quite a marathon.'

'It's going to be on a banner. We told you. With St Branwalader,' says Liv impatiently. 'When can we start, Mummy?'

'After tea,' says Julia, 'unless you want to watch *Jackanory*.'

Liv hesitates but Andy is already getting down, shouting

'Jackanory' and rushing into the sitting-room. Charlie immediately scrambles down after him and Zack sets up a wail from
the high chair in which he is propped with a rug so as to hold
him upright.

'Sorry, darling,' Julia says to Liv. 'It's nearly time for his
bottle. The knitting might have to wait until a bit later. I
promise we'll have a try before you go to bed.'

Liv sighs heavily and stomps away behind her brothers whilst
Julia picks Zack up and sits down with him opposite Pete. Zack
stares around him, eyes wide; presently his gaze rests on Pete
and suddenly he beams. Pete grins back.

'Hello, old son,' he says. 'Welcome to the circus. You'll get
used to it after a while.'

'He's already used to it,' says Julia, eating a neglected finger
of bread and butter. 'Can you believe he's nearly five months
old? I suppose,' she hesitates a little, 'I suppose we might have
another one ourselves sometime.'

Pete's face falls. 'Come on, love,' he protests. 'I think that
four kids are more than enough. Oh, I know we were hoping
for another girl, and of course it's really sad that we lost our
baby, but even so . . .' He shakes his head. 'I think we might
have to be content with this fellow. He's a splendid little chap,
Julia.'

'I know he is,' she says quickly, not wanting to start an argu-
ment on this last evening. 'It's not that. It's just, you know, I
was wondering about it, that's all.'

Pete watches her. 'I'm sorry,' he says gently, 'but I think you'll
find that four children under six are going to be an awful lot
for you to cope with. You've already said that you didn't know
how you managed these last few months, especially when I
was at sea. That's why we're getting Linda up from the village
to help in the house. Why don't you give it a bit longer before
you worry about having any more?'

'I expect you're right.' She smiles, hoping to restore the earlier cheerful atmosphere. 'Anyway, I'm going to have my work cut out teaching Liv to knit.'

'What on earth does she mean? How the devil can anyone knit Rough Tor?'

'I think the idea is that they make up a collage with each child doing its own little piece and then they're all sewn together to make the banner. Be grateful you're going back to sea, that's all.'

'I think I am,' he says. 'Well, not really, of course. Six weeks in the North Sea isn't exactly my idea of fun.'

'It'll be better than trying to teach Liv to knit,' promises Julia grimly.

When he's gone off down the drive with Uncle Archie next morning, the children waving and shouting their goodbyes frantically from the front door, Julia feels strangely bereft. She glances down at Liv whose eyes are brimming with tears, her mouth turned down at the corners, and knows exactly how she feels.

'Daddy gone,' says Charlie thoughtfully.

'Why does he have to keep going away?' asks Liv mutinously, repeating a question asked earlier but still unable to grasp the point of the vital importance of the defence of the realm. 'Yes, but *why* does he? It's not fair.' Julia stretches out a comforting hand but Liv shakes it off. 'Pee po piddle bum,' she shouts crossly.

Julia leads them all back into the house. 'It's horrid, isn't it?' she agrees cheerfully. 'But he'll be back soon and we'll make a lovely picture to send to him. We can do St Branwalader the Raven Lord. I'm going to make some porridge. Who wants some?'

Gloom as heavy and dull as an Atlantic depression hangs

over the breakfast table. Everyone is out of sorts and edgy, and the twins go off to school decidedly glum; the prospect of Branwalader the Raven Lord and the knitting of Rough Tor no longer excites them. Even sunny-tempered Charlie, who is rather enjoying the extra attention now that the twins are at school, grizzles and runs his car across Zack's head, making him cry. By late morning Julia feels the familiar lowness of spirits pressing in and wonders why she ever thought she'd be relieved when Pete had gone. She sees now that the need to keep cheerful for his benefit has had certain advantages. After lunch and the children's nap she bundles Charlie into his out-door clothes, puts Zack into the pushchair, and sets off with the dogs, down the drive and up along the narrow moorland road.

Charlie shouts joyfully as he stumbles amongst the rocks; climbing the smaller boulders, jumping off again, splashing in the puddles and pools. Zack cranes from his seat to watch him whilst Bella and the Turk race away over the moor, barking excitedly, tails waving. Julia plods doggedly on, head bent against the north-westerly wind. She's lost enough weight in the last few months to be able to fit into Tiggy's long sheepskin coat and she wears it gratefully, not only for its warmth but for the comfort she derives from it having been Tiggy's.

She pulls the collar more closely around her neck and catches the faintest whiff of scent: Tiggy's Arpège. It is as if Tiggy is beside her, thrusting her hand under her arm; so strong is the impression that Julia instinctively presses her elbow against her side in response. The remembrance of those happy days with its comradeship and silly jokes assails her and, without warning, tears stream from her eyes. She bends low over the pushchair handle, blind with silent weeping, but when she raises her head she looks into Zack's puzzled eyes and the sight of the small, trusting face pulls her up short.

With an effort Julia smiles at him. She wipes her eyes and blows her nose and turns the pushchair, glad to have her back to the chill wind. A swoop of starlings passes overhead, a dark trembling cloud that forms and re-forms against the dull, grey backdrop, before plunging suddenly in a fluid waterfall of flight to the small fields in the valley below. There is no hint of spring in the moisture-laden air; no sign that these short dark winter days will ever end. Yet far out to the west, over the sea, a gleam of sunshine suddenly pierces the sullen clouds and strikes downwards; a shaft of light that irradiates the silvery horizon and touches Julia's heart with faint hope. Calling to Charlie and the dogs, smiling at Zack, she begins to walk briskly home.

CHAPTER FIFTEEN

2004

It was the newspaper, flung down casually on the kitchen table, that reconnected Julia's memory. 'GIGANTIC ART FRAUD' announced the headline, printed in bold type alongside the photograph of an elderly man. Julia glanced at it, turned away and then swivelled back to look at it more closely. She remembered that it was Charlie's newspaper, lying just so on the table at breakfast, that had first aroused the uneasiness: but why? She bent forward, both hands resting on the table, reading the newsprint. A medieval bronze bought by an American museum had been discovered to be a fake; further investigation now showed that this was simply one of several frauds. Tristan Stamper, the owner of a famous French gallery, had copied the originals, which he had kept for his own private collection.

Tristan Stamper. Julia bent closer, heart hammering, peering at the photograph. It must have been the name that had first alerted her subconscious. Was it possible that there could be two Tristan Stampers who had art galleries in Paris? Julia's thoughts darted forward, this way and that, trying to see how the arrest of Tiggy's father might have any effect upon them. Only she and Pete knew that he existed; he had no knowledge of his grandson. As far as he was concerned Tiggy had died in a car accident and that was the end of it. He couldn't have known about the baby: not even Tiggy's grandmother had known about the baby. Julia stared at the photograph of Tristan Stamper. The eighty-year-old man bore no resemblance to the young father she'd occasionally seen at school events. She thought about Zack. There was nothing to connect him to this; nothing. Yet, her heart raced and her stomach churned as she imagined how Zack would feel if he were to be confronted with this article and told that the man was his grandfather. All his life he'd assumed that Tiggy and Tom were orphans; how would he react to the truth?

She told herself that he need never know; who would tell him? There was nobody who would make the connection. Nevertheless, she had the feeling that she was missing the point; that there was something she'd overlooked that could give the game away. There was something nagging at the back of her mind: ever since she'd seen the headlines in Charlie's kitchen, and then the old VW camper at Eype, she'd been conscious of Tiggy at her elbow.

'For God's sake,' she said aloud, 'get a grip. This is crazy.'

She wondered if she dared confide in Aunt Em.

'Don't tell anyone,' Pete had said long ago. 'If only you and I know who Tiggy was then nobody can spill the beans by mistake.'

It was as if Tiggy was trying to tell her something, to warn her; Julia sat down at the table and put her head in her hands.

1977

January passes slowly with spells of drenching rain and blustery winds; skies of uniform grey cloud lour, pressing down upon the land, rolling in from the Atlantic and drifting in the valleys and across the moors, enveloping the house and misting the windowpanes. On a particularly bleak morning, Julia has a visitor. She's been on her knees, fishing with the broom handle for one of Charlie's little cars which has run beneath the dresser, when the bell trills. She climbs to her feet, dusts off the little car and gives it to Charlie, then goes through to the front door, pushing her hair behind her ears.

She stares at Angela and Cat in horrified disbelief. Angela laughs, openly delighted at Julia's expression.

'Don't look so thrilled to see us,' she says, enjoying her discomfiture. 'We're on our way to Minions and couldn't resist dropping in on the way through.'

Cat, welded as usual to her mother's leg, fist crammed into her mouth, stares up at Julia, who experiences the usual instinctive dislike. The dogs, who rushed out expectantly, lose interest and go back to their baskets.

'I thought you were in Faslane,' Julia says lamely.

'We are,' answers Angela airily. 'Only, we've got tenant problems so Cat and I are with my parents at Rock for a few days while I sort it out. Any chance of a cup of coffee?'

Julia stands aside reluctantly and they go past her, through the sitting-room and into the kitchen. Zack, supported with a rug, is propped in the high chair and Charlie stands beside him, staring warily at the newcomers.

'You've grown,' Angela observes to him. 'And so this is Tiggy's baby?'

She studies Zack intently and Julia has a strong desire to

stand in front of him and protect him from Angela's scrutiny and Cat's cross-eyed stare.

'Yes,' she says. 'That's Zack.'

'Such a tragedy,' says Angela. 'And how noble of you to take him on. Pete's finding all four of them a bit much, I gather.'

'Do you?' asks Julia after a moment.

'Oh, well, Martin spoke to him last week.' Angela sits down at the table, fishes her cigarettes out of her bag. 'Said that leave had been a bit like a five-ring circus.'

Julia is silent; hurt that Pete should have implied any criticism of his family, trying to be rational.

'And I thought you said you were pregnant last summer.' Angela lights up and flips the packet across the table. 'What happened?'

After a moment Julia takes one. She hasn't smoked for several months but suddenly the craving is too great.

'*You* said that I was pregnant,' she says. She pushes the kettle on to the hotplate. '*I* didn't say so, if you remember.'

Angela shrugs, amused. 'I still think it's amazing to take on someone else's baby. Didn't Tiggy have any family of her own? I remember she said she hadn't but surely there must have been someone. Some aunt or a cousin or someone.'

'No,' says Julia firmly. 'There was nobody else. That's why she was with us. So what's this about your tenants?'

Angela groans. 'Honestly,' she says, 'it's such a bore. We thought we were so lucky getting a naval couple to rent the cottage but they've been unexpectedly posted to Portsmouth. I've got to do the going-out inventory and find someone else. You don't know anyone I suppose who'd like to rent a nice little cottage?'

'Sorry, no.' Julia makes coffee and puts a mug beside Angela. 'Would you like some juice?' she asks Cat, who stares at her with the familiar inimical look but refuses to answer. 'She's still not speaking then?' Julia says lightly to Angela. 'However does she manage at school?'

'She can talk when she wants to,' replies Angela, unperturbed. 'She ought to be at school now, actually, but I couldn't leave her in Faslane, and my parents wanted me to bring her with me. Would you like some juice, sweetie? Or some milk?'

Cat shakes her head, fingers still stuffed into her mouth. She reaches out, seizes Charlie's little car and with a violent shove sends it spinning from the table. He cries out in distress, hurrying to pick it up, and she watches him with satisfaction. Julia bites back a reprimand whilst Angela simply smiles.

'How on earth are you going to manage with four?' she asks idly. 'Stuck out here miles from anywhere and with Pete at sea so much. One's more than enough for me.'

'I think Cat would be more than enough for anyone,' Julia answers unguardedly.

For a brief moment Angela's habitual expression of wry amusement fades and Julia sees her true feelings: antagonism and dislike. The look vanishes in a second and the usual cynical half-smile returns.

'Did Pete tell you that he's coming to stay with us when the boat's in Faslane? No? He *is* naughty, isn't he? Should be fun. I wonder why he didn't mention it to you.'

'Perhaps he didn't think it was important,' Julia suggests, controlling an urge to smack that smug face. 'I'm sorry to hurry you but I'm going to have lunch with a friend and I ought to get a move on.'

Later she writes angrily to Pete:

So why didn't you tell me that you're going to stay with them? You know how she likes to wrong-foot me and you always manage to give her the ammunition. And why did you tell them that leave was like a five-ring circus? You're so disloyal sometimes . . .

As soon as she's written this, part of her is tempted to tear the letter up but Angela's words rankle and her heart is still sore. Quickly she puts it in its envelope and seals it, and when she goes to collect the twins from school she posts it, though part of her still regrets writing it.

All through the evening, exhausted by the bedtime routine, she struggles with the familiar demons of guilt, jealousy and despair that Angela's visit have disturbed. Zack begins to cry and she brings him downstairs lest he should waken the others. She switches off *Starsky & Hutch* and settles Zack in the corner of the sofa whilst she puts more logs on the fire. Sitting at the other end of the sofa, turned towards him, she studies his face as he gazes about him; quite quiet now, he stares at the flickering flames. Watching him, Julia feels a strong desire to weep; she wonders if Tiggy might be hovering in the shadows, just out of sight, and she remembers how they sat here together, talking about the future. All those plans Tiggy made; all her fears for her baby; yet neither of them foresaw the reality. Julia thinks about her own child, wondering whether it would have been a boy or a girl, and desperately swallows down tears of anguish. She simply mustn't give way: she has the suspicion that if she were to start crying, really crying, she might never stop.

The Turk stirs and jumps up on to the sofa, curling herself down into a ball beside Zack. Julia puts out a hand and strokes the rough coat. She feels unbearably lonely: she misses Pete terribly and now wishes with all her heart that she hadn't sent him such an unloving letter. Misery swells in her breast so that she can barely breathe. Bella comes to sit against her legs, head on her knee, and Julia passes her hand over and over the heavy head and thick soft ears. Gradually the rhythmic smoothing action soothes her and she stands up.

'I'm going to make a sandwich,' she tells Zack. 'I shan't be a sec, so don't cry, there's a good fellow.'

By the time she returns he is peacefully asleep and she sits quietly beside the fire, eating her sandwich. Presently she picks him up gently and carries him upstairs to his cot.

When Pete's letter arrives it carries news so important that his reply to Julia's caustic observations is relegated to second place:

> The captain's recommending me for Perisher. He told me this morning. You can imagine how relieved I am. I was beginning to think I'd never make it. He's given me a pretty good report and he says he's confident I'll get through unless I do something really stupid. It's fantastic news . . . As for staying with Martin and Angela, it just slipped my mind. Honestly, darling, I <u>do</u> wish you wouldn't get so uptight about Angela. You should tell her to wind her neck in when she upsets you. I know Trescairn is a bit off the beaten track but you need to make some new friends. I worry about you being so far from all your old chums around Tavistock but, more good news, David and Pam are buying a cottage in St Cleer. Not too far away, and I know how well you get on with Pam and the kids love young Will . . .

Julia feels light with relief. It is terrific news that Pete should be recommended for the Commanding Officers Qualifying Course, known by submariners as Perisher; even more wonderful that, if he were to pass it, he will be given command of a submarine. His negligent reaction to her angry remarks brings her an equal amount of delight; it seems that her own response to Angela had been the right one: he didn't consider it to be important. She is so thankful that she's been able to make her feelings known without starting a row that she feels happier than she's been for months – since before Tiggy died.

Pete is right too about making friends. They weren't at Trescairn long enough to make new friends before Tiggy arrived. It was such a perfect spring and summer that she didn't feel the need for other friends. How quickly the months passed; what fun they had. Julia realizes that, ever since Tiggy died, she's been caught in a web of mourning, like a fly in amber, paralysed with shock and grief. Yet now, since the twins have started school, she is meeting other young mothers of her own age and friendships are beginning to flourish.

When Aunt Em telephones mid-morning, suggesting that she might come to see her, Julia readily agrees.

'Pete's been recommended for Perisher,' she says jubilantly. 'Yes, it's great, isn't it? We must celebrate. See you later then.'

Driving out from Blisland, Em is surprised at her own delighted reaction to Julia's news. It takes her a little while to realize that it is the joyfulness in Julia's voice that is giving her so much pleasure. It is a long while since she's heard that note of real happiness and she wonders if, at last, Julia might be beginning to recover from her grief. She drives slowly, mentally recording small scenes that might be useful to her painting: that magpie, for instance, glossily debonair in his monochrome feathers as he forages on the stone wall, sharply marked against the flowering furze.

The open moorland on Kerrow Downs lies drowned beneath a stretch of shallow floodwater on which flocks of lesser black-backed gulls float so that it looks like some great estuary. A dog appears, a farm collie out alone, lean belly to ground as he follows a scent, and the flock suddenly take flight, great wings beating, crying hoarsely as they wheel above the wind-rocked surface of the water.

Em pauses on Delford Bridge to watch the De Lank, racing down from its source high up on the moor, streaming out over its banks and pouring between the granite piers of the clapper bridge. The sandy shallows where the children play in summer have vanished beneath the flood and the submerged grass streams out, just below the surface; undulating green tresses in the clear, tumbling water.

She drives on, light-hearted in the slanting winter sunshine, making a mental note of the dramatic backdrop made by Rough Tor and Brown Willy, clear-cut against the chill blue sky. She catches sight of some new catkins clustered on bare, brittle twigs and her heart lifts even higher; soon spring would be here, the cold, sweet spring; that magic time of healing and regeneration.

CHAPTER SIXTEEN

2004

'We could have let the cottages ten times over this month,' said Liv, putting down the telephone. 'If I say it myself, the website's really pulling in the punters. I made a pretty good job of it.'

'The photographs are very good,' Chris agreed. 'You made the courtyard look very attractive.'

'Well, it *is* attractive, but I think it was good to do some of the interior shots as well as the views, of course. I keep wondering how I can improve it.'

'It doesn't sound as if you need to if we're turning people away.'

'If the weather sets in fair then people suddenly think, let's dash down to Cornwall for the weekend. I always knew we'd be able to pick up some of that trade. I just didn't realize we'd be so booked up from day one.' She glanced at him, frowning. 'I'm just sorry that Val seems still to be so anxious. I thought she'd come out of her slough of despond for a while. She seemed positively effervescent. Now she's right down again.'

Chris didn't look at her but continued to stare at his screen. He made a resigned face. 'You know how it is. She's subject to mood swings and that's about it, I suppose.'

'Well, we're all a bit like that,' admitted Liv. 'Depending on the time of the month . . .'

There was an odd little silence; Chris stared more intently at his screen and Liv stared at him, an idea slowly dawning. She couldn't bring herself to ask the question but she could see a pattern now in Val's behaviour over the last two months and it also explained Chris's strained, almost embarrassed manner.

'I'm going to make myself a sandwich,' she said, getting up. 'See you later.'

In the annexe she walked up and down for a while, staring out at the sea.

What difference did it make, she asked herself, if Val and Chris were trying for a baby? She'd made her own vow never to come between them – never to be like Angela – so what difference? The little pain in her heart told her that it mattered very much. Clearly there was to be no future for her with Chris. The miracle that she never quite dared to imagine fully – Val throwing in the towel of her own accord and flouncing back to London – was not going to happen. It occurred to her again that she'd allowed Penharrow and Chris to become a kind of comfort zone: there was something attractive about being with someone who knew you inside out and accepted you totally, though no emotional demands were being made. It was fun and exciting; and dangerous.

Liv cut a slice of bread, took out some cheese, but her appetite had deserted her. She sat down at the table, opened her laptop and logged on. There was an email from Andy:

To: Liv
From: Andy
Did you see the news last night about the fraud trial in
Paris? There was a picture of a bronze that's just like
one we had at home. Do you remember, I mentioned it
ages ago after seeing the *Antiques Roadshow* but then
I forgot all about it? Did you ask Mum where ours is?
Cat remembered it from way back. It's called *The Child
Merlin*. Apparently the one in the museum in America
isn't the original but a copy. The old boy up for trial
denies keeping the original in his private collection
and nobody can trace it. I'm sure you'd recognize it.
Odd, isn't it? Perhaps we've got a masterpiece hidden
away. Ha ha! Cat thinks we should check it out. How's
Cornwall?

Liv stared at the message, confused. She remembered that
Andy had mentioned the little Merlin weeks back but clearly
they'd both forgotten about it. As for the trial, she'd been too
busy to watch the news or read the papers, and she resented
the way Cat's name always cropped up in Andy's messages to
her now. Dispirited, she returned to her sandwich.

Chris sat on after she'd gone; not seeing what was on his
screen, thinking about Val. Her reaction when she'd discovered that she wasn't pregnant had been almost frightening;
she'd been so certain that, to begin with, she'd refused to believe it. Ultimately, she'd had to accept it.

'It doesn't matter, love,' he'd said – well, that was a bad start,
of course.

'It might not matter to you,' she'd cried angrily, almost weeping, 'but it does to me.'

'I didn't mean it like that.' He'd tried to put his arms round her, to comfort her, but she'd shrugged him off. 'I meant that it's only the first try. It could take ages. Nobody gets pregnant first shot straight off the pill.'

She'd given him a withering look. 'How would you know? Made a study of it, have you?'

He'd felt such a surge of antagonism that he'd had to take a tight grip on his temper.

'I think it's a fairly well-known fact,' he'd said quietly. 'Anyway, I see no reason to lose it just because you haven't got what you want immediately. Other people try for years.'

'I'm not other people,' she'd answered flatly.

Now, Chris got up from his desk, stuck his hands in his pockets; it was an intolerable position to be in and he was finding the obligation to perform at regular times extremely off-putting. Val's grim determined face and her mechanical approach roused no ardour in him and when he'd said as much she'd been particularly vituperative.

It was affecting his relationship with Liv too. Sworn to secrecy by Val, he found that he was uneasy with Liv, as if he were in some way deceiving her. Now, he was pretty sure she'd guessed at the truth.

He looked round quickly as the door opened and she came in. She grinned at him, offering a piece of chocolate.

'Honestly,' she said, 'a quick lunch break and there's twenty-four unwanted emails and a message from Andy telling me that the family's had a priceless work of art stuck up on the shelf for the last however many years, like you do, and isn't it fun? Since Cat got at him his brain is more scrambled than usual.'

'What?' Chris took the chocolate, grateful for her cheerfulness, his own spirits rising. It was so crucial to his wellbeing that he and Liv were friends. 'What are you talking about?'

She shrugged. 'Don't ask me. Ask Andy. Make some coffee, Chris. I think I'm losing the will to live.'

1977

The snow comes softly, gently; large flakes whirling slowly and settling only for a moment before melting on the boggy moorland. By teatime, as the temperature plummets, a light dusting transforms the stony tors and the roads are icy. The twins scream with excitement as they drive out from the village and Julia mentally reviews the shopping she's picked up from the Stores, wondering if she's forgotten anything, hoping she won't be caught out if they are to be snowed in for a few days.

'Will we be able to build a snowman?' asks Andy, peering hopefully through the windscreen. It is his turn to sit in the front, a treat the twins share whenever Charlie and Zack are with them on the school run.

'Not this afternoon,' says Julia firmly. 'Maybe tomorrow. We'll see.'

Quite suddenly she is transported back in time: a year ago, almost to the day, Tiggy had arrived. On just such a day as this she'd driven down from Herefordshire in the camper, braving the elements, her one idea to protect her unborn child.

'What's the matter, Mummy?' Liv asks anxiously, leaning between the front seats. 'Don't you like the snow?'

'I'm fine,' answers Julia quickly, pulling herself together. 'Just being careful, that's all. It's getting a bit slippery and I shall be glad to be home.'

It is much later that the telephone rings; another naval wife, an acquaintance more than a friend, now living at Faslane in Smuggler's Way. Julia is rather surprised to hear from her but quite glad to have the evening's routine broken, to chat and exchange news.

'It was seeing Pete that made me think of phoning,' the friend says at last. 'I saw him leaving Martin and Angela this morning at breakfast time, in a taxi. Well,' a tiny laugh, 'leaving *Angela*, to be accurate. Martin's at sea at the moment but I expect you knew that. Anyway, must dash. Keep in touch.'

Julia replaces the telephone receiver; she feels sick and her brain refuses to function properly. She moves slowly round the sitting-room, trailing her hand along the sofa's back, mechanically patting the cushions.

Words repeat themselves in her head: That's it then. That's it. I can't stand any more. That's it.

It seems important to keep moving; walking to and fro, putting more wood on the fire, going out into the kitchen to put the kettle on. The dogs follow her anxiously, puzzled by her restlessness. She makes coffee and stares at it: how can she swallow anything? As she pours it away she hears footsteps on the stairs and Liv appears in the sitting-room.

'I had a bad dream,' she says fretfully. 'It was a really horrid dream, Mummy. I dreamed you'd gone away and left us.'

Her small face is distraught and Julia goes to her swiftly, pulls her on to the sofa and cuddles her. The dogs crowd at their knees and Julia talks to them and to Liv, comforting and soothing them all. That night she breaks the rules and allows Liv to sleep with her in the big bed; she takes up most of the room, her limbs disposed at angles, warm and heavy with relaxation. Julia listens to her regular breathing and is grateful for her company; the child's presence is holding her together for the moment. Julia dozes and wakes again, her heart hot with resentment and fear, wondering how much longer she can carry the weight of her burden.

CHAPTER SEVENTEEN

2004

The telephone rang just as Julia came in from hanging out the washing.

'Julia?' Aunt Em's voice was almost a whisper and Julia's stomach jolted. 'Have you seen the newspaper this morning?'

'No. I haven't been down to the village yet. Why?'

'Have you read anything about this French art fraud trial or seen it on the news?'

A tiny silence. 'Yes,' said Julia, casually. 'Yes, I think I have. Why?'

'There's a photograph today showing some of the pieces involved. One of them looks like your little Merlin . . . Julia? Are you there?'

'Yes,' said Julia at last. 'Yes, I'm here. What exactly are you saying, Aunt Em?'

'This man, Stamper, used to sell valuable pieces to museums and art galleries. It seems that on several occasions, having made the transaction, he copied the piece and gave it to the unsuspecting curator, keeping the original hidden away in his own collection.'

'But why?' asked Julia, puzzled. 'I can't see the point of that if it has to be hidden.'

'The point is, if you are a true collector you don't care about that. You simply have the original piece to gloat over. Like a miser with his hoard of gold. One of the faked pieces looks identical to your little Merlin.'

'*What?*'

'Julia, where did the little Merlin come from? It was Tiggy's, wasn't it?'

'Yes,' said Julia reluctantly. 'It was Tiggy's. But it can't be . . . this piece. You mean it's the original? How could it be?' A terrible sense of dread filled her. 'Why should Tiggy have had it?'

'I spoke to her about it once. She said her father had a gallery full of stuff like it and that her grandmother had given it to her when she came down to the west. Have you got the bronze there, Julia?'

'Yes. No.' Julia stared vaguely round her. 'I don't know.'

'Listen carefully. This is important. When I saw the bronze it had a name carved on the side of the base in capital letters. Do you remember that?'

Julia shook her head. 'No. No, I really can't remember much about it except that the children liked it. Oh God, Aunt Em, what are you actually telling me?'

'I think that Tiggy was given the Merlin as a gift quite by chance. Neither she nor her grandmother had a clue about its value. My guess is that it was probably kept with other pieces well away from the public eye and that the owner had become almost complacent about its safety. Now this has all started up. Someone discovered that a piece that Stamper sold to the New York Arts Museum was a fake and now they are investigating him thoroughly. The Merlin is just one of several. Tristan Stamper is saying that he had no idea that *The Child Merlin* was a fake and denies ever having any other copy of it in his possession. Who is Tristan Stamper, Julia?'

'He's Tiggy's father,' whispered Julia. 'Oh God, Aunt Em. I'd seen the trial in the paper but I was too frightened that someone might connect him to Zack to think about anything else.'

'Is there any chance that a connection to Tiggy might be found? Didn't you tell me once that her father cast her off when she was still at school?'

'That's right. All he did was pay the fees and she spent the holidays with us or with her granny. After she'd left school she never heard from him. He completely abandoned her, though that was her wish too, and once she knew she was having a baby she made me promise that nobody would know that he existed. He . . . he molested her, Aunt Em, and she didn't want him to have anything to do with her baby. She made me absolutely promise. What else could I do? I've often felt guilty that we've lied to Zack but how could anyone break such a promise? Pete agreed with me that we must honour Tiggy's wishes, though we've been terrified that Zack might decide to try to find his relations, but luckily he's never seemed the least bit interested. When her granny died Tiggy changed her name to Tom's and as far as I was concerned, that was that. Of course, I never gave the Merlin a thought. I don't even know where it is.'

'You must find it. Hide it. I'll come over later.'

Julia put down the phone: her knees were trembling and her limbs were weighty. She sat down suddenly. This was the connection she'd missed in her anxiety for Zack: the little Merlin.

Em stood thinking; she took deep breaths to steady the uneven beating of her heart: she felt dizzy and sick. There was nobody except themselves, she told herself, to connect the Merlin to Zack. It was impossible to contemplate that now, just as he was about to become a father, this should ruin his life. She imagined the press coverage, the scandal: it mustn't be allowed to happen. The bronze must be got rid of somehow. Em wondered if, during the investigation, the police – or some zealous reporter – might dig deeper and discover a daughter from an earlier marriage. It was fortunate that Tiggy's father had cut her off so thoroughly and removed himself to France nearly forty years ago: the trail leading to Tiggy was a very cold one. And, after all, *The Child Merlin* wasn't a particularly important piece, apparently, not even of great value; but the fact that it had been copied made it notorious. Now Em remembered the name carved on the base of the little statue: Vischer. Many years ago, before the war, she'd seen Peter Vischer's statue of King Arthur in the court church at Innsbruck, and his *Madonna of Nuremberg.*

How odd that the scent of the *luteum* had recalled the little scene with Tiggy and the Merlin: and now this. Yet if the Merlin was not at Trescairn, where could it be? On cue, the telephone rang.

'I think Zack must have the Merlin,' Julia said. 'I gave him to Zack, Aunt Em, when he was little. It seemed appropriate. After all, it was Tiggy's to begin with and I thought it was right that Zack should have him. He used to keep it with his toys and play with it sometimes. I never guessed that it was anything particularly special. Oh, I know it was very charming and all that but it didn't *look* valuable. Not as if it had been silver or gold or anything.'

'I think you have to be a bit of a specialist to appreciate bronze,' said Em. 'So Zack has the Merlin.'

'Oh God, I hope so.' Julia's voice trembled. 'I haven't seen it for years. He must have taken it with all his stuff when he got married. My fear is that they've stuck it up on a shelf where any of their friends might go in and see it. And recognize it, now it's all over the papers and the television news. I've decided to go to look for myself. I can't see any alternative. I keep thinking how Zack would react if it were to become public. Imagine the shock of knowing we've lied to him all these years, apart from discovering what kind of man his grandfather is. It doesn't bear thinking about. Oh God, Aunt Em, I must get hold of it if I can and smuggle it away. Don't you think so?'

'Yes, I do,' said Em after a moment. 'Shall I come with you? I can act as a distraction.'

Julia began to laugh nervously. 'I can't believe this is happening,' she said. 'That we're actually planning to steal the Merlin from Caroline and Zack. It's crazy.'

'It's necessary,' said Em grimly. 'Let me know when we can go. Shall you phone Caroline?'

'I shall do it straightaway. I'm trying to think of a good excuse for an urgent trip to Tavistock tomorrow. I shan't relax until we've found the Merlin.'

Em put down the telephone, wondering how easy it would be to remove the Merlin from Chapel Street. Would Caroline notice its absence or was it just an odd little statue that belonged to Zack that wouldn't be missed? Em bit her lip: who could have imagined that Tiggy's little mascot should now be such a threat to her child?

'I shan't sleep a wink tonight,' Julia had said.

Her voice had been full of distress and fear, and it reminded Em of another crisis, long ago, six months after Tiggy's death.

1977

Em, stopping work mid-morning to make herself some coffee, sees the car pull up, glimpses the desperate expression on Julia's face, and hurries out to meet her on the garden steps.

'I think Pete's having an affair with Angela,' Julia says before she's even reached the top step.

Em gathers her into the house. She is fearful but determined not to let Julia see her anxiety.

'I don't believe it,' says Em. It's not quite true – but she sounds so strong and sure that Julia stares at her almost hopefully. Her blue eyes are drowned with tears, her cheeks bright red with rubbing. Her thick fair hair is pushed back behind a navy-blue velvet band and she looks just like Liv; Em's heart is pierced with pain.

'Come and sit down beside the fire,' she says. 'Where are Charlie and Zack?'

'At home with Linda.' Julia stares round her rather blankly, as if she doesn't quite know where she is. 'It's her cleaning day and she never minds keeping an eye on the children, and they adore her. I just had to get out for a moment. You know how it is?'

Suddenly her mouth twists uncontrollably awry, tears jump from her eyes and she sits down quickly beside the fire on a little stool, covering her face with her hands. Aunt Em is shocked by this distraught and frightened Julia. Such abandon is out of character. Even at that terrible moment when she and Tiggy arrived back at Trescairn in the storm, Julia was in control, distracting the twins, calling an ambulance; and after Tiggy's death she managed to control her own grief and guilt, keeping strong and courageous so as to be able to care for the children and for Zack. Looking at her now, Em wonders whether they've all been deceived by her show of strength; unaware that Julia's burden has been far too heavy for her.

'Tell me why you think Pete is having an affair,' Em says, sitting on the edge of the fender beside Julia. She touches her lightly on the head, smoothing the thick hair, noticing its dryness, and waits for Julia to blot her cheeks and blow her nose.

'He's been lying to me,' she says at last. 'When the boat went into Faslane he said he'd be spending the night with Martin and Angela. They've got a married quarter in Smuggler's Way. Only now it seems that Martin was at sea.'

'Even if that's true, it doesn't mean that Pete's having an affair with Angela.'

Julia stares into the fire, biting her lips. 'I asked him once before,' she says miserably. 'Just after Tiggy died and I was a bit emotional. He was very late home a few times and I knew Martin was at sea then too.'

Em's heart skips and bumps. 'What did he say?'

'He didn't answer directly. He lost his temper and said that I was neurotic about Angela and . . . other things.'

Em is silent.

'He wouldn't answer, you see,' says Julia into the silence. 'He just stormed about and made it sound as if it was all me. That I was jealous, unreasonable, that I didn't trust him. But he never actually denied it. Then Zack started crying, which set Charlie off, and Pete stormed out and said he was taking the dogs for a walk. It's so infuriating, having someone walk out on you in the middle of a row. I can never have the luxury of it because of the children.'

'Oh, darling, I'm so sorry,' says Em helplessly. 'It must be very difficult for you.'

Julia straightens up, wiping her eyes with the back of her hand and trying to smile. 'It's not altogether Pete's fault. I haven't been very easy to live with since Tiggy . . . since Tiggy . . .' The passionate storm of weeping takes them both by surprise and Em leans forward, holding Julia tightly until it passes.

'Sorry,' gasps Julia at last. 'Sorry. I've never done that before, you know. Never really cried, not properly. There's never seemed to be the right moment. Pete gets angry because he feels helpless and when I'm alone I'm always afraid that the children might hear and be frightened. Oh God, Aunt Em, I still can't forget it all.'

'You'll never forget it all,' says Em gently. 'How could you? But you can try to stop tormenting yourself uselessly. Julia, you couldn't have left her alone in the car.'

'I could have run home.' Her head is bowed; the tears stream ceaselessly down, soaking her knees. 'I'm sure it was making her walk all that way when she was already in labour. I could have grabbed your car and gone back for her. I've been over it and over it, how I could have done it differently. Anyway, it's not just that.'

Em sees that it is necessary for Julia to release the whole burden of her pain and says nothing: she waits.

'I lost my own baby at the same time,' Julia says bleakly at last. 'I have Zack, of course, and I love him, but that doesn't make up for losing my own baby. I sometimes feel resentful and then I feel guilty about that too. When I woke up this morning I just knew that today was the day she would have been born. I lost her and I can't get over it.'

Julia weeps again and Em swallows back her own tears. 'I didn't know,' she says sorrowfully. 'I had no idea you were pregnant.'

'Nobody knew. Only me and Tiggy and Pete. I was waiting to be absolutely certain. Pete tries to be kind about it but he doesn't truly understand. He thinks that because I was only three months' pregnant it's not so bad. But it was my *baby*.'

The last word is ragged, painfully screamed out as if Julia is torn inside with grief, and Em sits quite still, mechanically stroking Julia's hair.

Julia raises her head. 'The other thing is that I really miss Tiggy. I can't believe she's dead. In those last few months we were like sisters. I can't believe I'll never see her again. I really loved her. It's what gets me through the bad days when I resent Zack because he's not mine. I love him. I *do* love him because he was Tiggy's. But sometimes it's hard and I feel so guilty.' She scrubs at her face again. 'And that's why I don't know about Pete. I wonder if I am mad, like he said, or whether he's bluffing me. God, I hate Angela.'

'I can sympathize with that,' says Em, 'but you're playing her game, you see. You must stop.'

Julia stares at her, puzzled, momentarily distracted from her grief. 'How do you mean?'

'Fear is disabling, and Angela is controlling the game because you allow her to frighten you. First she sows the seeds of fear in your mind and then stands back to allow your distorted perception of the danger to enable them to grow. You become wary, get jealous and make accusations: Pete is hurt, grows resentful and feels misjudged. She wants to undermine the firm ground of your relationship so she keeps the topsoil fertile by scattering little juicy hints here and there and then showers allusions over it so that your terrors flower and blossom correspondingly. Instead of seeing them as a crop of rank weeds, you encourage them with a nice mixture of doubt and fear so that their roots spread, grow strong and invade your secure territory. Angela and Pete don't need to have an affair, Julia. Your marriage can be destroyed perfectly well without that, and Angela knows it.'

By now Julia is wide-eyed, longing to be convinced.

'You sound so sure,' she says wistfully.

'Oh, I am,' says Em. 'I don't believe for a minute that Pete feels anything for Angela except guilt. He dropped her for you and somehow she's made him feel just a bit of a heel about it.

Enough to keep him twitching a bit. She's clever, is Angela. She's the sort of woman who can't let any man go but likes to demonstrate her power by an ongoing flirtation. Men never seem to have the courage to resist this, probably due to some misguided idea of chivalry or maybe it's just vanity, but whatever it is their wives and girlfriends resent it. They should tell these women to sling their hooks.'

Julia manages a smile. 'First you were being horticultural and now you're being nautical, Aunt Em,' she says.

Em grimaces. 'Archie had one or two Angelas hanging around,' she says feelingly. 'Don't go along with it, Julia. Don't allow Angela to manipulate you.'

Julia sits hunched, elbows on knees, chin in hands. 'It's easier said than done.'

'Of course it is, but you can try. At least they aren't living nearby any longer.'

'Well, that's why I was so furious. I really thought she was out of my hair at last.'

'Who told you that Pete spent the night with Angela in Faslane while Martin was at sea?' asks Em curiously.

'A mutual friend who lives in Smuggler's Way. Well, she's not really a friend, more an acquaintance. She said that she saw the taxi outside Angela's house yesterday morning and Pete leaving. She made a joke of it, of course, but she thought I ought to know.'

'Ah. We all need friends like that.'

'Well, I *would* want to know,' says Julia defensively. 'If Pete was being unfaithful, I mean. Imagine the humiliation of discovering that everyone knows but you.'

'You said that she's a mutual friend – perhaps she's more Angela's friend than yours and she was put up to it. If she's not a close friend why should she phone you unless it was to make a point on Angela's behalf? Do you know, I should say nothing to Pete about this if I were you. Play a waiting game and see what happens.'

Julia is silent. Em watches her compassionately. 'Have you time for some coffee?'

Julia shakes her head. 'I must get back to the children. They'll be wondering where I am. It was a really bad moment and I needed to get out. I'm sorry, Aunt Em. When I woke up this morning I just knew that today would have been my baby's birthday. I don't know how I got through breakfast and the twins off to school without screaming. I simply couldn't bear it another moment and I knew that if I was going to break down I'd want it to be with you. Sorry.'

'Don't be sorry,' says Em firmly. 'I'm very glad you were able to do it, Julia. You can't keep things pent up indefinitely. Something cracks sooner or later.'

'It's just that you feel you have to be strong, don't you? Especially with children around all the time. And I miss Tiggy so much. I had no idea how grief takes you by surprise, Aunt Em. It's little things. Hearing Elton John and Kiki Dee singing "Don't Go Breaking My Heart". Tiggy loved that song. She used to dance round with Charlie, singing it to him. And every time someone comes to the door, the poor old Turk leaps up and goes rushing out hoping it's her. She comes back looking so miserable. The twins are much better now but it was awful to begin with, trying to explain. They wanted to keep the van but, oh God, every time I looked at it I remembered all those wonderful times we had.'

Her weeping this time is only a little less desperate and Em continues to sit beside her, feeling helpless and willing down her own grief.

'Tiggy was very special,' she says sadly. 'To all of us.'

Julia draws a deep uneven breath. 'Well, at least we have

Zack,' she says. 'He's special too. And I'd better get back and give him a feed.'

'Look,' says Em, 'if you can give me a lift, I'll come back with you. Archie can pick me up later when he gets home. I'll leave him a note. Why not? I think you need a bit of extra support today.'

Julia smiles gratefully. 'You give me masses of support,' she says. 'I'd never have managed these last months without you. But yes, please. I'd like that.'

CHAPTER EIGHTEEN

2004

Val lay in bed, waiting for Chris. It was a hot night and she was naked under the thin sheet. She could hear the hum of the shower through the half-open door and the hiss of water on the floor and tiles. When he came through to the bedroom, hair on end, a towel round his waist, she raised herself on one elbow. His glance was so wary that for a brief moment she saw the lighter side of their situation and began to laugh. He watched her almost suspiciously and she made a face at him, half rueful, half pleading.

'Don't look so alarmed,' she said. 'You can sit down. I won't jump on you.'

He sat down, propping himself with pillows, legs stretched out, and she edged in under his arm and laid her cheek against his damp skin.

'I know I've been a bit over the top,' she said. 'It's just that it means a lot. You can understand that, can't you?'

'I can understand it,' he said, 'but I hate the way it's become so mechanical. I can't believe you'll ever get pregnant while you're so damned tense about it.'

'I think you could be right,' she admitted, and felt his arm relax fractionally. 'But you know what my family call me: Mrs Manic.'

He gave an almost unwilling snort of laughter. 'I'm not arguing.'

She laughed too, snuggling against him. 'Anyway, it's much too hot tonight.' His relief was so palpable she wondered if she should be offended but she was determined to stay cool. Since the telephone conversation with her sister she'd decided on a whole different approach.

'You won't conceive,' she'd told Val, 'while you're all worked up. And you'll make Chris tense, which is the last thing you need. He'll smoke and drink more and that's fatal. I mean, come on! You've only been trying for a few weeks. It took us three years. I was like you, though. Once I'd decided to go for it I wanted it to happen first go. It was crazy, really, to expect it. I was working, stressed out, and when it didn't happen I just freaked. I wanted a baby so much I'd have stolen one. It just didn't pan out until we adopted a much calmer approach, but after all that time and so many disappointments it wasn't easy. You're just beginning so, for once, take my advice and chill.'

It was good advice: Val rolled away to her own side of the bed and picked up her book.

Lying beside her, Chris felt ill at ease. He was tired but not relaxed and he craved a smoke.

'I'm just going downstairs for a minute,' he muttered, pulling on his dressing gown. 'Something I've forgotten.'

He didn't look at her, not wanting to encounter the disapproval that showed that Val knew exactly what he was going to do. He slipped out and down the stairs, picked up his cigarettes from the kitchen table and went into the small garden. He hoped there would be no visitors about, taking a late stroll, and he remained close to the house behind the screening of fuchsia bushes and the escallonia hedge.

The soft air embraced him, overhead a dazzle of stars, and he inhaled deeply, struggling against a desperate need to go next door to find Liv. He could see the light from her kitchen window laying a square of gold upon the cobbles and he wondered if she were sitting at her table sending an email to Andy. Supposing he were to just knock on the window; go in and have a chat and a cup of coffee? Instinct warned him that tonight it would lead to much more than that. He knew that Liv was finding it difficult too; the atmosphere between them sang and trembled with their neediness.

His hands were shaking. He threw the stub down, trod on it, then bent and picked it up and flung it into the hedge because he knew how Val hated cigarette butts lying around. Damn Val, with her rules and regs and demands and requirements. Why on earth hadn't he stuck with Liv when she invited him to go travelling with her after uni instead of accepting the prestigious pharmaceutical company job?

He sat down on the small bench by the front door and had it out with himself at last. He hadn't gone to Australia with Liv because he'd wanted security; a good job that brought fulfilment and rewards. The prospect of backpacking, picking up work here and there, simply didn't appeal to him. He'd wanted responsibility, advancement, and Val, being of like mind, had been there just when he'd needed someone to share his future. Without Val there would be no Penharrow; they would never have managed to buy the London house without her hard work and substantial salary. When Val was made redundant they'd decided to start a new life – and that included a family whether he felt he was ready for it or not.

Liv represented freedom, fun; he wanted her not just because of her warmth and generosity but because responsibility and family ties were threatening him. Chris stood up and walked to the edge of the garden. Liv's door was open; light spilled invitingly out into the yard. He stood for several seconds fighting his instinct to go in to her; at last he turned back into the shadowy garden, closed the front door behind him and went upstairs to Val.

Liv waited. She knew he was there, his cigarette scenting the mild night air. She knew too that if he came to her tonight she would be unable to resist him; she simply had no strength left, she wanted him too much. Oh, she'd told herself she'd be no better than Angela and that she'd be betraying them all but – just now, just tonight – she didn't care. She simply wanted his arms round her.

Why, all those years ago, hadn't she simply gone with him to London; settled down and made a life together? Well, she knew the answer: even now the prospect of the rat race, the concrete jungle, the nine-to-five, filled her with absolute horror. No way – not even for Chris – could she have settled to the drudgery of the daily commute and the knowledge that this was it for the next however many years simply for the sake of bricks and mortar and a pension.

She shivered at the thought of it. Perhaps when she was old she'd regret it, but she refused to be a prisoner in order to provide for an old age that might not happen. She stood, leaning against the door jamb, wineglass in hand, listening intently; still waiting. Supposing he were to appear, standing before her, wearing that expression she'd seen several times in the last few days: what then? Could they simply turn back the clock and pick up where they'd left off ten years ago? Would a relationship that had foundered once because of their very different needs be able now to survive the break-up of his marriage and the crumbling of all their dreams?

What would have happened to her and Andy, to Charlie and Zack, if their father had succumbed to Angela's persistence? What would have happened to their mother? Of course, there were no children to worry about here . . . or might there be? Supposing Val were pregnant?

Silently, reluctantly, Liv turned her back on the soft dark night and closed the door very gently behind her. She picked up her mobile and scrolled down to Matt's number.

1977

Much to the children's disappointment the snow lasts less than forty-eight hours. For a few days the high tors retain a fairy-tale icing, pure and sparkling in the bright sunshine, but the lower slopes of the moor remain obstinately dun-coloured, squelching muddily beneath their gumboots and the dogs' feet. The wind continues to blow from the north-east, increasing in strength, pinching and nipping at cheeks and fingers, but these cold, dazzlingly sunny days raise Julia's spirits and give her new courage. Ever since her outburst, the unburdening of her pent-up grief for Tiggy and for her own unborn child, she's felt a sense of release that is enabling her to be more confident in herself and in the future.

She persuades herself that she should try Aunt Em's advice and give Pete the benefit of the doubt: play the waiting game. Sometimes she feels capable of it; at others she can only believe the worst. She tells herself that other people besides Pete might have been at Angela's that night, or that perhaps it hadn't been Pete getting into the taxi, but all the while the worm of distrust continues to gnaw at her new self-confidence. She remembers how, after Pete's letter, that brief moment of happiness had been smashed by Celia's telephone call, and she reminds herself of what Aunt Em said about fear being disabling. She sees now how much she has allowed Angela to manipulate her in the past – and how she is still allowing it – and she tries to take a firmer grip on her emotions.

She takes the twins with her to collect Pete from the dock-yard, knowing that their presence will help to keep their meeting on a light note. Aunt Em looks after Charlie and Zack and is in the middle of their bath-time routine when they all arrive back at Trescairn so it isn't until the evening that Julia finds herself alone with Pete. He is in high spirits, pouring wine for them both, drinking to his good news.

'Of course, it means being away for a bit,' he says. 'In *Dolphin* in the Attack Teacher to begin with, and then north to do it for real. Let's just hope that if I pass I get a submarine down here in Devonport.'

'I hope so too.' Julia speaks feelingly; the thought of moving to Faslane or Gosport with four children is a daunting one. 'Especially now that the twins have settled in so well at school.'

Pete grins. 'I gather Rough Tor is growing apace.'

Julia laughs. 'No thanks to Liv. Learning to knit is a long, slow process.'

He refills her glass, and kisses her. 'God, I'm just out of my mind, darling. I was really sure I wouldn't be recommended.'

Julia keeps smiling, though all the while she longs to question him about the night in Faslane. 'I bet Martin was pleased,' she says lightly. 'You must have had quite a celebration.'

He stares at her, the smile fading from his face, and her heart beat speeds anxiously.

'I didn't go,' he says. 'I changed my mind.'

She raises her eyebrows. 'Did you?'

'Martin was at sea,' he says abruptly. 'I thought under the

circumstances that it would be . . . well, foolish. Angela said that if I was that sensitive about it I could take her out to dinner instead but I thought, after your letter, that it would be disloyal.'

He slightly stresses the word she used in her letter to him and she is silent, eyes on her wineglass. He puts his own glass on the table.

'I think it was the right decision,' he says. 'I'm going to have a bath. Shan't be long.'

He goes out, through the sitting-room and up the stairs, and she remains sitting at the table, feeling desolate. He sounds so sincere and she longs to believe him, yet how can she now confront him with the fact that he was seen leaving Angela's that particular morning? Presently she goes into the sitting-room to make up the fire and sees his grip, half open with a shirt trailing from it. She opens it wider, so as to take out the clothes to be put in the washing machine, wrinkling her nose against the smell of diesel. A heavy parcel is wedged down in the corner and she pulls it out, puzzled: half a dozen paperbacks. Pete comes down as she is looking at them.

'That's my C. S. Foresters,' he says. 'I lent them to Martin last leave just before they moved. I couldn't believe he'd never read him, but he's an ignorant bastard.'

She looks up at him, still kneeling. 'But how . . . ?'

'Oh.' He grimaces irritably. 'I was a bit miffed, actually. Angela phoned the base the morning we were sailing to say that Martin had left this parcel for me and that she'd be in real trouble if I didn't take it. She made such a song and dance about. I felt a bit guilty about standing her up the night before so I just had time to grab a taxi out to pick it up. Only books, for God's sake. I think she was annoyed that I'd refused to take her out for dinner and was trying to make a point.'

Julia bends her head so as to hide her expression of relief. 'That explains it,' she says.

'Explains what?'

She stands up and, perching on the edge of the sofa, tells him about Celia's telephone call. He watches her with disbelief.

'But why?' he asks. 'The bitch. Why should she want to make trouble?'

'She's Angela's best friend,' says Julia.

'Honestly, love.' Pete shakes his head disbelievingly. 'That's a bit strong, isn't it? It's a poisonous thing to do.'

Julia shrugs. 'Angela *is* poisonous,' she says. 'I've told you that lots of times but you haven't wanted to hear it. She resents the fact that you dropped her for me and she tries to make me as miserable as she can. You know it really. Why do you go along with it?'

He sits down on the arm of the chair opposite, his face serious in the firelight. 'I suppose part of it is vanity,' he admits. 'You feel a fool not responding to her, and the other chaps egg you on a bit. That kind of thing. Part of it is guilt. I didn't treat her very well. We were pretty nearly engaged when I met you and I just dropped her like a brick. None of it meant anything, you know that.'

'It did to me,' Julia tells him angrily. 'This last time, when she came here, and then when I had that phone call, I very nearly decided that I'd had enough and that if she was so important to you that you could keep ignoring how I felt about it then you could have her.'

He stares at her, shocked. 'You're not serious?'

'Yes, I am.' She stands up, fists clenched. 'You don't know what it's like, Pete, to have that kind of poison dropped in your ear at regular intervals, and you encouraging her publicly and doing nothing to support me. I've felt utterly humiliated.'

He gets up too and holds out his hands to her, his face contrite. 'I'm sorry, love. Really, I am. I never believed you could ever take anything she said that seriously. Honestly, Julia.'

Julia ignores his outstretched hands. 'Do you know that she told Tiggy that there was a story going round that her child was yours and that's why she was here with us "all so cosy together", as she put it?'

This time he is angry. 'She actually said that to Tiggy?'

Julia nods. 'She just wanted to add to her humiliation, I suppose.'

'But *why*?'

Julia shrugs. 'Tiggy assumed that it was because Angela hated me and her hatred extended to Tiggy as my friend.' She remembers what Aunt Em said. 'I let her get away with it all for too long. I was afraid, I suppose, that her sly little hints and allusions might have some basis of truth in them. You always behaved as if she had rights over you. She implied once that Cat might be your child.'

'You couldn't believe such rubbish. For God's sake, Julia.'

'That's the whole trouble. Angela's clever. She manipulates people and works on their fear. I've hated you sometimes when you've been all over her at some party or Ladies' Night and she looks so triumphant and then she comes here a week or so later and drops her little poisonous hints.'

Pete looks so shaken that Julia feels a wave of sympathy for him, yet she holds firm for she knows that she's been given her chance at last; it is the opportunity to be free of Angela's influence for ever. She crosses her arms so as to stop herself reaching out to him.

'You should have said something,' he mutters.

'I *did* say something,' she cries. 'You know I did. Often. You just laughed it off.'

255

'Women are such bitches,' he says. 'Oh, I don't mean you, darling. But honestly . . .' He shakes his head. 'It was nothing. Just a silly jokey habit we'd got into. And, like I said before, I suppose my vanity was tickled. I thought you were just being oversensitive. I still can't believe she made me go out for the books so as to start a rumour but I did wonder why she made such a song and dance about them. And she hung about on the doorstep keeping me in silly conversation.' He colours, looking uncomfortable, remembering her overaffectionate farewell hug. 'And to say that to Tiggy! I wonder who else she said it to. Good grief, the woman's crazy!'

'Tiggy thought she was mad,' says Julia. Suddenly she relaxes. It is clear from Pete's reaction that none of her fear has been justified and that Aunt Em is right: she's allowed that fear to colour her imagination and feed her suspicions. Now, Pete has been given an insight into the results of his readiness to go along with Angela's behaviour and Julia knows with a deep conviction that Angela's hold over him has been dissipated. 'It's OK,' she says. 'I had to get it out of my system, that's all. From now on I shall be able to handle her.'

'From now on I hope you won't have to,' he says grimly. 'Sorry, love.' He holds out his hands again and this time she responds.

She goes into his arms and hugs him tightly. He kisses her, drawing her closer, slipping his hands beneath her jersey. Neither of them hear the footsteps come pattering down the stairs and into the room.

'That's what they call a lip-lock,' says Andy, observing them closely and with great satisfaction. 'Daddy woke me up when he had his bath, Mummy, and now I can't get back to sleep. I could hear you arguing. I hate it when you argue. Why do you?'

'For the same reasons that you and Liv argue,' answers Julia, freeing herself reluctantly. 'And Daddy and I hate that too.'

Andy made a face. 'OK,' he concedes. 'Will you read me a story?'

Julia grins at Pete's frustrated expression. 'Daddy will read one very short story while I get his supper ready,' she says. 'Your penance,' she whispers in Pete's ear, and gives him a quick kiss. 'Don't forget where we'd got to, though.'

Pete sits down on the sofa and pulls Andy down beside him. 'I see you've come prepared,' he says resignedly, taking the book. 'What is it? *Mrs Frisby and the Rats of NIMH.* OK. Five minutes and that's it and no arguing.'

'OK,' Andy says again, settling himself comfortably.

CHAPTER NINETEEN

2004

'I remembered something last night,' Julia told Aunt Em next morning on their way to Tavistock. 'All that summer of nineteen seventy-six the little Merlin was out in the tent. The twins took it out to stand on their little table to make it seem more like home. Do you remember? When the weather broke I put it into a box with all the other bits they'd had out there and carried it into the porch. It was there for weeks.'

She glanced sideways at Aunt Em and they both burst into horrified laughter.

'To think of it,' murmured Aunt Em. 'Vischer's *Child Merlin* in the bottom of a toy box in the porch. And then you gave it to Zack?'

'When the wretched Cat spilled the beans about his adoption to Zack we gathered up all Tiggy's stuff and gave it to him. All except for the jewellery, which I kept for some special occasion; perhaps to give to his wife, if he had one. I gave the garnets to Caroline on their wedding day. Now I'm thinking that if they have a daughter I shall give the locket to her when she's old enough to appreciate it. Tiggy had very little, of course, but Zack was given the photographs and her books, and the Merlin went up into his bedroom. When he got married and we were clearing the room up he must have taken it with the rest of his things. To be honest, I can't remember when I last saw it. Once the children grew too old to play with it none of us was particularly interested in it, apart from its sentimental value. Oh dear. It makes us all sound such philistines, doesn't it?'

'Obviously you've never noticed it in Chapel Street?'

Julia shook her head. 'They haven't been there very long and it's taken Caroline a while to unpack everything. Anyway, I wouldn't have been looking for it, you see. Let's hope I find it quickly. I've told Caroline we're having lunch with one of your old chums at Mary Tavy so we're just dropping in for a cup of coffee.'

'Have you got a good size bag?'

Julia jerked her chin in the direction of the back seat and Aunt Em glanced over her shoulder. A big black and red tapestry bag with cane handles lay there, capacious and strong; it usually contained Julia's knitting. Aunt Em settled back in her seat.

'I'm terrified,' she said conversationally. It was true; her heart was behaving very oddly and her head felt as if it were filled with cotton wool. 'What about you?'

'I feel sick with terror,' admitted Julia. 'I couldn't sleep at all last night, thinking about it. I'm frightened at the thought of taking it but not as frightened as imagining that I shan't find it. I keep wondering what Pete would say if he knew. He'd be horrified. I suspect that he might feel that the time had come to tell Zack the truth, but how can I? I *promised* Tiggy. If she wanted to keep her father's existence secret then, how much more would she want to *now*? Not only a child molester but a forger! At the same time I can't believe what I'm doing. Honestly, Aunt Em! What *are* we doing?'

'Protecting Zack,' she answered calmly, 'and keeping your promise to Tiggy.'

Caroline led them through the house, down the garden to the shady pergola; Julia carried the tray.

'Poor darling,' she said, momentarily distracted from her terrors by Caroline's size. 'Are you very uncomfortable?'

'I shall be very glad to get it over with,' answered Caroline, pouring coffee. 'I just hope that Zack will be home in time. I feel it might be any minute.'

'And the boat's due in on Sunday?' Julia let Caroline put her mug on the table; her hands were trembling slightly. 'You should have come to Trescairn for this last week.'

'Perhaps I should have.' Caroline smiled warmly at Julia. 'It was sweet of you to invite me, and Mum offered to come down, but I've been fine and I'm sure that Zack will make it in time now. I'm sure you can understand how I feel. I want to be here when he gets back.'

Julia nodded. 'Of course you do. I'd feel exactly the same. At times like these one's own home is always the best place to be. Goodness, it's hot. We left poor old Frobes at home. He's feeling the heat almost as much as you are.' She took another quick sip of coffee and stood up, clutching the tapestry bag. 'I'm going to the loo,' she said. 'Shan't be a sec.'

She crossed the garden, hearing Aunt Em say to Caroline: 'So you'll be going into Derriford to have the baby?' and went into the house. She paused in the narrow, fitted kitchen, looking round; no Merlin here nor much room for him except on the windowsill. Julia hurried along the hall, into the sitting-room. No sign of him in the glass-fronted alcove cupboards on either side of the pretty Victorian fireplace, nor in the room across the hall which they used as a combined dining-room and study. This room was more untidy than the sitting-room and Julia moved round it slowly, checking out the crowded bookshelves, the small bureau, the big table.

Upstairs she hesitated, looking down into the garden from the landing window. Aunt Em and Caroline seemed engrossed in conversation but she was filled with anxiety and her palms were damp as she opened the bedroom door and looked into the warm, comfortable untidiness of Caroline's bedroom. The Merlin was not among the dressing table's clutter or on the bedside tables; he wasn't in the neat and tidy spare room or in the nursery.

Downstairs she took several deep breaths before going out into the garden. Aunt Em and Caroline were laughing beneath the pergola and Julia sat down, keeping the bag on her lap, picked up her mug and took a long draught of the lukewarm coffee. One quick glance at Aunt Em, a tiny shake of the head, and then she was glancing at her watch, telling Caroline that they really mustn't stay much longer but, yes, perhaps another half-cup of coffee.

Aunt Em was amusing Caroline with an anecdote about Uncle Archie arriving back unexpectedly early from sea, allowing Julia time to gulp her coffee and try to control her shaking hands. Presently they were standing up, kissing Caroline goodbye.

As they drove out of Tavistock up on to the Launceston Road, Aunt Em gave a great sigh. 'No luck then.'

Julia shook her head. 'That was awful,' she said. 'I feel like a criminal. There was no sign of it anywhere. So what do we do now?'

'Just because you couldn't see it doesn't necessarily mean it wasn't there,' said Em. 'Maybe it hasn't been unpacked yet.'

Julia shook her head despondently. 'There was no sign of any tea-chests, and the nursery looked all ready for action. Zack's old teddy was sitting on the bed.' She smiled reminiscently. 'He always went everywhere with Zack when he was little. When she knew she was pregnant Caroline insisted that teddy should be with them but there are quite a few toys left at home. Some of them have come into their own again now Charlie's two are old enough to play with them – the little trolley with the wooden bricks in it, and the rocking horse and things like that – but there are a few special ones that the children couldn't quite bear to part with. I put the soft toys into a sealed plastic bag but the other things are in the toy box in the attic.'

Em turned to her sharply. 'But didn't you say that Zack and the others sometimes played with the Merlin? Might he have been put away with the other toys?'

'Oh my God,' said Julia slowly. 'What a fool I am. Yes, that's where he'll be. The children wouldn't necessarily have considered him as an ornament. Why ever didn't I think of that first? I suppose it was because the toy box has been in the attic for years and Zack only cleared out his room eighteen months ago. That's why it was uppermost in my mind. Damn!'

'But that's much better,' cried Em with relief. 'Don't you see? It means that Caroline has probably never seen the Merlin and that Zack hasn't given him a thought for years. The fewer people to have seen it recently, the better. How easy is it to get up into the attic, Julia?'

An hour later Julia was in the attic at Trescairn, on her knees before the toy box with its torn stickers and faded, peeling paint. As she lifted the lid the smell of the past, musty with a thousand memories clinging to it, assailed her nostrils. Here were Andy's roller skates, wrapped in a twenty-year-old copy of the *Daily Telegraph*, his tattered collection of *Mad* magazines and his Evel Knievel motor bike. There was Charlie's little blue plastic suitcase specially constructed to hold two tiers of Dinky cars, each in its own small compartment, and most of which were still intact, if very battered. A group of Zack's grim-faced Action Men were bundled together, each wearing his own special uniform, whilst Liv's Sindy doll smirked vacuously at them across James Bond's Aston Martin from her bed on a pile of Mr Men books.

The Child Merlin stood upright, wedged into a corner; chin up, hurrying forward into the future with that familiar swirl of his tunic and the falcon on his wrist. With a tiny sob of relief, Julia reached and took him into her hand, feeling the smooth weightiness. She looked at him, turning him, examining him with fresh eyes. Memories stirred; she swallowed, biting her lips, and then called down softly: 'I've found him.'

She turned round, still on her knees, scrambling to the hatchway, and handed the little Merlin down to Aunt Em, who received it carefully. She held it in both hands and Julia closed the toy box and came clambering down the ladder to stand beside her. They gazed at it together; at the intricate workmanship and the soft sheen of the bronze.

'Beautiful,' murmured Aunt Em, turning him gently. 'Quite beautiful.'

Julia touched *The Child Merlin* with one finger. 'He *is* beautiful,' she agreed. 'I never really noticed it before. I just sort of took him for granted. But what shall we do with him?'

'We must lose him,' said Aunt Em calmly.

'But it seems so terrible,' said Julia anxiously. 'Now that we know, I mean.'

'Terrible but necessary if you are to keep your promise,' said Aunt Em.

CHAPTER TWENTY

2004

Liv was sitting with Chris and Val in their kitchen sharing an early lunch. She felt an odd detachment, as if a glass sheet had been slipped between her and the two who sat opposite. The emotional excitement of the last few months had been quenched with determination, though bittersweet tremors still shook her heart, rather as an amputated limb might twinge long after its separation.

'I'm still wondering,' Val was saying, 'whether we need to be quite so generous. I mean, do we really need to leave cakes and bread and stuff for the visitors? Rush about putting milk and butter in the fridge and all the fiddly bits in the bathroom? That kind of thing.'

Chris was silent. He didn't glance at Liv as he would once have done, just to check out her reaction, but continued to eat his sandwich thoughtfully with his eyes on his plate.

Liv made an effort and brought her professional judgement into play. 'Yes, I think we do,' she answered firmly. 'You only have to look at the visitors' books to see how much it's appreciated. I know there are shops fairly close at hand but if you've driven a long way the last thing you want to do is go out again because you've forgotten your shower cap or the soap. It's the kind of thing people remember afterwards when they're about to book a weekend away. Boxes of tissues in the bedrooms, kitchen towels. I think the details are crucial. Does it affect the profit margin that much?'

She spoke directly to Chris and he looked at her at last, and then at Val.

'No, it doesn't,' he said. 'We're not cheap, which is reasonable given the location, but I think those small extras make the punters feel they're getting their money's worth. After all, Debbie bakes every day anyway, so the cakes and bread aren't a problem, and we bulk-buy everything else. I think it's a positive approach that will pay us in the end.'

Val shrugged, still dissatisfied. 'OK. But I think your idea of preparing a meal for each arrival is going much too far, Liv. It would be a nightmare.'

'I agree with that,' said Chris. 'After all, think how much you'd have to liaise. There could be problems with vegetarians or nut allergies and God knows what. It's a nice idea in theory but I think that *is* going over the top.'

'You're probably right,' said Liv. 'I read about a complex in the Cotswolds that does it and apparently it's a huge success but I agree that it's probably more trouble than it's worth.' She paused; now was the moment she'd been dreading. 'By the way, I hope this doesn't come as too much of a shock but I've been offered a rather exciting job beginning in the autumn so I think I ought to warn you that I shall be moving on. You don't really need me now and you'll find the extra revenue for the annexe very useful. The way we're booking up I think you'll be glad of the extra space very soon.'

'Oh.' Val was disconcerted, even embarrassed; she wondered if Liv could have guessed her feelings, or if Chris had voiced them, and she experienced a little flare of irritation that Liv should have got in first. 'Well, we don't really want to turn you out.'

Liv grinned at her, knowing that Val would have liked to be the one in control here. 'You've always looked on the annexe as an extra bit of income, we all know that. I think you're quite ready to manage without me and I shall only be in Truro. It's not a million miles away if you have a problem.'

'Truro?' Chris tried to hide his shock so as to match her cheerfulness. 'So what exciting thing will be happening in Truro this autumn?'

'An acquaintance of mine has bought a wine bar and he's extending it. He seems to think I'm the right person to get the new extension up and running and I agree with him. It's certainly a challenge but, hey!, so was Penharrow.' She looked away from the bleakness in Chris's eyes and smiled inwardly at the expression on Val's face: relief battling with indignation. 'It's just a warning shot across the bows, as my dear old dad would say. There's plenty of time to get used to the idea and make adjustments. And now I'm off for an hour. See you later.'

She went out and Val looked at Chris. 'Why didn't you say something?' she demanded. 'I felt a bit of a fool. Did you know anything about this?'

Chris shook his head. 'Not a thing. But it was on the cards, wasn't it? She wasn't going to spend the rest of her life with us. And you've been saying that we could use the income from the annexe.'

'I know, but it's still a bit of a surprise. I think she should have consulted us before accepting this new job.'

Chris shrugged. He was shocked but strangely relieved:

Liv had let him off the hook and he was grateful to her. He wondered about this acquaintance with whom she would be working, and felt an odd stab of jealousy.

'I thought it was what you wanted,' he said.

'It is,' said Val after a moment. Her indignation at being wrong-footed was tinged with a slight anxiety. 'Well, in a way it is. But, if I'm honest, I shall miss knowing she's there. There's something reassuring about having Liv around. I know I go on sometimes about her but you were right when you said that we wouldn't have coped so well without her. There is much more to it than I'd imagined.'

Chris pushed back his chair. The prospect of managing without Liv was a desolate one but he knew it was the right decision: it would encourage him to be whole-hearted.

'Well, we'll have a few weeks to get used to it,' he said. 'I'd better get on, I suppose.' He paused and then, to Val's surprise, he put his arm round her shoulders and gave her a hug. After a second or two she responded.

'What's all that about?' she asked lightly, slightly embarrassed by such an uncharacteristic gesture.

'I think we've been getting our priorities a bit confused just lately, that's all,' he answered. 'We need some "us" time.'

The sharp retort with which she would have replied a few days earlier seemed unwise; some instinct warned her that, without Liv around, Chris's love and support would be crucial to her and to Penharrow.

'Sounds good to me,' she said casually. 'When do we start?'

'I think we might book a few days away sometime at the end of summer, before Liv goes anyway. Not too long for starters but I'm sure Myra and Debbie could manage for a long weekend. I think it would do us good.'

Once again a sarcastic rejoinder trembled on Val's lips but she swallowed it down. She sensed some kind of change in him; a new concentration on her and a commitment to their bond that had been lacking lately. Whatever it was, the same instinct warned her to nurture it and she nodded agreement.

'OK, then,' he said cheerfully. 'Have a trawl on the Internet and see what you can find.'

He went out and she began to clear away the lunch things with an unusually light heart.

Julia just had the time to thrust her knitting into the bag on top of the Merlin and hang it on the back of the kitchen chair as Liv came into the kitchen.

'Hello, darling,' she said, flustered. 'I wasn't expecting you.'

'I passed Aunt Em at the bottom of the road,' Liv said. 'She said you'd been over to see Caroline.'

'We had coffee with her and we haven't been back very long. Is everything OK?'

'Oh, I just needed to get away for a minute.' Liv bent to pat the recumbent Frobisher and then sat down at the table. 'Driving around calms me down. You know the feeling?'

'Yes,' said Julia. 'Yes, of course I do. As long as nothing's really wrong . . .'

'No. Well, I've decided to take up Matt's offer and I can't decide whether I'm deliriously happy or scared to death.'

'Oh, darling.' Julia sat down opposite, almost forgetting the bag hanging at her shoulder in her delight. 'But that's wonderful news.'

'I hope so. After all, Penharrow was never going to be for ever, was it? To be honest, I think the time's come for us to make the break. And Val and Chris will need the extra income from the annexe.'

'Well, it's a very wise move. You know how I felt about you being a bit too close . . .' Julia paused rather awkwardly, wondering if there had been a particular problem. 'You can always come here, you know, until you find somewhere of your own. I imagine you'll go on working at Penharrow for a little while yet?'

'Oh, yes. Until the end of the season. Thanks for the offer. Are you OK, Mum? You sound a bit breathless.'

'I'm fine. Of course I am. I told you, we've just got back from Tavistock.'

'My decision to come and see you was a bit sudden.' Liv smiled reluctantly. 'Like I said, I'm having a fit of the wobbles. By the way, what's all this about the little Merlin? Andy keeps going on about it. Something to do with an art fraud, apparently, and one of the pieces looks just like ours. He mentioned it weeks ago and asked me to ask you about it but I forgot all about it, I'm afraid. Have you seen anything about it in the papers?'

Julia kept her eyes fixed on Liv's; carefully she assumed an expression that combined faint surprise with a casual indifference.

'I don't think so.'

'I've told him he's nuts.' Liv snorted. 'He must be to be going out with Cat. Apparently it's her idea that our Merlin is this missing treasure. It's just so likely, isn't it? Where is the Merlin, by the way? I don't remember seeing him around for years.'

'I've no idea. I expect he was some kind of cheap copy. Like one of thousands of Michelangelo's *David* or the Madonna and Child. He probably got lost when we went out to Washington. Is Andy still seeing Cat? I hoped it might have just been a flash in the pan thing. He can't be serious about her.' Julia shivered slightly at the prospect of Cat as a daughter-in-law. 'I hope she hasn't been back to Penharrow, causing any more trouble?'

Liv shook her head. 'It was embarrassing, though. It really worries me that I can dislike someone as much as I do her.'

'I think it must be genetic.' Julia tried for a lighter note. 'I felt exactly the same way about her mother, though with some cause. Cat's a troublemaker. From childhood onwards she's had a destructive gift for upsetting people and she enjoys the results. I think we both instinctively fear that aspect of her character. I've always felt guilty that Zack found out the truth from her rather than from me. That was my fault. Nevertheless, I know that even at eight years old she would have really enjoyed telling him. I suppose that's why neither of us wants to see Andy involved with her. We fear that she'll hurt him. Well, there's nothing we can do about it. Have you had some lunch? Would you like something?'

'I had a sandwich with Val and Chris. A kind of working lunch. Thanks, Mum, but I have to get back. I've just told them I shall be moving on and I thought we all needed a short breathing space.'

'Well, I'm absolutely thrilled at your decision,' Julia told her. 'Matt sounds great and he's obviously got some very good ideas for The Place. And so have you. It's certainly clever of him to ask you to help him.'

Liv smiled. 'You couldn't be the least bit prejudiced, could you?'

'No,' answered Julia firmly. 'You're perfect for the job and I just know it's the right thing. You'll be great.'

'I've never taken on such a big commitment.' Liv made a face. 'I suppose it's about time, though. At least Dad'll be pleased.'

'He'll be over the moon. We'll text him.'

They went out together and Liv climbed into her car and drove away. Some instinct made her pull over into a gateway and fish out her mobile: no signal. She drove on slowly, keeping one eye on her phone, and then stopped again as soon as the signal showed. She keyed Matt's number, waited. At the sound of his voice she was seized with a mixture of relief and excitement.

'Well, I've finally done the deed,' she told him. 'I've given in my notice.'

'That's fantastic.' His voice was jubilant. 'You won't regret it, Liv. I just know that this is going to be so good.'

She laughed at his delight. 'It had better be. So what happens next?'

'Champagne,' he answered at once. 'Soon. Where shall we meet?'

'You tell me,' she said. 'Cornwall's crawling with emmets. Have you any ideas?'

'Yes,' he said. 'Actually, I have. Somewhere very special. I shall take you to Aqua. It's a restaurant owned by a friend of mine, Richard Smithson, down on the Welsh Back in Bristol and you haven't lived until you've tasted his Done to Death Duck. As a matter of fact, I'd like to talk to Richard. He's planning to open a second restaurant in Walcott Street in Bath. It's going to be called Aqua Italia. Rather like us calling our new project The Place Upstairs, isn't it? Richard might be able to give us a few ideas.'

'Fine. But Bristol? Isn't that rather a long way to go for champagne?'

'Not a bit. You'll love Richard. And it'll be fun driving back in the dark. I love driving in the dark, don't you? Lovely empty, quiet roads. I get my best ideas driving about in the car.'

'So do I,' she said, surprised. 'OK. Let me know when Richard can fit us in.'

'I will. And thanks, Liv. I can't tell you how very pleased I am.'

She switched off her phone. Filled with excitement and with new resolve she drove back to Penharrow.

CHAPTER TWENTY-ONE

2004

Julia went back into the house and ran upstairs to the loo. She was washing her hands when she heard the car: perhaps Liv had forgotten something. Frobisher barked and she dried her hands, combed her hair and went out on to the landing. Someone was moving about downstairs.

'Hello. Is that you, Liv?' she called as she came out. At the bottom of the stairs in the sitting-room she came face to face with Cat. 'Oh, my God,' she gasped.

'Hello, Mrs Bodrugan.' Cat smiled, easy and friendly, as if she were in the habit of wandering in without knocking. 'Just thought I'd see if anyone was around. Andy said to send his love if I saw you. I called but you didn't answer and the back door was open so I came in. The dog barked but he didn't seem to object too much.'

She touched Frobisher lightly on the head but he was already turning away, going back to the kitchen. Julia's heart jumped and hammered. She hadn't seen Cat since the children's schooldays and it was as if time had swung backwards and Angela had walked in: thin as a pin, chic in black linen. Julia believed that she'd seen a ghost.

'I didn't hear you,' she said. 'Well, I heard the car. I thought it was Liv coming back. Didn't you see her? You must have passed her.'

Cat's smile widened but she didn't answer and Julia felt inexplicably frightened. In her mind's eye she saw the bag still hanging on the chair in the kitchen; Cat had walked straight past it. She knew exactly why Cat had come and she swallowed in a suddenly dry throat whilst managing to smile.

'You should have telephoned,' she said. 'You're looking very well. Would you like some coffee?'

'Thanks.' Cat followed Julia into the kitchen. 'Mum said to say "Hi" if I saw you. I'm staying with her for a few days. When I said I was going over to Rock she said to drop in, just in case you were around, to say hello.'

Julia pushed the kettle on to the hot plate and got down the mugs, and all the while the bag hung on the chair with the bundle of knitting on its thick wooden needles sticking out at the top. Out of the corner of her eye she saw Cat was scanning the dresser, the windowsill, looking for something. Julia made the coffee and sat down.

'How's Andy?' she asked. 'We haven't seen him for a while.'

'Andy's fine. Actually he sent a message. He asked me to pick something up for him.'

'Really?' Julia looked surprised. Her hands were locked in her lap and she didn't attempt to pick up her mug of coffee.

'I don't know if you've seen all the fuss in the art world at the moment?' Cat waited, watching for a reaction. 'No? Well, it's all a bit silly but Andy asked me to ask you if I could bring back a little statue. I remember I saw it when I was a child. It's Merlin as a boy. Andy thinks that there's a very faint chance that it

273

might be a copy made by this man who's on trial in Paris. If that's so it would make it an interesting piece and he said he'd like to take it to an expert to have it checked.'

Julia frowned. 'I think I can remember it,' she said slowly. 'But I haven't seen it for years.' She shook her head. 'It was a silly little thing, as I remember, but the children liked it. I've no idea where it might be. Tell Andy I'll have a look for it if he's really serious. Sounds crazy to me.'

Cat watched her. 'I was wondering if it belonged to Tiggy.'

'To Tiggy?' Julia shrugged, as if puzzled by the question. 'Why should it have? To be honest, I simply can't remember much about it. There were always so many toys and odd bits and pieces when the children were small.'

'I was talking to Mum about it this morning and we were remembering a big scene right here in your kitchen when I picked it up and Tiggy came in and screamed at me for touching it. That's why we wondered if it might have been hers. Mum said she had no family but everyone has a family, don't they?' A pause. 'Who was she?'

Julia's gut churned; her hands were icy. 'She was a school friend of mine,' she answered. 'Her parents died young in an accident when she was very small and she had no brothers and sisters, just a grandmother. She was Tiggy's only relation. She died just after Tiggy came to stay with us. I was her best friend, that's why she came to Trescairn. And she was Charlie's godmother, of course.'

'And Zack's mother.'

'Yes. She was Zack's mother.'

Cat's watchful slant-eyed stare was disconcerting. She finished her coffee and put down her mug. 'Is it OK if I use the loo before I go, Mrs Bodrugan? I'd better be getting on.'

Julia watched her go out; she unclenched her hands, drank her coffee quickly. Putting her hand down behind her she felt the reassuring weight in the knitting bag. She heard the creaking of a board and light footsteps in the bedroom overhead: she waited. Presently Cat reappeared.

'Finished?' Julia asked brightly.

Cat stared at her. 'I'll tell Andy I saw you,' she said, 'and that you'll look for the Merlin.'

'*I'll* tell him,' said Julia. 'I'll phone him tonight.'

'The newspaper report says that this man who's on trial is a widower but there's a son called Jean-Paul who lives in Switzerland,' said Cat as she went out to the car. 'What did you say Tiggy's real name was?'

'Antigone,' answered Julia promptly. 'Antigone Dacre. Her father was a classics tutor or something at Oxford, I think. Goodbye, Cat.'

Watching her drive away, Julia was reminded of Angela's visits all those years before. She went back into the house, took the bag from the chair and put it back again. Aunt Em had suggested that she should drop it down a mine shaft or throw it off a cliff but now Julia had an irrational fear that Cat might be watching her; parked up somewhere waiting for her to go out. Perhaps she'd arrived earlier, when she and Aunt Em had been with Caroline, and had parked higher up on the moor watching for the car to come back. She'd have seen Aunt Em driving away and Liv arriving almost immediately afterwards and had waited for her to leave; which is why she hadn't passed her on the road.

Julia was suddenly seized with a fit of nervous laughter: all that stuff about Tiggy's name being Antigone had come from nowhere. And they'd sat drinking coffee with the little Merlin within touching distance. Clearly *The Child Merlin* knew how to look after himself.

1977

It is nearly Easter before Angela comes visiting again at Trescairn. Unannounced as usual, with Cat in tow, she appears just after lunch one wild, windy afternoon, with lambs crying in the fields below the house and an untidy party of rooks circling above the church tower.

Julia opens the door, Zack astride her hip, and Charlie following behind, pushing himself along on a small wooden tricycle. She'd seen the car pull up on the drive and experienced the familiar twinge of apprehension but now, standing at the door, looking at that narrow, slant-eyed face, she feels a new, unusual surge of confidence.

'Hi,' she says amiably. 'Have you ever heard of the telephone, Angela? Isn't it rather a bit off your road to come all this way only to find that I'm out? Trescairn isn't exactly on the direct route between Minions and Rock.'

'Oh, but you're never out,' observes Angela, smiling. 'You're always here, doing your motherly thing. The original earth mother, Pete once called you. The prototype. Such a good example to us all.'

Julia stands aside to let them come in but she smiles too. 'I suspect you've often called when I've been out,' she says. 'And you've peered through all the windows and then driven away again. Isn't that so, Cat?'

The question is so quick and natural that Cat answers automatically. 'Yes,' she says, 'and Mummy gets cross and drives very fast afterwards. But she looks in through the windows like you said.'

Julia laughs, genuinely amused. 'Just to make certain we're not all lying on the floor trying to avoid you, like Uncle Matthew in *The Pursuit of Love*.'

Angela puts her bag on the kitchen table and takes out her

cigarettes; she is disconcerted but still in control. 'Nonsense,' she says lightly. 'I think that happened once. I banged on the window in case you hadn't heard but I was in a hurry anyway so it didn't matter. So how are you? Great news about Perisher. Pete's just so thrilled, isn't he?'

'Oh, yes. Pete's thrilled. We're all thrilled.'

'When he came to see me he could hardly stop talking about it. He was really worked up. Mind you,' she gives her subtle, secret smile, 'Pete gets worked up pretty quickly, doesn't he? Anyway, that's my experience. He's hoping to get a boat in Faslane, did he tell you? He hardly talked about anything else the whole time he was with me.'

'Well, given you must have had barely five minutes on the doorstep it's hardly surprising, is it? Not long for an in-depth discussion about anything. He was pretty irritated to have to get a taxi that morning simply to collect some books that Martin could have dropped off here any time. And as for Celia phoning up specially to tell me that she'd seen him, well, I thought Pete was going to implode when I told him.'

It is clear that Angela is taken aback; for the first time in their relationship the balance of power shifts. Julia knows quite surely that Angela suspects that she's lost control, that her subtle hints and allusions no longer have the power to hurt, and Julia's own feeling of triumph contains an unexpected tinge of compassion.

'Do you want some tea?' she asks, putting Zack into the high chair and giving him his brightly coloured teething ring. 'I can't be too long because I've got to fetch the twins from school.'

'Thanks.' Angela sits down. She looks thoughtful, as if she is already planning a new line of attack. 'I've been seeing the new tenants in. Nice couple, no kids, thank God.' She glances at Zack, as if this has triggered an idea. 'Zack's grown. You know that rumour is still going round that he's Pete's. I suppose it just seems so amazing that you should be prepared to bring up someone else's baby.'

Julia begins to laugh. 'You don't give up easily, do you? I told Pete that you'd said that to Tiggy and he was disgusted. Anyway, Zack's not someone else's baby. He was Tiggy's baby and now he's *our* baby, just as much as the twins or Charlie, and you can think what you like about it.'

In that moment she is struck by a different kind of exaltation. By saying the words she's made them true: Zack *is* their baby, hers and Pete's. She is filled with relief yet, almost immediately, she is seized with misgiving. Cat is watching her slyly. She's taken Zack's teething ring away from him, holding it just out of his reach, and she's put one foot on the handlebars of Charlie's bike so that he can no longer push it forward. Zack grizzles; reaching for the teething ring that jiggles so tantalizingly just beyond his grasp; whilst Charlie, shouting frustratedly, strives to pit his weight against Cat's restraining foot. Her look dares Julia to comment on the power she has over the two smaller children and Julia has an instinctive feeling that the battle is not yet over, but that the lines are drawn up against a different protagonist.

'It's a pity Cat doesn't have any brothers and sisters,' she says sharply. 'Perhaps they'd teach her to grow up a bit and be less tiresome.' She takes the teething ring from Cat and puts it back on the high chair's table, lifts her sharply to one side and gives Charlie an encouraging push. 'She must be so popular at school.'

As soon as she's made the sarcastic remark she regrets it. It's cheap, trying to score points over a child: foolish to feel frightened of her, but her irrational fear remains.

'Do you want some juice, Cat?' she asks, trying to overcome it. 'Or milk?'

Cat shakes her head, refusing to answer, reaching up to the

little Merlin, who stands on the lowest shelf of the dresser. Julia swiftly puts it out of reach on to a higher shelf and Cat begins to whine. Charlie watches her curiously.

'What is that thing?' asks Angela, irritated. 'There was a fuss over it once before, if I remember. Why can't she play with it? Is it valuable?'

'Not particularly,' Julia answers, making the tea. 'Well, it has a sentimental value. It's pretty heavy and if she drops it on her toes, or on Charlie's, it could be very painful, that's all.' She puts the mugs on the table and sits down. 'So tell me about the new tenants.'

Later, after they've gone, she takes Zack out of the high chair and cuddles him, her cheek pressed against his silky head. As she holds him she thinks about Tiggy: the schoolgirl, lonely and uncared for, longing for a family to which she might belong. How she hated the big London flat, empty of any love, inhabited by the series of au pairs who were harassed by her father. Julia holds Zack more tightly: he must never, never know the ugly truth about his grandfather's behaviour. She remembers that first frantic telephone call; Tiggy's flight to Hampshire, and the story she told about her father. It was difficult to comprehend such a betrayal. The weight of so terrible a secret was such a heavy one that, in the end, she told her mother Tiggy's tragic little history, swearing her to secrecy. Her mother became quite rigid with horror.

'Poor child,' she said. 'Poor little Tiggy. Don't forget, Julia, that she's welcome here at any time during the holidays. Keep an eye on her, darling, won't you?'

And she *did* keep an eye, watching over Tiggy, taking her home for holidays when she wasn't with her grandmother. Even after Tiggy's father moved to Paris, and severed all except financial connections, she remained watchful. By the time they left school their friendship was firmly fixed and, when Julia married Pete, Tiggy was a bridesmaid and, later, Charlie's godmother. Then there was that second phone call, and another flight, this time to the west.

'I don't want my father to know about my baby,' she said. 'Not ever. Promise me, Julia, that you'll never say a word to anyone.'

Poor Tiggy; despite all her fears for the future, she never imagined for a moment how it would be for her or her baby.

Julia kisses Zack, smooths his downy hair: Zack beams gummily and waves his fists. Smiling back at him she suddenly has the conviction that she is capable at last of separating the grief for the loss of her own baby from her feelings for Zack. There will still be difficult moments, and it will take time to allow the grief to be contained, but she knows now that the words she spoke earlier are true: Zack is their baby, just as much as Charlie and the twins.

CHAPTER TWENTY-TWO

2004

Later, Julia telephoned Aunt Em.

'Listen,' she said. 'You'll never guess who's been here. Cat . . . Yes, amazing, isn't it? She said that Andy asked her to bring back the Merlin to check it out, though she was very careful to say that it was probably a copy, not the original . . . Honestly, it's true . . . No, it was still in the knitting bag hanging on the chair. I'm afraid to go out now in case she suspects something and is waiting somewhere but I'm probably being silly. She had a very good look round so I don't think she'll come back here. I shall phone Andy and put him off the trail . . . Yes. I know exactly what I'm going to do but I shall wait until tomorrow just in case Cat's still around . . . Well, if you could come up that would be great. It'll be a great comfort to have you here. Thanks, Aunt Em. I'll see you in the morning then.'

She put the telephone down. Quite suddenly, talking to Aunt Em, she'd known exactly what she would do with the Merlin.

She would drive to Tintagel, to Tiggy's favourite place on the cliff, where they had scattered her ashes, and throw the little Merlin into the sea in full view of the entrance to Merlin's Cave. Tiggy had loved Glebe Cliff, looking away to The Mouls in the west and back towards Tintagel Island.

Standing in the kitchen with Frobisher asleep in his basket, Julia remembered those happy months with Tiggy and the children, and their fear of Angela and their obscure dislike of Cat. Her own mistrust of Angela had been fairly reasonable but the depth of their joint antipathy towards the child, despite her tiresome behaviour, had seemed unfair and they'd felt guilty.

'I can't think why I felt like that, especially about a child. I just disliked them both on sight,' Tiggy had said after that first meeting when she'd found Cat with the Merlin. Perhaps some sixth sense had warned her that, one day, Cat would be a threat to her own child.

Supposing the newspapers were to get hold of the full story? Supposing those au pairs from Tiggy's childhood should come forward to tell stories of abuse and ill treatment at the hands of their employer? Now she, Julia, and Aunt Em were the only people alive who knew that he'd tried to force himself on his own daughter but she could imagine very clearly Zack's shocked reaction to the whole truth and she felt duty-bound to protect him from the knowledge that his grandfather was something far worse than an art forger. She'd promised Tiggy. Julia shivered: she was deeply relieved that Pete was away; she knew that, in the light of this new evidence, his natural instinct would be to go to some higher authority, to explain the situation and hope that some kind of justice would prevail. Her own instinct, and Aunt Em's, was to act quickly and destroy the evidence. Zack's wellbeing was very much more important to them than abiding by a set of rules and regs that took no regard for personalities. Pete might be happy to stand by Tiggy's wishes that her father was denied access to her son but he'd have drawn the line at throwing priceless works of art over a cliff. Thank goodness that Pete eschewed any kind of communication with the world when he was sailing and probably hadn't seen a newspaper, let alone a television.

She wondered if even Pete would make the connection, though. After all, he'd never known Tiggy's father and she doubted if he'd recall his name; he might recognize the Merlin, of course, but it was difficult to guess just how well he'd remember it. It had probably been in the attic for the best part of twelve years and before that would have just been one item amongst the collection of Zack's toys: the Action Men, the James Bond cars, the aeroplanes. Even so, she was sad that she'd have to keep this secret from Pete. Julia tried to imagine how difficult it would be; she suspected that she'd never feel really secure ever again, always wondering if someone might remember that Tristan Stamper had once had a daughter called Tegan and make connections. How many of her friends might recognize the photograph of *The Child Merlin*? After all, Cat had remembered, although that was probably because it had been the cause of a major scene and had made a deep impression, and afterwards Cat had always made a beeline for it and created a fuss when it was denied her.

Julia dithered: should she take the Merlin now, risking being shadowed by Cat, or should she wait until later? The idea of being out on the cliffs at night filled her with trepidation but so did the prospect of spending the night alone at Trescairn with the Merlin. She wished that Aunt Em was with her.

'Don't be a fool,' she told herself. 'Nobody's going to come creeping round. Get a grip!'

Nevertheless, she kept the doors locked and each time she left the kitchen she took the knitting bag with her. She telephoned Andy but got no reply and eventually she left a message asking him to call her. She'd just finished supper when Caroline telephoned.

'The ETA's been changed and the boat's in later tonight,' she told Julia jubilantly. 'Great, isn't it? If I haven't popped by Monday we're going to Boscastle to see some friends and we might dash up to see you about teatime. Will you be around? . . . That's great. Oh, I nearly forgot. It was really odd this afternoon. Andy's girlfriend dropped in. It was a bit embarrassing, actually, because I didn't even know he had a girlfriend. Cat, is it? . . . She was so friendly and really loved the cottage. Wanted to see all over it. She apologized for giving no warning but she was meeting up with friends in Tavistock and Andy had told her to drop by. She's only down for the weekend, she said. She's driving back to London on Sunday evening but couldn't resist the chance to meet me. Rather sweet, I thought. She's so thin I could have killed her . . . Anyway, see you Monday afternoon, if all goes well. I'll text you. Bye, Julia.'

Julia rested her elbows on the table and put both hands over her eyes. Quite suddenly she was shaken by a surge of fury: how dare Cat go to spy on Caroline, whom she'd never met and con her into showing her round her home? The telephone rang, making her jump; this time it was Andy and she was in exactly the right mood for him.

'Mum,' he said. 'Sorry I missed you earlier. How are things?'

'Things are OK,' Julia answered, 'but I could do without Cat harassing the family. Perhaps you could do something about it, love.'

A short silence. 'How do you mean?'

'I mean that I can't really imagine that you told her to drop in unannounced on me and then make a search of the house for a little statue she insists that you want, nor, when she couldn't find it, to do the same to Caroline, who doesn't know her at all and was expected to give her a guided tour of the house, presumably for the same reason. She's already been to Penharrow and made insinuating remarks to Val about Chris and Liv, which really caused trouble.'

More silence. 'The thing is,' Andy said defensively, 'there's been all this stuff in the news about the art fraud and there was a photograph of *The Child Merlin*, and I have to say that Cat's right. It looks just like the one we had when we were kids.'

'So?'

'Well, Mum, it might just be that somehow we've got hold of an art treasure, that's all. It could be worth a fortune.'

Julia laughed derisively. 'That funny little statue you all used to play with? That's just so likely, isn't it! Is that really why Cat came to spy on us all?'

'I had no idea that she'd come to see you or Caroline,' he said indignantly. 'In fact, I had no idea she was in Cornwall until she phoned this afternoon to say that if she went to Tavistock she might drop in on Caroline and Zack. She asked what the number was in Chapel Street but it was all very casual. She said Liv had told her they were in Chapel Street. I knew she'd been to Penharrow a few weeks ago but I didn't realize that she'd made trouble for Liv.'

'And what's in it for Cat? Why is she so keen to lay her hands on this statue that she comes prowling round like a burglar?'

'I can't think why you all dislike her so much.'

'Can't you, love? Well, you'll just have to use your imagination and your memory. As for the Merlin, Liv said that you'd mentioned it in an email, and I've had a quick scout round but I think the best thing is for you to come and look for it yourself. It's probably one of a thousand cheap copies of this statue you're so excited about, otherwise we would never have let you play with it when you were children. Can you honestly believe we'd have allowed you to use even a slightly valuable statue as a toy? Liv says you need to get real and I agree with her. Anyway, I suspect that it must have got lost during the move to Washington because none of us can find it. Feel free to come and search. You, not Cat. Will you do that, Andy?'

'OK,' he said reluctantly, after another silence. 'But if you're really sure it's just a cheap copy there's not much point, is there?'

'Not really. And, Andy, keep Cat off our backs. If you can't resist her that's your bad luck. We don't want to know, perhaps because our memories are better than yours. She's always been a troublemaker. She's lied to me and to Caroline, prowled round our houses and nearly got Liv the sack. And don't tell me that she's changed. I've just met her again and I'm not impressed.'

'OK,' he said again, sulkily. 'You've made your point, Mum.'

'Good,' she said lightly. 'Zack's home tonight and Caroline's about to pop so I'll telephone when I've got some good news. Night, love.'

Julia sat for some moments, still holding the telephone. She hated to pull the heavy mother act, though sometimes it was necessary; but had it succeeded this time? She'd felt it was important to make the point strongly even though it was fairly clear that Cat had been working off her own initiative.

'Please don't let him be in love with her,' she prayed.

She raised her head, saw her reflection loom at her in the windowpane, and realized with a little shock of fear that it was getting dark. Jumping up quickly, she hurried to draw the curtains, something she never did in the summer. When she let Frobisher out, she hooked the bag on her arm and took the torch. She strayed hardly any distance from the door but stood waiting anxiously until he returned and they both went back inside. Every window was checked, the doors locked before she took Frobisher upstairs with her, the bag still hooked over her arm. How empty the house felt; how silent. Frobisher padded round the room and then settled down at the end of the bed.

Julia bundled the Merlin into the bedside cupboard and undressed, alert to any noise: was that the creak of a floorboard beneath a stealthy foot or simply the wind rising? Quickly she climbed into bed and picked up her book but she was too anxious, and her head was too full of memories, to be able to concentrate.

1977

'You were right,' Julia says to Aunt Em a few days later. 'Pete and I have had it out but I didn't accuse him. I waited, like you said, and I didn't say a word about the phone call. In the end it all happened very naturally.' She explains about Angela and the books and Pete's reaction once he'd heard the other side of the story. 'He was furious,' she says. 'Something changed in him. Once we'd talked about it properly, not me accusing and him defending like we usually do, it was all different. We were on the same side at last. Honestly, I felt so good, and when Angela turned up I just saw her off. It was amazing. I almost felt sorry for her. I could see exactly what you meant about my fear allowing her to manipulate our marriage. I felt so confident.'

'But?' prompts Em, seeing her frown.

'Well, it's nothing really. It was just that, even while I was feeling that new confidence, I had a strange sense that it wasn't all over. But the weirdest thing was that the threat seemed to come from Cat rather than Angela. She was teasing Charlie and Zack and I was afraid for them. Why should that be?'

'I suppose nothing is ever truly finished,' says Em reflectively. 'Everyone living happily ever after never actually happens, does it? Our lives continue to unfold; some end, others begin, and our journeys take different directions. Paths cross and recross, and whether we're stuck fast in the Slough of Despond or enjoying the view from the Delectable Mountains depends on which bit of the journey we've reached. Apollyon can appear at any moment and try to drag us back in the Valley of Humiliation. Old Bunyan knew his stuff. Do you remember that he said that there was a way to hell even from the gates of heaven? I suspect that Angela and Cat will continue to impinge on your lives but I believe that you've come through the most difficult stage, Julia. Enjoy the sunshine while it lasts.'

Julia laughs. 'I'm not sure that I find that particularly reassuring.'

'It was meant to be. I can't prophesy for the next generation but I feel certain that Angela will never be able to make trouble between you and Pete again. That's a good start. And spring's nearly here. The cold, sweet spring, oh, how I love it.'

'It's exactly a year since Tiggy came to Trescairn,' Julia says. 'A *year*. I can hardly believe it. Time passes so quickly. Poor Tiggy. She was only twenty-five. I wonder where we'll be in twenty-five years, Aunt Em. The twins will be older than I am now and Zack will be preparing to celebrate his twenty-sixth birthday. I could even be a grandmother.'

She looks so shocked by the prospect that Em grins. 'Well, I shall certainly be a septuagenarian,' she says cheerfully. 'Now there's a sobering thought. Shall we drink to it now before we become too old and feeble to lift our glasses?'

CHAPTER TWENTY-THREE

2004

'I'm glad you're here,' Julia said when Aunt Em arrived next morning. 'I hardly slept a wink last night.'

Before Em could answer, the telephone rang. It was Zack: the visit to Boscastle was still planned and he and Caroline would be at Trescairn in time for tea. He sounded cheerful, happy to be home in time for the birth of his child, and Julia felt sick inside at the thought of him discovering the truth.

'I must do it today,' she said to Aunt Em once she'd said goodbye to Zack. 'But I've only just realized how difficult it will be to throw something off Glebe Cliff with crowds of holidaymakers looking on.'

Aunt Em looked serious. 'I hadn't thought of that,' she admitted. 'Yes, that's a problem. We don't want some busybody interfering because they think you're trying to get rid of a puppy or a kitten.' She glanced out of the window at the bright sunshine. 'What's the weather forecast?'

'Scattered showers late morning becoming heavy this

afternoon. I checked it for obvious reasons. Do you think I should wait a bit?'

Aunt Em nodded. 'Heavy rain will drive any but the most indefatigable of walkers off the cliffs. If Zack and Caroline aren't coming until teatime you've got plenty of time and it means that Cat will be well on her way to London.'

'I should have done it really early, before anybody was around,' said Julia. 'I thought about it but I wanted to feel certain that Cat had really gone. I know it's fanciful but I wouldn't put anything past her and I have a horrid feeling that she'll try to catch me out somehow. Of course, it might be a trick, anyway, about going back this morning. She might have said that to Caroline hoping she'd tell me and put me off my guard. I wonder how much trouble she could really make, Aunt Em? Supposing she dropped a hint to a journalist or something?'

'There's hardly anything in today's paper,' Aunt Em told her comfortingly. 'A tiny paragraph three pages in. I think you'll find that the big moment has passed and we can just be thankful that the trial is taking place in France and not here. The great British public isn't all that interested in art fraud and it isn't headline-grabbing stuff. And, after all, what could Cat tell anyone? That when she was four she remembers seeing something that looked like *The Child Merlin* at a friend's house? A valuable bronze knocking about in the kitchen or in a tent in the garden? Not much to go on, is it? Even Cat would fear looking a bit of a twit. I agree the risk is there but all we can do is get rid of the evidence and stonewall everything else.'

The morning passed slowly.

'I think the forecast for scattered showers might be right,' Julia said just before lunch. 'There are some rather black-looking clouds over the Camel estuary.' She frowned; the words seemed familiar.

The sunshine dimmed, disappeared, and the day grew eerily dark: brilliant stabs of lightning forked to earth and distant thunder grumbled.

'I think I shall take a chance,' Julia said as soon as lunch was over. She pushed back her chair, picking up the tapestry bag, holding it for a moment. Aunt Em watched her, eyebrows raised. 'No,' said Julia firmly. 'You're staying here and so is Frobes. I'm not taking any unnecessary risks and, anyway, Zack and Caroline might turn up early.' She looked apprehensively at the darkening sky. 'I rather wish they'd stayed put. I think there's bad weather coming.'

They were both startled by a sudden tattoo; a hollow drumming on the roof of the back porch. For a moment they stared at one another, puzzled, until Aunt Em said: 'It's raining. It's absolutely pouring,' and Julia felt another tremor of déjà vu. She seized her bag and the car keys from the hook on the dresser, patted Frobisher, who opened an eye and thumped his tail.

'I'm going now, Aunt Em,' she said, and bent to kiss her.

'Be careful,' said the older woman anxiously.

She saw her go out, heard the back door slam, and just briefly she was transported twenty-eight years back in time and it was Tiggy and Julia going out together into the storm. Em stood at the window watching; she felt helpless and old and frightened.

Julia came out of the house and closed the door behind her. The little Merlin, wrapped in the handkerchief, was at the bottom of the bag. How heavy he was. She climbed into the car and put the bag into the well on the passenger's side. The rain came down in torrents, sizzling and bouncing off the earth so that soon the bare moorland looked as if it were covered in a low cloud of steam. Rain hammered on the roof and clattered on the leaves of the rhododendron bushes; it dislodged stones and washed the loose, dry topsoil away in rivulets of muddy water that poured down into the lanes. As she drove she was aware of Tiggy beside her, urging her onwards. She remembered that other fateful journey and was suddenly filled with terror.

Through the lanes and villages, she drove, glancing from time to time in her mirror to check that no small sports car was following her. The windscreen wipers thrashed rhythmically across the glass, yet she could barely see through the streaming water and she hunched in her seat, the tapestry bag a bright splash of colour at the edge of her vision. Through Tintagel where tourists fled for shelter, down the narrow little lane beneath the high stone-buttressed wall, past the rain-lashed church, and out on to the cliff. Once out of the car she was soaked in moments. Clutching the bag to her chest, slipping and stumbling, she made her way cautiously out to the point where once, on a bright September day, she'd scattered Tiggy's ashes.

At the edge of the cliff she sat down lest she should overbalance, glanced over her shoulder along the path, and took the bronze from its hiding place. The wind howled over the cliff, sweeping the heavy rain eastwards and the sun burst with startling brilliance from behind the clouds. Tunic swirling, chin up, with the little falcon on his wrist, *The Child Merlin* stared unafraid into the future.

Julia looked at him with sorrow and with love. 'I'm so sorry,' she whispered. 'So sorry.'

Taking him in a firm grip she swung her arm as far as she could and the bronze sailed out over the edge of the cliff and arced down into the surging seas. She thought she saw a flash of light and a spray of water as he disappeared, though her eyes were full of tears and she couldn't be certain. The sun vanished. Rain and tears poured down her cheeks, her hair was plastered to her head. She stood up uncertainly, taking small careful steps away from the edge of the cliff.

As she made her way back along the path she was gripped with a fearful premonition. Back in the car she took her mobile and dialled Zack: no reply.

'Darling,' she said, her voice trembling, 'just to say that I'm worried about you. The weather's awful. Don't think of coming out to Trescairn. If you've got to Boscastle then just go back home. Will you do that?'

She switched off and sat in silence, staring out through the streaming rain; she could barely see Tintagel Island or the entrance to Merlin's Cave but with her inner eye she saw them all; she and Tiggy and the children, with the two dogs and the van, on a summer's day long ago. She wept then; unrestrainedly, head resting on her wrists crossed on the wheel, she wept for them all.

CHAPTER TWENTY-FOUR

2004

It was Liv who telephoned later with the first stories of the disaster.

'Are you OK?' she asked anxiously. 'Did you have that thunderstorm?'

'We've had everything,' said Julia. 'The roads are dangerous. Please stay put, Liv.'

'I shall. The café's packed. There are some scary stories coming in about a flood at Boscastle.'

'A flood?' Julia could hardly speak for terror.

'The Valency's burst its banks,' said Liv. 'I hope Zack and Caroline changed their minds when the rain started and went home.'

'They were supposed to be here for tea but they're very late. I can't get hold of them on their mobiles but I think that might be because they're out of signal. They're not at home.'

'Shit,' said Liv. 'We'll just keep trying their mobiles. I'm sure they're fine, Mum. By the way, I've had an email from Andy. I gather you spoke last night? Well, he's feeling a bit of a twit and he's absolutely furious with Cat for harassing us all. He had no idea she was coming down to Cornwall and he's beginning to realize that she's still the same old Cat. I think we can feel pretty safe that it's all over.'

'I was horrid to him,' said Julia remorsefully. 'I did my voice. The one you all call my captain's wife thing.'

Liv laughed. 'He'll survive,' she said cheerfully. 'And try not to worry about Zack and Caroline.'

'Let me know if they get in touch with you,' said Julia anxiously. 'Bye, darling.' She put down the telephone. 'The Valency's burst its banks and flooded Boscastle,' she said to Em. 'It sounds like Lynton and Lynmouth all over again. Oh my God, I wonder where Zack and Caroline are. I do hope they won't risk coming out here. The lanes are in a terrible state.' At last she spoke her fear; the premonition that had been with her all day. 'It couldn't happen again, could it, Aunt Em? Life couldn't be so cruel.'

She picked up her mobile and keyed in Zack's number: still no reply. Simply because she needed something to do, she put the kettle on the hotplate ready to make more tea. Em watched her, seeking for some kind of reassurance but finding no words that were adequate. When the phone rang Julia seized it anxiously: Zack's voice.

'Mum,' he said. 'Just to let you know that we're at Derriford. Caroline's in labour.'

'Oh, darling.' She was weak with relief. 'Oh, thank God. You didn't go to Boscastle after all?'

'Yes, we did. And we managed lunch at The Wellington but then Caroline began to get pains so we just leaped in the car and headed for Plymouth. It all happened so quickly and the weather was appalling. I was terrified we weren't going to make it. I should have phoned but I'm afraid everything went out of my mind. I'm sorry, Mum. Look, I must go. I'll be in touch.'

'Give Caroline my love,' she said. 'Oh, darling, I'm so glad you're safe.'

'Where are they?' asked Em. 'I gather they're not in Boscastle.'

Julia sat down, closed her eyes, and took a deep breath. 'They were there for lunch but Caroline's pains started and they shot off to Derriford. Caroline's in labour but they're safe.' Tears spurted from her eyes and she put her hands over her face. 'I was so afraid,' she cried. 'I thought it was going to happen all over again. Just like me and Tiggy. I've felt Tiggy with me ever since I came back from Hampshire, as if she was trying to tell me something. Oh God, it's been awful. And the real problem is that we can't draw a line under it, can we? We'll never know whether something else might pop out of the woodwork all the while this trial is running.'

'Probably not, but we've done everything we can do to protect Zack. We can't legislate for every eventuality but we've done the best we can. You can't win with this one, Julia. By keeping your promise to Tiggy you have to keep the truth from Zack.'

'But supposing he were to find out from someone else? It's like the adoption thing all over again, isn't it? Too soon and it might be damaging; too late and someone else might get in first. But this time I really feel I have no choice.'

'If Cat hadn't jumped the gun, you and Pete would have told Zack he was adopted when you judged that he was old enough to deal with it, and maybe one day you will be able to tell him about this too, but there are times when the truth is better left untold. This is one of them.'

There was a little silence.

'When I was out there on Glebe Cliff,' Julia said, 'I

remembered the day we went there together, me and Tiggy and the children. It was such a wonderful day and we were all so happy.'

She fell silent and Em got up and went round the table to her. She put her arm about Julia's shoulders and laid her cheek against her head.

'My poor darling,' she said compassionately. 'What a week it's been. I think the worst is over now. I'll make the tea and then we'll phone Liv and tell her that they're safe and ask her to send an email to Andy. After that you could text a message to Pete to tell him he's about to become a grandfather for the third time.'

They watched the news; silent in shocked horror at the images of the Boscastle flooding. The scene was one of devastation: the swollen river, with trees and rocks jammed in its roaring throat, and a bright red car that bobbed like a Dinky toy and wedged upended, lights still on, beneath the bridge; a father with his daughter, clinging together in mid-air, rescued from the rooftops by helicopter; a caravan, fragile as a cardboard box, bouncing backwards on the floodtide. The noise was terrific: the thundering of water and the thrashing of helicopter rotor blades, the shouting urgent voice of the reporter.

'There were two miracles last night,' Em was to say the next morning to Liv. 'One was that no lives were lost in the Boscastle flood and the other was Zack's baby.'

Zack phoned at a quarter to seven whilst they were still watching the news. His voice was jubilant.

'It's a little girl. Seven pounds two ounces. She's lovely and Caroline's fine.'

'Oh, Zack.' Julia could barely speak for relief. 'Oh, thank God.' She made joyful signs to Em. 'And Caroline's really OK?'

'She did wonderfully well and she's so excited. She's spoken to her mother and they're travelling down tomorrow. She's resting now but if you want to come in to see her she says that she'd love to see you, Mum. The staff sister says that'll be all right but just you for this first visit and not for too long, if that's OK.'

On the journey into Plymouth Julia could still feel Tiggy beside her but this time there was no tension. With Zack's news all the doubts and fears of the last week had miraculously vanished, and Julia was filled with an exhilarating mixture of peace and excitement.

'Our granddaughter,' she murmured aloud to Tiggy as she turned north on to the A30. 'Yours and mine. That's how I feel about her because Zack is yours and mine, isn't he? It was hard to begin with, because I resented losing my own baby and I'd imagine you were watching and feeling sad because I found it so difficult. But it wasn't because I didn't love him, you know that. It was just because I was always fighting the guilt and the sadness, and each time I looked at Zack those feelings resurfaced. And then, that day with Angela, I knew that it was different. My grief for my own baby and my love for Zack could be separate. And the amazing thing was that, very gradually, it was as if they merged into one person: Zack and my baby. The other odd thing was that, though I missed you so terribly and I still do, because of him you've always been around.'

The car passed over Hendra Downs, fled past Launceston, turned eastward on to the Tavistock road.

'I felt so guilty, Tiggy. I went over it and over it, reliving it and doing that awful "if only" stuff, but in the end you just have to get over it, don't you? All the time he was growing up I just longed for you to be there, really there. When he made the first fifteen and got good grades for his A levels, and the passing-out parade at Dartmouth, that's when I really missed you. The weird thing was that I often had such a strong feeling that you were beside me. Like now. I remember you telling me once that when you were out on Glebe Cliff you had the feeling that all the earthly barriers dissolved and you felt close to Tom. At the time it seemed a bit scary; a bit fanciful. But there have been times when I've understood what you meant. I mean, this is crazy, isn't it? Talking to you as if you were here in the car with me.'

Julia laughed; she was so happy, driving fast through the gathering dusk, crossing the River Tamar at Greystone Bridge, passing through Milton Abbot, heading for Tavistock.

'Do you remember the way we were that spring and summer, Tiggy? We had no idea what was ahead, thank God, but that year we had so much fun. For a while I thought it had all ended on that awful day; everything seemed finished. And now here I am, driving to see our granddaughter; Zack's child. I suppose there are no ends or beginnings, not really. It's only that we're so wrapped up in our tiny view of life that we can't see the whole journey.'

In the west, the last gleams of watery golden light flooded the cloud-laden horizon. Through Yelverton, over the open moor and down into Roborough: it was nearly dark as she approached Derriford Hospital, parked the car and ran in through the doors of the maternity wing.

Caroline was in bed, cradling her baby; Zack sat beside her, his face bright with love and pride. He smiled up at Julia, such a special look, and it seemed to her that Tiggy was still beside her, slipping her hand under her arm; Julia instinctively pressed her elbow against her side, her heart bursting with joy.

Caroline lifted the child, holding her up towards Julia,

whose arms went out to receive her. She took the little girl and held her, looking down at the tiny crumpled face.

'We've been thinking about names,' Caroline was saying, 'and after Liv told me about the Celtic names we wondered if we might call her Tegan. But the minute we saw her we knew, didn't we, Zack?'

Zack nodded, his arm tightening about her, and they both smiled at Julia.

'Her name's Claerwen,' Caroline said happily. 'Clare for short.'